The Accidental Text

BECKY MONSON

The Accidental Text
Copyright © 2021 Becky Monson
Cover Art by Angela Talley Smith

This book is a work of fiction. The names, characters, places, and incidents are the products of the author's imagination or are used fictitiously. Any resemblance to actual events, business establishments, locales, or persons, living or dead, is entirely coincidental.

All rights reserved. Without limiting the rights under the copyright reserved above, no part of this publication may be reproduced, stored in, or introduced into a retrieval system, or transmitted in any form or by any means (electronic, mechanical, photocopying, recording, or otherwise) without prior written permission of the copyright owner. The only exception is brief quotations in printed reviews. The scanning, uploading, and distribution of this book via the internet or via any other means without the permission of the copyright owner is illegal and punishable by law.

Other Books by Becky

Thirty-Two Going on Spinster
Thirty-Three Going on Girlfriend
Thirty-Four Going on Bride
Speak Now or Forever Hold Your Peace
Taking a Chance
Once Again in Christmas Falls
Just a Name
Just a Girl

*To my mama.
I love that you can still inspire me.
Miss you always.*

Chapter 1

Maggie: So, here's the deal, Mom. I don't want to do this.

I know it's what you wanted, I know we're only honoring your wishes. But honestly, what kind of mom asks her family to spread her ashes while jumping out of a plane?

You. You're that mom.

I was prepared to do it, even willing to. But now that we're here …

I know I've done this before. Seventeen times, to be exact. But today I want to keep my feet firmly on the ground. Going up there seems reckless … and foolish. I mean, I've already lost you.

Why couldn't you have asked to have your ashes spread under some tree or in the ocean like a normal person?

"Who are you texting?"

"What?" I flop the phone facedown on my lap, my face instantly heating. My belly churns, but I suspect that's because there's a mixture of feelings going on inside me right now.

"You seemed really engrossed," my sister Chelsea says. She's standing in front of me, holding a paper cup of coffee in one hand and looking down at me, seated on a rather uncomfortable wooden bench that's pushed up against the wall of a mostly nondescript airplane hangar. I'm tasked with keeping track of all our rigs.

She's wearing a white jumpsuit with black-and-pink detailing, the top half zipped down to the waist, a black cotton T-shirt on underneath. Her highlighted brown hair is in a bun atop her head.

"I was just … texting Hannah." This is my standard excuse—this isn't the first time I've been caught. It's only a matter of time before someone figures me out. Or boots Mom's phone up. So far no one's bothered to do that. The phone has sat in one of the cubbies of my dad's dark oak credenza desk for the past three months. I've been safe so far.

In any case, the Hannah excuse is a good one since I text back and forth with my best friend on a daily basis and have been doing so for years. Sometimes even from our separate bedrooms in our shared apartment. What a time to be alive and lazy.

"You looked very serious," Chelsea says, her brows pulling inward.

I reach up to grab my necklace, the one my dad bought for both Chelsea and me after Mom died, and remember that I didn't wear it on purpose. It's become such a comfort to me, I almost feel naked without it.

"It was a serious text," I say, suddenly feeling warm in my own jumpsuit. February in Phoenix isn't all that hot, but it now feels stifling. I unzip the top of my teal-and-black suit, feeling the cool air hit my undershirt as I do.

Chelsea looks at me with eyebrows raised, expecting an answer. I'm not actually going to tell her. I haven't told anyone I've been sending texts to my dead mother's phone. Not even Hannah, and I tell her everything. I've kept it to myself because ... well, it sounds mental. And I'm not ready to explain or answer questions ... or be committed.

It started out simple. I had the thought that I wished I could text my mom. She'd been gone for a week and I knew she'd never see my message, but the phone felt like a connection to her. A tether. Also, I'd begged my dad to keep the number. It just felt so final to get rid of it. I also knew the phone had died and was sitting in my dad's desk.

So, I sent her a text. All it said was, "I miss you." That was it. And then the next day I sent something similar. Then the day after that, the text was a little longer, and this kept going until the texts starting becoming thought dumps that I'd send to her. Or ... I guess, to her phone. Three months later, it's now become a habit—a part of my daily life.

I know she can't read them. I don't actually need to be committed. I know there's not some direct messaging service to heaven, even though that would be an excellent idea and I think someone needs to make that a thing. Who has an in with God that could ask for a favor? The pope? Oprah?

It's my dirty little secret. I don't have a lot of those. This is probably the only one. And how dirty can it be? It's not hurting anyone, and I really think it's helped me work through all the feelings I've been having. There are so many. Twenty-six is much too young to lose your mom.

"What are you texting Hannah about?" Chelsea asks, and then takes a sip of her coffee.

I jerk my head up, bringing my mind back to my older sister, still standing in front of me with her signature I'm-not-giving-up-until-you-tell-me facial expression. It's a look I'm quite familiar with.

I stare down at my phone, still lying facedown in my lap, the silver sparkle case glinting in the overhead lighting of the hangar.

"I was just venting," I say to Chelsea. It's the truth. Just not the *whole* truth.

Chelsea dips her chin once, letting me know I should continue. Or rather, *expecting* me to continue.

Part of me wants to lie. I could tell her I have a stomachache or a serious case of diarrhea … but in an effort to be more honest about my feelings, I decide to tell her the truth. "Fine," I say. "I'm just … not … feeling this."

"Not feeling what?" She raises just one perfectly shaped eyebrow. It's an exclamation point on her well-practiced judgmental look.

"This." I throw my arms out, gesturing around the space. I look over to see a group of people heading toward the big hangar door, getting ready to load a plane. Some have a skip to their step, but it's clear by the rigid posture of one particular man that this is his first time. I'd love to tell him that it's not half as scary as it seems, but even after jumping many times, I'm currently struggling myself.

Chelsea's eyes go wide, the one eyebrow rising even higher, and I could put money on what she'll say next. "But it's what Mom wanted," she says, sounding exasperated.

Yep. Those were the exact words I knew would come out of her mouth.

"I realize that." I hold back an eye roll.

"So then, what's your problem?

I look to the side, away from Chelsea's penetrating gaze.

"I just feel ... anxious. Like something could happen ... to you, or Dad, or Devon, or me."

Chelsea moves to sit next to me and puts an arm around my shoulders. She has the ability to go from judgmental to compassionate in a split second. It's impressive. The comforting gesture, combined with my still-churning stomach, makes tears well up in my eyes.

"Mags, it's going to be fine."

"I know," I say, adding a sniffle. "I was totally on board until we got here. I'm just—maybe I'm not ready or something."

"Ready for what?" my dad asks. He'd been standing some feet away from us engrossed in something on his phone, the white cylinder urn filled with my mom's ashes tucked under his arm. I hadn't realized he'd moved closer to us. Now he's looking at me with concern in his blue eyes, deep crow's-feet in the corners. Chelsea has his eyes, minus the crow's-feet. Devon too. I got my mom's green ones.

"Maggie's having second thoughts about the jump," Chelsea says.

"Oh, Magpie." My dad uses the nickname he's called me since I can remember. He takes a seat on my other side, setting the urn next to him. He's wearing a black jumpsuit with gray detailing. He wraps an arm around my waist. I'm now in a very public family sandwich. I just need Devon to come over here and pull us all in a big hug. Not that Devon would ever do that.

I feel my dad reach up and run his hand down my ponytail, then he tugs lightly on my dark-brown locks. I may not have gotten his eyes, but I did get his hair, except that his is now mostly gray.

"What's going on?" he asks.

"I feel ... anxious, I guess."

"We don't have to do this today," he says.

My heart skips a tiny beat at this idea, and the churning in my stomach starts to slow.

"What?" Chelsea says, sitting tall next to me, her back rigid. "We have to."

"Why?" Dad asks. "There's no rule."

"But it's—"

"Your anniversary," I finish Chelsea's sentence for her. My shoulders slump, and a weight drops inside my gut.

"So what?" my dad says.

"Well ... I mean ... I ..." Chelsea trails off, and I feel her stiff posture falter next to me.

THE ACCIDENTAL TEXT

Today, February eighteenth, would have been thirty-three years for my parents. That's why we picked this date. It has significance. My parents had a marriage for the ages. Something I've hoped my whole life to find. They met through mutual friends when my mom was twenty-four and my dad was twenty-six. It was love at first sight, according to my dad; my mom needed a little more convincing. It didn't take much, because they were married less than a year later.

All my life, I've had this movie in my mind of being walked down the aisle by my dad and looking over to see my mom crying tears of joy. I've dreamed of this since the day I decided boys were no longer gross and smelled like sweaty feet. Well, sometimes they still smell like sweaty feet—I'm just able to overlook it.

But my mom didn't even get to see me in a long-term relationship. Not anything that went beyond six months. I've never really been in love, I'm pretty sure. At twenty-six, my dating history has been sparse, to say the least.

I realize I'm still young, and I hopefully have a lot of life ahead of me, but my wish to have what my parents had looks so far away, it seems unobtainable.

So far my parents' relationship has only rubbed off on Chelsea, who, at nearly twenty-nine, is married and has two kids. The most adorable girls in the world, in my doting-aunt opinion.

Devon seems to be more on my track. Only he's too big of a player to look for anything lasting. He's a year and a half younger than me, so he's old enough that it's starting to be concerning.

"I don't care about dates," my dad says. "We can do this anytime." He runs a hand up and down my back.

"I think we should just do it today," Chelsea says. "We're already here."

"Not if Maggie isn't feeling it."

"Why's everyone sitting here?" Devon asks, walking toward us, the top half of his jumpsuit unzipped and hanging around his hips, the arms swinging back and forth as he approaches. He's got a white T-shirt on that shows off all the time he spends in the gym.

"Maggie doesn't want to jump," Chelsea says.

"I didn't say that." I whip my head toward her.

"Oh, sorry." She purses her lips. Her eyes move to Devon. "She's 'not feeling it.'" She uses air quotes for the last part.

"I don't sound like that," I say, referring to her whiny imitation of me. "And only old people use air quotes."

Chelsea's mouth drops. "I'm not old!"

"Girls," my dad says, his voice chastising.

"What's going on, Mags?" Devon asks, his eyebrows pulled so low they hood his blue eyes. "Why are you freaking out? You were fine in the car on the way here."

"I'm not freaking out," I say defensively. "I'm just having second thoughts."

"Why? We've jumped out of a plane plenty of times. You know what Mom says about jumping—"

"It's safer to jump out of a plane than to get behind the wheel of a car," I say, finishing the quote my mom pulled out when people couldn't understand why this was a family pastime of ours. It wasn't like a weekly thing or anything. But it was often enough that it caused concern for some people.

"Exactly," Devon says, a smug smile on his lips.

"I know all that. I just ... I can't shake this feeling." I look down at the floor.

"So we'll wait," Dad declares, his tone carrying a finality to it.

"No," Chelsea protests loudly.

He holds out a hand to Chelsea. "If Maggie isn't feeling like doing this now, then we'll wait for another day when she is." He picks up the urn in his hands, his eyes perusing it reverently.

Devon holds out a hand toward my dad. "We're already here. If Mags doesn't want to do it, I'll do it. Give me Mom." He flexes his fingers back and forth at my dad.

"No," my dad says, pulling the urn in toward his chest in a protective stance. "We do this together. It's what your mom wanted. We can wait."

I want to tell them that we should just do it, that I can suck it up, but the relief I feel from the thought of not going up in that plane is so overwhelming, I can't even bring myself to say it. I can't fake it.

"When will we do it?" Chelsea asks, her obsessive need to have things planned out—to know all the details—making an appearance. When we were kids, she used to schedule time to play with me and our bubblegum-pink Barbie DreamHouse.

"When Maggie is up to it," my dad says definitively.

Devon runs a hand down his face, his frustration evident. "Fine."

"Sorry, guys," I say, feeling tears building in my eyes. It's from a little regret and a lot of relief. "I'll get it together, I promise." A tear escapes and falls down my cheek. Devon reaches over and rubs my shoulder, proof that, while irritated by the scenario, he still loves me.

My dad wraps his arm around me, pulling me toward him, and I lean my head on his shoulder. "Take all the time you need," he says. "Mom's not going anywhere." He holds the urn up as proof, a joking smile on his lips.

"Dad," Chelsea chides, the corner of her lips curled upward. "That's totally inappropriate."

"It's the truth, though," he says, with a shrug that makes my head bob up and down on his shoulder.

Chelsea stands up from the bench. "I better go, then. I can salvage the rest of the day with Mark and the girls. He took the day off, you know."

Her intentional jab is felt in my gut, but not enough for me to change my mind. "I'm so sorry, you guys. I'll be ready the next time, okay?"

My dad stands up and offers his hand to help me up. "You let us know when that is, Magpie."

Chapter 2

"You choked?" Hannah asks me, her dark-brown eyes wide with disbelief. Her nearly black, perfectly straight, long hair tossing back and forth as she shakes her head at me.

"I didn't choke," I say, my tone defensive. "I just ... freaked out."

"That's choking," she says, dipping her chin to her chest.

"Fine. I choked."

We're currently sitting at the oak dining room table at Hannah's family home, a modern light fixture hanging above us, giving the room a warm yellow hue.

It's the first time I've seen Hannah in person since the ill-fated ash spreading incident yesterday. She's been extra busy at work and came home late last night after I was asleep and was gone this morning by the time I woke up.

We're only two doors down from the house I grew up in, the house where my dad still lives. Even though we have our own apartment in downtown Scottsdale, you can regularly find us around here, in one of our childhood homes. We mostly hit up Hannah's because her grandma likes to make us dinner and it's a thousand times better than anything we could make on our own. Hannah and I both lack in the cooking department.

"What's wrong with you?" Hannah asks, tilting her head to the side.

"Sorry?"

She shrugs one shoulder. "You've gone weird on me. The Maggie I know would've jumped out of that plane."

I look down at the table, the soup Hannah's grandma prepared in front of me.

I let out a breath. "I just ... don't feel like myself right now."

"Why?"

"Well, I mean ... my mom just died."

"Of course." She nods her head, her eyes crestfallen. "And we all miss Katherine Cooper very much."

Hannah loves calling my mom by her first and last name. I'd once thought it was a Korean thing, but it turns out it's because she enjoys the alliteration so much.

We've lived down the street from each other since I was six and Hannah was five. We bonded our first day of first grade, and the fact that we lived so close only sealed the deal. We were instant besties, always together, only separated during the summers when Hannah would go with her grandma to South Korea to visit family, and also during college, when Hannah went to Stanford and I stayed here and went to ASU.

After college and a year back at our parents' houses, we finally got an apartment together, where we've been for the past four years. Hannah has a real job now, working at her mom's law firm, and can no longer do a full summer trek to Korea, much to her grandma's chagrin.

"What I mean is," Hannah says, "the Maggie I know would have honored Katherine Cooper's wishes, no matter what."

"I know. That's what I mean about not feeling like myself," I say. It's hard for me to get people to understand how I'm feeling when I don't even understand it.

"How did Chelsea take it?" Hannah asks. She takes a sip of broth from the dumpling soup her grandma made us from leftover *mandu* she'd made for the Lunar New Year celebration last weekend.

"She was … annoyed." I look away from Hannah and over toward the contemporary decor of the living room. The space has changed a lot since we were kids. Some pieces are still here from when we were younger, like the modern-looking grandfather clock in the corner and the painting that hangs over the fireplace. Hannah's mom is very particular about keeping things nice. Hannah didn't get that gene, since her room in our apartment usually looks like a tornado hit it. In her defense, sixty-hour workweeks don't leave a lot of time for cleaning.

Hannah snort laughs. "I'm sure she was." She adds an eye roll for emphasis. "What about Devon? And what about your dad?"

"Devon was irritated, of course, but was fine after my dad offered to buy dinner. And my dad was … supportive."

"Good ole Nick," she says.

"Yeah," I say, resting my spoon by my dish, having just eaten the last bit of the soup.

It's at this moment that Hannah's grandma comes over and sees that I'm done. She nods her head as if to ask if I want more, and when I tell her no thank you she eyes me, a scowl on her face. She says something to Hannah in Korean and Hannah just stares at her. She says something again and Hannah says something back. Hannah turns to me with a frustrated expression.

She lets out a breath. "Halmoni wants me to tell you that you've gotten too skinny."

I look down at myself and then back up at Hannah and her grandma. Sure, I've lost a few pounds since my mom died. But it's not like I'm sickly skinny or anything. I've always been on the thin side, never having had to work too much on my physique. But to say that I'm overly thin seems like a stretch, even with my recent unintentional weight loss.

Still, Halmoni, as we call Hannah's grandma, keeps up the scowl and has now added verbal tsking, along with one pointer finger rubbing atop the other, the universal sign for "shame on you."

Halmoni doesn't speak much English, and both Hannah and her mom are fluent in Korean, so she's never really had to learn. Although this doesn't stop her from lecturing me via Hannah.

"Well, I guess I need more *manduguk*, then," I say, most likely butchering the word.

THE ACCIDENTAL TEXT

Halmoni walks over to me, her graying permed curls bouncing around her face, her countenance now one of approval. She pats me on the head and grabs my bowl to get me more.

"So what now? Are you going to find another place to leave her ashes?" Hannah asks after her grandma walks away.

I sigh and slump in my seat. Halmoni tsks me from the kitchen and I sit up straighter. The woman has eyes in the back of her head, I swear. Hannah and I could never get away with anything when we were younger. Not with Halmoni around. Sometimes she'd scold us for things we *didn't* do, just in case we ever dared consider doing it.

"I don't think I could convince my family to spread them anywhere else, since that's what my mom wanted," I say.

About a year before my mom started having trouble with her legs and her balance, we did a jump in southern Utah. On the same plane as us was a group of guys who'd recently lost a friend in a car accident. They went first, and we watched as they jumped together. They must have been experienced, because they knew how to jump in a formation—something my family and I had been practicing—linking arms together as they fell. Then one of them released their friend's ashes into the sky.

After we landed from our jump, my mom informed us through teary eyes that that was how she wanted her ashes spread after she died. She said if we were too old to do it, then we'd have to send her grandchildren up there to jump.

When she got her official diagnosis and we found out it was terminal, one of the first things she did was remind us of that.

"So when will you go again?" Hannah asks.

"Not sure," I say. "My dad says it's up to me."

"And how will you not choke next time?"

"I have no idea. Maybe I won't. Maybe I'll be just fine." Even as I say this, though, I feel tendrils of fear twist around my insides. What is wrong with me?

Halmoni sets down a fresh bowl of steaming hot soup in front of me. She points to it and says, "Eat." And then pats me on the head again before walking away.

"Can you like, practice?" Hannah asks.

I scrunch my face. "I don't think practicing will help. I've been doing this for years."

She twists her lips to the side as she thinks.

"What about building up to it? You could start smaller or something. Go bungee jumping."

My eyes go wide. I hate bungee jumping and always have, and she knows this. "Jumping out of a plane is not the same as bungee jumping. That's like apples and … something that's not apples."

Now it's Hannah's turn to scrunch her face. "Oranges?"

"I'm really tired." This is the truth. Grief is draining.

Hannah looks down at her nearly finished bowl of soup, twisting her lips again. "What about those indoor jumping places?"

I shrug. "I guess. Also not the same. The truth is, I just need to get over myself."

THE ACCIDENTAL TEXT

"I've been saying this for years." She gives me a smirk.

"Yes, I know," I say flatly.

"So what if you can't do it? What's your plan?"

I look to the side, contemplating. Hannah always asks the hard questions. I know I need to think about this, but I don't really want to. What if I can't do it? What if I'm forever Maggie the Chicken? I suppose I could strap myself to Devon and go tandem, since he's certified to take other people. But it's impossible to even out your jumps when you go tandem and others are going solo. You fall much faster when there are two of you strapped together. It won't work for what my mom has asked us to do.

"No plan, really. I just have to do it. I think I just need time. I'll figure it out."

"Because it's what Katherine Cooper wanted." Hannah looks at me with soft eyes, the corners of her closed mouth upturned slightly.

I think about the phone in my pocket; the last text I sent to my mom was me apologizing to her for failing her. I'm sure if she were here, she would tell me that I could never fail her, but it feels like I did all the same.

"Hi, Dad," I say as I walk into the cluttered home office where my dad's sitting at his desk, his eyes glued to his computer screen.

"Hey, Magpie." He doesn't even look in my direction.

After finishing my second bowl of soup at Hannah's, for which I got a nod of approval from Halmoni, I popped over to my parents' house—the place I've called home since I could barely say the word—to see what my dad's up to. I also wanted to make sure that my mom's phone is still sitting in its same location.

It's the first place my eyes went when I entered the room, and sure enough, it's still there. Second shelf down, in one of the cubbies. It's an older iPhone, with a case that has a cover attached to it. I never knew why my mom liked having a cover on her phone. It always seemed like an inconvenience to me—an extra step. The red faux-leather of the cover now has a dull look to it, with a thick layer of dust on top.

Never have I ever felt appreciation for a layer of dust. But I do right now. It's proof that the phone has sat there, untouched. My secrets are safe. It's hard to believe that my mom will never hold that phone again. She'll never answer a call, never send a text.

"What are you up to?" I ask my dad as I take a step closer to him and look at the screen he's been studying intently.

I take a sharp breath inward. "Silver Match?" I say, my voice taking on a scratchy sound from my instantly dry throat.

My dad is looking at a dating site. For old people. I knew this kind of thing existed, having looked at dating sites myself, but I didn't know he'd have a clue about them. He's not all that internet savvy. And he's only been single for three months.

My dad, who has been mostly in a trance since I got here, whips his head toward me, realizing what he's looking at and that he just got caught looking at it.

"It's not what you think," he says, the words spilling out of his mouth.

"Well, it looks like you're scrolling through single ladies on the internet," I say, unable to keep my tone from sounding horrified.

"Okay ... then it *is* what you think." He reaches up and rubs his jaw. Like he's always done when he's been caught.

"Dad?"

He sighs. "I'm not dating anyone. It's just ... well, you know June?"

I almost laugh when he says that. Do I know June? Our neighbor down the street? The one who's been in our neighborhood almost as long as we have?

I nod my head. "Of course I know June," I say. Her oldest son, Shane, used to pull my pigtails in the second grade.

"Well, she's been doing the single thing for a while now."

"Right," I say.

June has been single since my junior year of high school, when her husband, Roger, passed away unexpectedly.

"Anyway, we got to talking," my dad continues. "I told her I was curious what was out there, and she told me to have a look. So"—he motions toward the screen—"that's what I'm doing."

"Why?"

He shrugs one shoulder. "I mean, I don't want to date anyone, but it's ... more informational, that's all."

My dad leans back in his seat, folding his arms. For nearly sixty, he's in quite good shape. He'd probably look even younger if it weren't for the almost-all-gray hair. He started graying early, right around the time that Devon was born. Although he's not sure if it was something genetic or if Devon was the cause. I'd put money on the latter.

"I thought you said you never wanted to date again?"

"I did say that. And I still feel that way. It's just ... lonely."

I reach over and put a hand on his shoulder, feeling my heart do a sudden twisty thing. "I'm sorry, Dad."

"I have you kids, of course, but ... it's hard to come home to this big empty house sometimes."

Even though Mom has been gone for only three months, Dad has been coming home to an empty house for more than six. Since my mom went into the hospital and never came home.

I swallow audibly, wanting to ask him a question but not sure I want the answer. "Did you find anyone ... interesting?"

My dad gives me a small smile. "No. Probably because no one compares to your mother. It was just out of curiosity mostly."

I feel relief wash over me. I want my dad to be happy. I just want him to be happy being alone for the rest of his life. Which is very selfish of me, I realize. But I've only just lost my mom; I don't need to add a new wife for my dad into the mix. Would it be like a stepmom thing? I'm too old for that, right? Oh gosh. I hope it never gets to that.

My dad stands up from his chair. "Don't worry, Magpie. No one can replace your mom."

"I know that," I say, feeling a lump in my throat make an appearance. This is a familiar feeling, unfortunately. I've cried so much throughout the past year, it's become an unwanted companion of mine.

"Well, that was enough looking around for me," my dad says, pushing his chair back from his desk and standing up. "Ice cream?"

"Sounds perfect."

I take one last look at my mom's phone before leaving the room. I have *a lot* to tell her in my next text.

Chapter 3

Maggie: Well, I started my period. Thanks, womankind, for this oh-so-precious gift of menstruating.

It's days like today that it really feels like you're gone, Mom. I'm cramping and my boobs hurt and there's no one to complain to that will actually listen or care. We both know Chelsea isn't that person. And Dad and Devon are no help. Hannah and I cycle together, so she gets it but offers no support. As we all know, sympathy is not one of Hannah's gifts.

Here's a tiny silver lining: my freaking out at the jump last week? It must have been PMS. Which makes me feel better, honestly. I'd thought I'd snapped or something. And obviously I still don't want to do it because I'm on my period. Once it's over, I'll be back to the old me. Ready to fulfill your wishes.

"Mom's birthday."

I scream at the sound of a voice. My phone slips out of my hands, and I bat it around like a cat, trying to get a hold of it, before it lands on my knees and rolls down my leg, landing with a plop on the top part of my foot and then onto the floor under my desk.

THE ACCIDENTAL TEXT

"Ow!" I say. The phone hit just the right spot—right on that bone on the top of my Vans-clad foot. It makes me want to both laugh and cry at the same time. I roll back my chair on the epoxy-finished cement floor of my office and reach down to pick up my phone, rubbing my foot before sitting back up.

I look the phone over to inspect it and, sure enough, there's a tiny little crack at the top of my screen protector.

First my period and now this? I *hate* this day.

"What?" I say to Chelsea, who's missed this entire sequence as she's staring at something on her phone. She's wearing jeans and a company polo that says *Cooper's* on the pocket. I never wear the polos from work, even though I have a bunch in all different colors. I like wearing my own T-shirts. Plus, I feel like polos make my shoulders look bulky. I've requested other shirts and even had some designed, but we haven't gotten around to ordering them.

Chelsea looks up at me, down at her phone, and then up at me again, like she's forgotten why she's even here. Mom brain, she calls it. I say it's her brain starting to misfire from all her multitasking. She does the books for our family-run business, manages a household with two small girls, runs a charity that we do called Drives for Dreams, and still finds the time to be an exercise addict as well.

"Mom's birthday," she repeats.

"Yes … May fifteenth." I wonder if I'm being quizzed or something. What an odd thing to say.

She shakes her head. "Put it on your calendar; we're jumping then," she says, impatience in her voice like I'm supposed to read her mind.

"What?" I ask, pulling my calendar app up on my phone and scrolling through three months to get to May. "Why so long? Can't we just do it in a week or something?"

I'm suddenly super annoyed. Didn't Dad say I got to pick? I reach up and tug on the *k* pendant on my necklace. It feels like taking a big deep breath. But I take one of those too, for good measure.

"We have so much coming up with the anniversary party, Drives for Dreams, plus Mark and I are taking the girls to see his parents in April." She ticks these things off on her fingers as she says them. Then she looks at me, wearily. "Last week really was the best time."

"Sorry," I say for the umpteenth time. I really do feel horrible about what happened.

I had a long discussion with Mom over the weekend, via her phone. And even though it was one-sided, I'm feeling better about the whole thing. Plus, like I was just telling her—before getting interrupted by Chelsea—the whole thing was most likely due to PMS. I'm pretty sure.

Chelsea shakes her head in quick movements. "It's fine," she says. "Anyway, Dad and I think May will be a good time."

"You've already talked to Dad?"

"Yes." She nods once. "He thinks it's a great day to do it. And …" she stops herself, her eyes moving around the room as if she's trying to think of the words she wants to use. "We both think it will give you enough time to … you know." She purses her lips. "Get your crap together. Devon used another word, but Mark and I are working on not cussing since Alice called Mark's mom an ass last time we were there."

I snort laugh out my mouth. I love that story. If only I had that kid's gumption. And in Alice's defense, Mark's mom *is* pretty terrible. At least, according to Chelsea she is.

My smile drops as I realize something. "Wait … Devon was there too? So, what … you all had a meeting behind my back?" Annoyance pools in my belly. I suddenly feel like a fragile person who's left out of conversations that might be "too hard" for me to handle. This is not who I am. I'm the middle child. The glue. Clearly, my family no longer sees me this way.

Sure, I've taken my mom's death the hardest of all of us. But that's because Mom was my person. I talked to her every day. I told her nearly everything. I don't have a family to keep me occupied, like Chelsea. And Devon is always busy doing whatever Devon does. Plus, boys don't stay as close to home as girls do, or so I've been told.

But now I feel like I look weak and pathetic in my family's eyes. And I don't like it. It sort of feels like everyone else is on the same page and I'm over here in my own corner, feeling all my own feelings. I feel like no one understands me.

Chelsea looks annoyed now. "It wasn't intentional. We just all happened to be in Dad's office and it came up."

"Well, I would've liked to be part of that conversation," I say, my voice full of frustration. "May seems so far away from now."

"Yes, well, I think it will work out for the best."

By "the best," she means the best for me. They must really think of me as fragile. I hate that so much.

I open my mouth to protest more, but then Devon appears in the doorway, next to Chelsea.

"You tell her?" he asks.

She nods.

"Are you gonna freak out again?" Devon turns toward me.

Chelsea punches him lightly on the shoulder. "Stop it. I've already talked to her."

"What did she say?"

"She's going to do it."

"Yeah, but will she really?"

"I'm right here," I say loudly.

"Right," Devon says, his face turning toward me again. "And?"

"It's fine. I'll be ready." Even as I say this, though, I feel nervousness swim through me. What if I can't do it? What if I choke? What if I'm Chicken Maggie indefinitely?

"Good," Devon says, and Chelsea echoes him with the same word.

"Are we done here?" I ask my siblings after a few seconds of quiet, both of them still standing in my doorway.

"Yeah," Devon says, and Chelsea nods.

THE ACCIDENTAL TEXT

"Good, because I need to tell you that I caught Dad on a dating site the other day."

"What?" Chelsea and Devon say at the same time.

They both walk into my office and stand near my desk. Without words, we are now in a sibling meeting. It's something we've always done.

When we were younger, we'd get together in Chelsea's room and sit on the floor, calling our meeting to order so we could discuss things we didn't like—like the chore chart our mom had started using—or we'd make plans to strike over our allowance (we never followed through with that one). We also used to make detailed, coordinated plans to get our parents to take us places. Like to dinner, or the zoo, or even Disneyland. And it worked, most of the time.

As we grew older, the meetings were less and less frequent, and when we'd have them, they'd mostly be about Mom and Dad. For the past nine months, our meetings had been about health care for my mom, and then what hospice we should use ... and eventually funeral planning. My dad wasn't in a place to make huge decisions, so we'd gather the information, present him with all the options, and let him choose.

Then, after Mom was gone, there were meetings about Dad and what we were going to do for him. How we would take care of him, fill our mom's shoes as best we could.

"Dad was on a dating site?" Chelsea says, her voice a hoarse whisper, as if saying it fully out loud will make it real.

"Yep," I say, raising my eyebrows as I look between the two of them.

"Why?" Devon asks.

"To check the weather," Chelsea says sarcastically.

He looks at her, hands resting on his hips. "I know what a dating site is, believe me."

Chelsea wrinkles her nose at this information.

"I mean, why would Dad be on one?"

"Apparently, our neighbor June told him to check it out. To see what's out there," I say.

"Why would Dad even want to see what's out there?" Chelsea asks.

"He said he's lonely."

We just look at each other, no words, our concerned and questioning eyes doing the talking.

"Maybe I should ask him to move in with me and Mark?" Chelsea says, her voice ending the silence.

"He's fifty-nine," Devon points out. "He's not going to want to do that."

"Could we get him a dog?" I ask, the idea coming to me just now. A dog would definitely help with loneliness.

We had a dog once. Butch was his name and he was a golden retriever/boxer mix. He regularly ate my mom's shoes, and I suspect there wasn't a lot of love lost on her end when he finally passed away at thirteen years old. I, on the other hand, didn't think I could ever be more sad about a death. Until my mom died. That was much, much worse.

"Yeah, a dog might work," Chelsea says. "I'll look into it."

THE ACCIDENTAL TEXT

"We probably shouldn't spring a dog on him, though. Maybe we should ask first?" Devon says.

"Right," I agree. But already my heart is feeling a little less heavy. A dog would be a perfect way to keep my dad from feeling alone at the house.

"Okay, I'll let you know what I can find," Chelsea says.

Devon and Chelsea both turn to leave, the meeting over. Gone are the days when we used to stand in a circle, put our hands on top of each other's, and yell "Coopers!" at the top of our lungs before releasing our hands and shooting them up toward the ceiling.

Just as they're walking out the door, I hear two taps on the wall outside my office and someone saying, "Knock, knock."

I would know that voice anywhere. The low, soothing, extra sexy tones of Dawson Hargrove.

"Dawson," Devon says when he sees him, in that "bro" way guys talk to each other. He gives him a fist bump. "What's up, man?"

Chelsea also offers a greeting—a more professional one—and then leaves.

I watch as Devon and Dawson start up a conversation about something car related. I appreciate this, as it gives me time to get myself together. I've got a sweaty palms and pits situation happening right now.

Dawson is the operations manager at Cooper's—my family's shop. He's worked for my dad for about a year now, and he's been the object of my affection since the day he accepted the position and said those fateful words to me: "You're stepping on my toes."

I was literally wordless when I first met him—seeing that perfect chiseled jaw of his and those stark blue eyes. It took my breath away. It was like he'd stepped out of a magazine.

My dad introduced us, Dawson went in for a handshake, I went in for a hug—because I'd temporarily lost my mind—and toes were stepped on. He was very nice about it, and my embarrassment wasn't enough to put me off him. I don't think much could, really.

My crush has ebbed and flowed throughout this year and had become nearly nonexistent with all the things in my personal life, but recently there's been a new development: he's *single*.

This is significant. Dawson has been dating Natasha since I met him. *Natasha*. I've only met her a handful of times, but I could never figure the two of them out. She just seemed all wrong for him. Natasha is super wannabe Instagram famous, and Dawson is more reserved ... more introspective.

He's also the most gorgeous man I've ever seen in real life, with that beautifully thick, dark-blond head of hair and that gorgeously structured face. He shouldn't be wasting that face at Cooper's; he should be an actor or a model or something. That face is God's gift to the world. But I'm grateful he's not any of those things. Because, his looks and my sweaty pits aside, Dawson is a great asset to Cooper's. He works hard and is dedicated to the company, and he runs the shop better than any other hire we've had.

THE ACCIDENTAL TEXT

My dad thinks the world of him. My mom too. She'd told me more than once that if the day ever came that Dawson was single, I needed to make something happen with him.

Well, he's single now. Sexy and single. The day has come. And I'm going to go for it, since this is the first time we've been alone in my office since the breakup.

"I've got a situation for you," Dawson says when he enters my office after finishing his conversation with Devon.

"Sure," I say. My heart does a strange skipping thing again—clearly the extra time I had while he was talking to Devon did not help.

He's wearing charcoal-gray coveralls, a white T-shirt peeking out underneath. His hair is perfectly styled—combed back with some gel to hold it all in place. His blue eyes crinkle on the sides as he smiles at me with perfectly straight, white teeth.

"Have a seat." I put on my best professional demeanor, gesturing toward the black mesh guest chair facing my desk.

Dawson takes a seat, very cool-like—casually, where he does that thing that guys do, leaning back in the chair, legs spread apart. With his Converse-clad feet and coveralls he looks like someone from the past. James Dean, reincarnated.

"What did you need to talk about?" I ask after Dawson doesn't say anything.

"Right." Dawson clears his throat. "Your dad's not here, so I thought I'd run this by you. I think we have to redo Andy Lawrence's car ... for free," he says, his smile falling.

My smile falls, too, with this news. "Why?"

"The wrap looks bad. There's some bubbling and the edges were done poorly."

"Who did it?"

"Chad," he says, with a knowing look on his face.

"Right."

Chad is Devon's friend, and Devon begged us to give Chad a job here. Actually, Devon never begs. He just told us that we were hiring his friend Chad and that was the end of it. Only Chad has no clue what he's doing, and it's becoming more and more apparent that whatever training Devon gave him, it was either half-hearted or, most likely, not much training at all.

We've been wrapping cars for nearly fifteen years now—even before it became a popular thing to do. My dad had been doing vinyl decals for cars—business cars and race cars were his bread and butter. But since the invention of the full-body car wrap, we've been working on all kinds of vehicles. Some customers want to save the original paint for value, and some just want something different and original—for their car to stand out. Whatever they want, Cooper's can do it. That's our motto: "Whatever you want, Cooper's can do it!"

This isn't exactly true, since there are state laws and limitations for what can and can't be put on a car. Like naked people. Or even cartoons of naked people. This has been requested. A lot.

It's a family affair at Cooper's. My dad does most of the selling and runs the shop, I help run the day-to-day when he's not here and I do all the HR, Chelsea does the books, and Devon ... well, we're not entirely sure what he does. He can sell like no other and wrap too. He's kind of all over the place. My mom, when she was alive, liked to pop in and visit, but she mostly stayed away from the business. She liked to have her own thing, which up until her diagnosis was real estate.

"So what do you want to do, Boss?" Dawson gives me a wink.

I'd allow my stomach to throw confetti if this were a new thing. But Dawson has been a winker since day one. It clearly means nothing. The "boss" thing isn't new either. But I get a little pang of butterflies every time he says it. I'm not technically his boss. My dad is the main guy around here.

"I guess we have to do the wrap again."

"I figured. Just wanted to run it by you."

"And give him ten percent off his next wrap too," I say.

"Will do."

"And we should probably give Chad an easier job."

Dawson rubs his chin, his fingers running over the tiny bit of stubble there. I'm feeling envious of a jaw. This is a new low for me.

"I think I can train him; let's give him another chance," Dawson says.

My heart does a little stutter. See? Even knowing that Chad has cost us time and money, Dawson still wants to give him another chance. He's the perfect man ... Dawson, *not* Chad.

"Okay, then." Dawson leans forward in his seat, placing his hands on the tops of his knees. "If that's all, I guess I'll get back to work."

He stands up and then turns to walk out the door.

"Wait," I say, the word coming out extra breathy sounding. I stand up from my chair as Dawson turns around, his eyebrows raised expectantly.

This is it. My chance. We're alone in my office. I can ask him. I can make a move.

"I was wondering," I start, but then my mouth runs dry. The blood between my ears is making a loud whooshing noise.

I don't continue. I just stare at Dawson, suddenly feeling fear and doubt course through me. It's instant. There's no preamble or warning—it just happens. A lot like what I experienced before I ruined the jump last week.

"Yes?" Dawson asks, pulling his eyebrows inward, his look now one of concern.

"Well ... um ... I was thinking that ..."

Oh dear, my heart is pounding. I can hear it in my ears. I feel my face flushing as panic rises.

"Are you ... is everything okay?" Dawson asks.

"Ya-yeah," I finally choke out. "I'm fine. Everything's fine."

"Well, what were you wondering?" he asks.

THE ACCIDENTAL TEXT

"You know"—I shake my head and then give him the first excuse that comes to my mind—"I forgot," I say, and then laugh awkwardly.

Dawson's mouth moves as if he's going to say something, opening and closing, and then all he says is, "Okay," and with a wave and a smile, he walks out of the room.

Chapter 4

"Oh, my gosh," Hannah says after an exaggerated gasp. "You choked again."

"I totally did," I say, putting a hand to my forehead.

"What's going on with you?"

"I don't know," I whine, letting my hand drop to my side as dramatically as possible. "I mean, he was right there, it was the perfect timing. And … I couldn't do it. The words wouldn't even come out of my mouth."

"So what did you do?"

I let my face fall. "I pretended that I forgot what I was asking."

"You didn't." Hannah shakes her head, looking utterly disappointed. She's sitting with me on the tan upholstered couch in our apartment. Remnants of the curls she put in her hair before work hang loosely over her shoulders. She's still got on her work attire: a white flowy blouse and a black pencil skirt. Even after a full day of work, Hannah is stunning.

I'm not so stunning myself right now in a pair of cotton shorts I threw on after getting home from work. I paired it with a pink tank top that still has a pizza stain on it, right smack-dab in the center of my chest. I wanted my outsides to match my insides. Messy.

I had to drag myself up the three flights of stairs to get to our apartment, and it about did me in. I feel so drained.

"I totally did," I say, repeating myself. I do a full body sag, letting everything droop. I'm grateful we're not at Hannah's place right now so I can do this without another Halmoni lecture.

"Is this part of you not feeling like yourself?" Hannah asks.

Tears prick behind my eyes. "I don't like this new me."

Hannah reaches over and pats me on the shoulder. It's almost farcical the way she does it. Like she's patting a piece of paper. Comfort does not come easily for Hannah. She tries, like right now as she taps me with a mostly rigid hand as if to say, *There, there.*

My mom was the best at offering comfort. She gave the best hugs of anyone I've ever known. They were tight and warm and protective. She felt 100 percent present when she hugged, like you were all that mattered in that moment—the most important thing in her life. It wasn't just me who felt that way. At her funeral, many people commented on how they would miss her hugs.

If she were here right now, she'd be hugging me and comforting me with words of wisdom and encouragment. Giving me a kiss on the cheek for good luck. Instead, I've got Vulcan-like Hannah patting my shoulder. *There, there.*

Of course, if my mom were still here, I don't think I'd be experiencing all these new feelings. I hate how different I feel in my own skin since she died. I'm sure anyone who loses a parent does. I don't know how you could *not* be changed by something like that. But what I wasn't expecting was my confidence waning. Like my mom's death put a large crack in its shiny veneer. It doesn't make any sense, really.

Hannah gives me a warm smile. "I think you're making this all too hard on yourself. Maybe you just need to dumb it down."

I pull the bottom of my tank top up and wipe my eyes and nose with it. "How's that?"

She points an index finger at me. "Take all the formality out of it. You walk up to Dawson, grab him by those sexy coveralls he wears, and just plant one on him."

I give her my best side-eyed glare. "I may have recently lost some of my confidence, but even when I had it I wouldn't have done that."

Hannah purses her lips in thought. "Hmm ... that does sound more like something I'd do. At least before I swore off the species."

Hannah swore off men last spring when she broke up with her ex, Ben. He did a number on her. She doesn't call him the "Cheating Douchewaffle" for nothing.

"Well, if you have any better ideas, let me know," I say, and then rub a hand over my face.

Hannah sighs. "Listen, KFC—I might start calling you that—I know you're sad. And I know you're still in the midst of your grief. But you've got to pull yourself together. That boy will not stay single for long. Men like that don't."

"Gee, what a pep talk," I say, my voice flat.

"You're welcome," she says extra cheerfully.

"It would be so much easier if he made the first move."

She puts a finger to her chin. "This is true, but I have a theory with Dawson."

"Do tell."

"Your dad is his boss."

"So?"

"So, that complicates things. Because if he flirts with you or asks you out, and it's unwanted, that could affect his job."

I tilt my head to the side. "I guess?"

"So that's why you have to make the first move—so he knows you're interested and that the door is open."

I let out a breath through my nose. "Maybe the problem is that I've never made the first move before. Not outright."

"Oh, you poor, poor creature," Hannah says sarcastically. She puffs out her lips and shakes her head. "Poor sweet Mags, never had to make the first move. I feel so sad for you."

"Shut up," I say. "I've made moves, just not the first one. Plus, it's not like I've got some long list of lovers in my life."

She scrunches her nose. "Gross. Never use the word *lover* again in my presence."

"Oh yay, another word to add to the list," I say. Hannah has a long list of words she hates. *Panties* being the top offender. I don't know why she tells me—it only makes me want to say them more.

"So tell me, oh wise one, how do I make Dawson my *lover*," I over-accentuate the word and then give her my best smirk.

Her eyes shoot daggers at me.

"Fine, sorry. Just ... tell me what to do."

"Make a move."

I let my shoulders slump. "Yeah. I tried that, remember? And it kind of felt like not being able to jump out of a plane."

"Maybe this will be good practice then. If you put yourself out there for Dawson, then maybe it will make you feel more daring and you'll be able to jump."

"That seems a little far-fetched. And besides, what if he rejects me? That would probably set me back."

"Maybe," she says, lifting her shoulders briefly. "But you'll never know unless you try."

"I guess," I say, and then move to stand up from the couch. "I think I'll go sleep on it."

"Okay," Hannah says. "I mean, it's only ten thirty, but you do you, Grandma."

In my room I lie down in my bed, pull out my phone, and start texting my mom. I tell her about Dawson and what a chicken I've become. I ask her if she has any sound advice she can offer.

I know what she'd say if she were here. Something like *Seize the day* or *What have you got to lose?* I can hear her voice so clearly in my head. I remember what she sounds like, what her skinny fingers felt like in my hand. The smell of her auburn hair. I hope I never lose those memories.

THE ACCIDENTAL TEXT

I scroll through my phone, looking at my one-sided conversation that goes back and back. As my eyelids start to feel heavy, I make a wish that she could write me back, just once. Even so, I'm grateful I have this little piece of her still.

Chapter 5

Maggie: Hi, Mom. Today is a new day, right? I never appreciated when you used to say that. Sorry about that.

I'm feeling a little lost this morning, and a little angry if I'm being honest. Maybe I've entered that anger phase of my grief. I don't know what to think. I just don't feel like me anymore. I know I've told you all this before. Sorry for the repeat. But it feels like no one understands. That might be the hardest part. I feel sort of alone in all this.

I know you'd tell me I'm not alone, if you could talk to me right now. I know you'd tell me to be strong and all that. But you're not here. And no matter how hard I try to channel your strength, it doesn't seem to be working.

Miss you, Mom. So much.

I hit send, feeling tears sting my eyes as I toss my phone toward the end of my bed and then lie back and stare up at the textured ceiling of my bedroom. My eyes move to the part that looks like a heart, right next to the fan. My eyes go there a lot. I often wonder if someone did it on purpose. I don't know much about texturizing a ceiling, but it seems like it was more by chance.

THE ACCIDENTAL TEXT

I never noticed it until the first night I slept in my bed after my mom died. I'd been staying at the hospital with her, and then in my old bedroom at my parents' house after she passed. I was trying to be a comfort to my dad, but really it was more comforting for me to be there. Devon stayed with us, too, for a while.

When I finally came back to the apartment, I lay down in my bed and just stared at the ceiling, and that's when I saw it. That perfectly shaped heart. I wondered if it was meant to be—a little token from my mom, silly as it was.

But this morning I'm feeling a little cynical. And I'm seeing it for what it probably is. Just a happy mistake from a texturizing gun ... or machine ... or whatever the heck they use to do that.

It all feels contrived. All this texting I've been doing, all these signs I've been seeking. It feels like she can't hear me. I believe in heaven; I believe she's moved on to another place where she's whole and no longer suffering. But right now, it all feels a bit far-fetched. Maybe I *am* in the anger phase.

I feel my phone vibrate at the end of my bed and I sit up to grab it, wondering what Hannah needs in the next room.

But it's not from Hannah. My screen says I have a text from ... my mom.

My *mom*? I scream and throw the phone down on my bed, watching as it bounces a couple of times before landing facedown.

I know it's not from her, because even as hard as I've wished for that to be a thing, I know it's not a thing.

Who could it be? Someone from my family, obviously. Only one of them would have access.

My dad, maybe? He might have been missing my mom and booted up her phone. But he doesn't know her passcode—he could never remember it. It's my grandma's—my mom's mom's—birthday, which is why my dad can never remember. But also, my dad is terrible with all dates and numbers. Anytime he'd needed to open the phone when my mom was in the hospital, he'd have me or Chelsea do it, or call one of us for the passcode if we weren't there. He said he didn't need any more numbers in his head. Maybe he remembered? Or figured out how to bypass it? That doesn't sound like him.

But it must be him. And that means ... oh gosh, that means he's read my thought dumps—the texts I've been sending to my mom. And he thinks I need mental help, which, let's face it, I probably do.

He's now texted me back to tell me we need to talk. He'll probably never look at me the same. From now on, I'll be the daughter that texted her dead mom's phone. This is how he will always think of me.

I need to take a breath—take a moment. If I really think about it, nothing here points to my dad. He's not very tech savvy, and he really is so terrible at remembering numbers. It's possible that it's not him.

Which means, even worse ... it's Devon. Or Chelsea. Oh, please don't let it be Chelsea. *Anyone* but her. I take it back. I hope it's my dad.

THE ACCIDENTAL TEXT

I feel sick to my stomach as I reach for the phone. I need to know. I have so much damage control to do. So much explaining.

I pick up the phone, put in my passcode, and click on my texting app. The one that now has a little "1" in the corner, notifying me that I have a message.

I puff air out my mouth and click on my mom's name, highlighted at the top.

> **Mom:** Hey there. So, I'm not sure how to tell you this, but I just recently changed my number, and this is the number they gave me.

What? I look down at my phone, and then up at my white farmhouse-style dresser across the room, and then down at my phone again. I quickly text back.

> **Maggie:** This must be a mistake. This number belongs to my mom.

It *belonged* to my mom, I guess. But it's still hers. My dad told me he kept the number. I asked him to keep it for a while, and he said he would. It's only been three months since she passed. He didn't cancel her line, did he? Surely this must wrong.

My phone vibrates in my hand.

> **Mom:** I figured that, but I just got a new phone and a new number, and this is the number they assigned me.

I swallow, feeling confused. My brain suddenly feels like it's waterlogged.

My phone vibrates again.

> **Mom:** I'm really sorry about your mom, by the way.

I put a hand to my chest, my breaths coming in rapid succession. How can this be? This must be a mistake. How could this person have my mom's number? And if my dad did, by some awful chance, cancel her account at some point, wouldn't my texts start coming back to me as undeliverable? I'm so confused.

I pick up the phone and text back.

> **Maggie:** I think there's been some kind of mistake. This number shouldn't have been given out.

I look up again at my dresser. My mom's dark wood jewelry box is sitting on the top. We all got to take something after she died. Something to have that was hers. I chose the jewelry box because she's had it since I was young. It's scratched and well used, but every time I look at it, it reminds me of her. It's also where my necklace, the one with her initial, currently hangs.

I take a few cleansing breaths, using the jewelry box as a focal point. There's clearly been a mistake.

I pull up my dad's number and call him.

"Magpie," he says when he answers.

"Did you end Mom's phone contract?" I begin with no preamble. I don't have time for small talk.

There's silence on the end of the line.

"Dad?"

"I'm here," he says.

THE ACCIDENTAL TEXT

"Did you get rid of Mom's phone number?" I ask again, with an unmistakable accusatory note in my voice.

"I did," he says on a breath. "It ... it was a waste, Mags. There was no reason to keep it."

"Dad!"

"I'm sorry."

"I asked you to keep it." I feel tears prick my eyes.

"Why did you want to keep it so badly?"

There's too much to explain and, honestly, I don't want to tell him right now. I may never want to tell him.

"It's ... nothing. When?"

"When?"

"When did you get rid of it?"

Silence again.

"Dad?"

"Um ..." I can see him in my head, rubbing his chin the way he does when he's been caught.

"Dad?"

"About three months ago," he says.

I let out a gasp, throwing my phone on my bed again.

I can hear him saying my name, his voice sounding tiny and far away.

Damage control. *Must do damage control.*

I pick my phone back up and hear him say, "How did you find out?"

"I called it. To hear her voicemail." The lie rolls off my tongue.

I hadn't actually done that yet, because hearing her voice felt like too much. I have a bunch of her voice mails saved for a rainy day but haven't been able to bring myself to listen to any.

My dad takes a breath. "Oh, Magpie," he says, his voice cracking just slightly.

"I don't understand why you got rid of her number," I say, trying to keep the wobble out of my voice.

"I didn't understand why you wanted to keep it, honestly. She couldn't take it with her. Seemed … kinda silly."

I exhale slowly, a single tear falling down my cheek. I focus again on the jewelry box.

I know it didn't make sense, even when I asked for him to keep the phone. But it felt too soon to get rid of it. It felt so final. Chelsea and Devon agreed with me. At least I thought they did. Now that I think of it, it could have been only me petitioning to keep the phone.

"It's … I just …" I stammer over my words, not sure what to say.

"It's just a phone, Mags."

I know this; I know it's just a phone. But it was *her* phone. My mom's. And now it's not. No one really understands.

"You're right," I say. "It's just a phone."

I tell my dad that I love him and that I'll see him at work. I hang up and lie back dramatically on my pillow. After a bit, I pick up my phone and text the question I really need an answer to.

Maggie: How long have you had this number?

Mom: …

THE ACCIDENTAL TEXT

I wait, watching the three dots stare at me. They appear and then disappear, only to reappear again.

I stare up at the ceiling while I await the answer. After a minute of this, my phone vibrates in my hand and I look down at the screen.

> **Mom:** For about two weeks now

"TWO WEEKS?" I screech and cover my mouth with the hand not holding my phone.

Two weeks is a long time and *a lot* of texts. At least one a day. And maybe sometimes more, depending on how I was feeling at the time.

I think about all the things I could have talked about in the past two weeks. It's so much my addled brain can't even narrow it down right now.

My phone vibrates in my hand.

> **Mom:** I'm so sorry. I should have told you before. I just felt bad. You seemed like you needed to vent.

I was definitely venting. What the hell did I tell this person?

I start scrolling back through the most recent texts I've sent to my mom. Seeing words pop out like *worst period ever*, and something about my boobs, and oh my gosh—an entire text yesterday about Dawson's butt.

And for the past two weeks I was texting all this to a stranger. There was someone on the other end.

My phone vibrates again.

> **Mom:** So, I thought I should tell you. I'm sorry it took me so long.

I stare at the phone. I have no idea what to say back. Do I get mad and say, *Yeah, you should have said something, you stalker!* Or *No worries! Happens to us all!* But this doesn't happen to people. And this person isn't really a stalker, because it's not like they searched me out ... even if they were reading my texts without saying anything. My secret texts to my mom who can't even read them.

I decide to take the high road. It's not this person's fault I'm having a crisis.

> **Maggie:** Thank you for telling me. Sorry for the mix-up.
>
> **Mom:** No problem

I let out a breath. Everything is fine. I'll never see this person. It's probably some middle-aged woman or something. Or maybe a grandma. I don't owe them any explanations. Although I'm sure whoever it is can gather exactly what was happening.

I look down at my phone, and the three dots are back. My phone vibrates as a new text comes in.

> **Mom:** Just FYI—from a guy's perspective, I think you should definitely tell Dawson how you feel.

My eyes go wide. I drop my phone, pull the pillow from under my head, and scream as loudly as I can into it.

THE ACCIDENTAL TEXT

So, not a grandma. Not even a woman. A guy. A man. I've been texting my deepest thoughts ... to a man. A stranger man.

That's it. I need to escape. I need a plan. I've been living the past year like a nun—I might as well be one. Sister Maggie has a ring to it.

My phone vibrates again. I pull the pillow off my face to look at it.

> **Mom:** I hope that wasn't too forward. Sorry again. About your mom.
>
> **Maggie:** Thank you. Can you possibly delete all the texts I sent your phone? Please?
>
> **Mom:** Of course
>
> **Maggie:** Thanks. I feel super weird right now that I was texting a complete stranger.
>
> **Mom:** I'm Chase. Now you have a name. So, not complete strangers.

I shake my head at my phone, picturing what this guy might look like on the other end. What would a guy who reads texts from a stranger for two weeks before telling her look like? He's probably a computer genius or something. He wears short-sleeve button-up white shirts and knows every line of *Star Wars*. Not the prequels or the new sequels. Only the three originals. He's a *Star Wars* puritan. That's how I will picture this Chase person.

Like that show *Chuck*. No ... Zachary Levi is much too handsome to be on the other end of my texts.

Maggie: I'm Maggie. Thanks again for deleting the texts.

Mom: Sure thing. Take care, Maggie.

I set my phone down next to me. Well, that's that, then.

I feel so many things right now. Embarrassed would probably be the main feeling. But I also feel a bit betrayed by my dad. Well, betrayed seems a bit extreme. How about bamboozled? Although you can't really be bamboozled if the person doing the bamboozling had no idea he was doing it. Maybe it's more like disappointment.

I do feel some relief that my deepest thoughts aren't out there on someone's phone anymore, but along with that relief comes another realization: My mom's phone is gone. There's no more texting her. No more writing her in secret. The tether is gone.

Tears spring to my eyes. No more texts. How am I supposed to cope now? I guess I could journal. I could pretend like I'm still texting my mom on a journaling app or something. But even as I think that, I know it won't be the same. When I would write a text and hit send, it felt cathartic. It felt proactive, in a way. It felt like a connection.

And now that connection is gone.

Chapter 6

"That's hilarious," I declare to Dawson, laughing out loud.

We're standing in the lobby of the shop, by the check-in desk. He's wearing navy-blue coveralls and a bright smile. It honestly deserves awards, that smile of his.

He's been telling me about something ridiculous that Chad did, and while it was funny, it wasn't exactly hilarious. But this is me trying to flirt. I think. I'm rusty.

It's been two weeks since I found out I was texting a complete stranger. It's been hard. Harder than I thought. I've taken to talking to my mom in my head. But it doesn't have the same feeling.

I deleted the number from my phone so I don't accidentally send a text to that guy again. It felt like a stab in the gut when I hit that gray circle with the x in the center and deleted her number. It's not her number anymore. It's Chase's.

At least I get to keep all the texts I sent her. Not that I plan on looking at them anytime soon. I don't want to lose them, though. Or the texts she sent me before she died. I'm not ready to look at those either.

My dad tried to talk to me about it again when I saw him at work, but I just told him it was no big deal. Even though it was. I couldn't tell him that I've been spam texting some poor guy. I get a little uncomfortable chill up my spine when I think about it. So I try *really* hard not to.

I guess I understand why my dad didn't tell me he canceled the number. I would have thrown a fit. I still wanted to but had to stop myself from verbalizing my anger because there would have been too many questions. So I only told him that I would have liked to have known. He apologized again, and that was that.

Well, I wish that was that. It feels like there's another part of my life that's missing now, and the hole in my heart that formed when my mom died feels like it will never close.

But today I woke up and decided that despite this hole in my heart, I need to get back to my life. And since I'd like to have Dawson in my life—romantically speaking—I need to *make my move*.

Actually, last night over Korean food that Halmoni made us, Hannah made me swear on my favorite One Direction sweatshirt that I would do it. She promised to chop it into little bits if I didn't. She's always looking for reasons to get rid of that sweatshirt.

Threats aside, she's right. I can't keep shuffling my feet and doing what I'm doing and expect life to change.

So now I'm standing in front of Dawson, in the empty front lobby of Cooper's. I'd say it was fate or the universe, but I saw him walking by and asked him to come over and chat with me. I'm going to keep it simple and just ask him to lunch. No big deal. I've got this.

"So, Dawson," I say, after taking a big breath because I really *don't* have this. But I'm going to fake it until I make it. Which is something my mom used to say.

She also used to give us a kiss for good luck anytime we were doing something challenging or daring. If she were here right now, she'd kiss me on the cheek, probably pat me on the butt, and tell me to go for it.

Dawson looks at me, his eyebrows raised in question.

"I was thinking—"

"Hey, Dawson," Robin, our front desk girl, interrupts me as she takes a seat at the high-top desk we're standing in front of. She's a tiny thing, with straight blonde hair and crystal-blue eyes.

She'd asked me to watch the front desk while she used the restroom, which is why I was standing in the front lobby in the first place. It just worked out that Dawson happened to walk by.

I hired Robin. She's got a lot of energy and is a great fit for the front desk—the first representation of our company when clients come through the front door. What I didn't know is that she has the worst possible timing. Not that I would have asked her that in the interview.

Robin looks to me. "Thanks for watching the desk, Maggie. I appreciate it."

"No problem," I say. I turn to look at Dawson. He smiles and I swear his eye twinkles. It could be the overhead lighting reflecting in his pupil, but it seemed like there was an honest-to-God twinkle.

"You ... were saying something?" he asks, his lips still curving upward.

"Yeah, I ..." I stop myself and look at Robin and then back at Dawson. This just got weird. I can't ask Dawson out in front of Robin. She's my employee. And what if he rejects me? I don't want an audience for that.

I'll just ask him to come to my office, and then it will be go time. I tug on the *k* pendant on my necklace. Maybe it will give me courage.

You can do this, Maggie.

I open my mouth, but then Robin starts. "Hey, Dawson," she says, her eyes on him, giving him an award-winning smile. "Do you want to go to lunch today?"

Wait ... what?

"Sure," Dawson says, giving her a grin, those beautiful pearly whites fully exposed.

I look at Robin and then at Dawson. She just asked him out in front of me ... to lunch. Exactly what I was going to do only seconds ago—only I talked myself out of it because it would have been awkward. But Robin just said the words. No big deal. And he said yes, without flinching or even a momentary pause. Just like that. It was so easy.

I stand there, totally mouth breathing, stunned by what just transpired. Dawson looks to me and then back at Robin, and then back to me again.

"Do you ... want to come with us?" he asks, as if he could read my mind.

THE ACCIDENTAL TEXT

"I …" I start but then stop myself.

"Actually," Robin interjects, "who would watch the front desk if we both went?"

If Robin is playing some game and doesn't want me to come, she's just offered the perfect excuse. It's usually me that takes over front desk duties for her breaks.

"That's true," I say.

"We could find someone else?" Dawson throws it out there, nodding his head at Robin and then me.

We probably could, but lunch with Dawson *and* Robin doesn't sound all that appealing to me. I think I'd feel like a third wheel.

"You know, I think I better take care of the front desk," I say, and then give them a fake smile. "Rain check?"

"Of course," Dawson says, directing that gorgeous grin at me.

"Well, I better … get back to work," I say. "Give me a call when you're leaving, Robin."

What just happened?

Later that day after most of the staff has left for the night, I sit in my office and stare at my phone.

I called Hannah after Robin unknowingly stole my lunch date, and she lectured me for three minutes about how I'm going to miss my chance and how right she was and blah, blah, blah. Then she had to hang up really fast when her mom caught her on the phone. Sometimes Hannah working for her mom makes me feel like we're teenagers again.

Right now, I'd be texting my mom, telling her about my day. Venting about my feelings. Instead, I'm sitting here staring at my phone, feeling like there's no one I can talk to. I was getting so much off my chest with those texts to my mom. And now … now who do I have? My family is dealing with their own grief, in their own way. There's Hannah, of course, but it feels like she's not really getting it. How could she? She has both parents still, even if her mom and dad are divorced and her dad lives in California.

I feel like I'm in a big sucky club for one.

I hear a throat clear and look up to see Devon walking into my office.

"What're you staring at so intently?" he asks, with a chin dip toward my phone.

I put it facedown on my desk and lean back in my chair. "Nothing," I say.

He walks in, doing that Devon swagger he does, wearing jeans and a black T-shirt, and takes a seat at the chair in front of my desk.

"I've been tasked with checking on you," he says, leaning forward, resting his elbows on his knees.

"Checking on me?"

"Chelsea." He only needs to say one word.

I wrinkle my brow. "Why is Chelsea having you check on me?"

That's so Chelsea. Delegation is a strength of hers. She's so good at it, she sometimes delegates delegation.

Devon shrugs. "She thinks you're ... having a hard time with things."

I give Devon a confused look. "Aren't we all having a hard time?"

The corners of his mouth lift up just slightly. "Yeah, but ... you know, with the jump and stuff. She's just worried about you."

Ah, the jump. Yes, I've been trying not to think of it. It's not until May, anyway. There's really no need. Also, when I do think about it, nervousness creeps up my spine and my heart picks up its pace. Just a little, but it's enough to make me think maybe I should just *not* think about it right now. Of course, there's also another nagging part of me that keeps telling me I need to figure myself out now, before it's too late.

For right now, I'll go with avoiding. It's serving me.

"Are you worried about me?" I ask Devon.

He looks at me and shrugs one shoulder. "Not really. You know Chels."

I do know Chelsea. The thing is, she's not far off. I'm not doing so well. I thought I was covering it up ... faking it until I make it.

"I miss her too," Devon says, leaning back in his chair, looking over to the side as he does. Devin doesn't do eye contact while talking about profound things. I think it might be too much for him.

"I know," I say.

One of the things that's gotten me through this is my family. I thought we were pretty close before, but now we have this whole new bond. It's a shared grief, a shared comfort that we're all experiencing this together.

Which is why it makes no sense that I feel as alone as I do. It's just that I never relied on Devon or Chelsea to discuss my feelings, as close as we are. That's always been my mom's job.

But maybe if I tried …

I look at Devon. "I don't feel like myself."

He just nods.

"And I don't know how … to feel like myself."

Devon nods again.

"I really miss myself, you know? The … old me."

Devon nods yet again.

I look at him, and he looks back at me. I can tell by the look on his face that he's not here to offer me any words of wisdom or comfort.

Well. At least I tried.

I take a breath. "What have you been up to?"

I've learned with Devon, if all else fails, talk about *him*. It's probably his favorite topic.

Devon reaches up and scratches the back of his neck. "Just work."

"Any new women in your life?" I don't know why I ask this. I don't really want to know.

"Funny you should ask," he says, a mischievous look on his face.

"No," I say, knowing exactly where he's going with that. "Why?"

THE ACCIDENTAL TEXT

"We've already gone over this. You're not dating Robin. I told you the rules." I give him my death stare.

I knew when I hired Robin that she'd be on Devon's radar. She's his type: petite, blonde. So before she even started, I had words with him about keeping his paws off. Except for her being a lunch date stealer, I like Robin and she does a great job.

I think I made things worse, though. Devon has only had eyes for her since she started. It's like keeping her off-limits made her even more attractive. The forbidden fruit.

"Sorry, Devon, it's not happening."

"Fine," he says. "How's Hannah?" The corner of his mouth lifts up, a sly look.

I give him another death stare. Hannah is also off-limits. Although I should really let him try. She'd eat him alive. But there's that .0001 percent chance that he'd get through her walls and get past her dislike of men, and I'm not willing to take that chance. Don't get me wrong, I want Hannah to find someone, just not my player brother.

Devon holds his hands up, palms toward me. "I know, I know," he says. He stands up from his chair. "I'll keep your dumb rules."

"Thank you."

"See you tomorrow," he says as he leaves.

"Thanks for the chat," I say, my tone oozing sarcasm.

I'm not sure why Chelsea thought sending Devon to talk to me was a good idea. This time her delegation skills are sorely lacking.

Chapter 7

I'm getting ready for work when my phone beeps, telling me I have a text.

It's been a week since Robin snatched my lunch date, and now it would seem that Robin and Dawson are a *thing*. Yep. There is, without a doubt, a thing happening between the two of them.

So Hannah was right—he didn't stay single for long, and now I can go back to my regularly scheduled pining. It's fine. This is a more comfortable place for me, sitting on the sidelines.

The truth is, I'm not in the best place myself. So why was I even bothering? I'm still in the midst of my grief, still not feeling like myself, still being a chicken. I also still have to jump out of a plane in two months and haven't even tried to think about that lately.

I've got to fix myself first. I still have no idea how to do that.

I pick up my phone to see that it's from an unsaved number, but it's one I know by heart.

I have exactly five phone numbers memorized: my dad's, Chelsea's, Devon's, Hannah's, and ... my mom's.

THE ACCIDENTAL TEXT

I let my phone see my face for recognition and then watch as it opens up. I click on my texting app and then click on the number.

(480)555-1058: Hi

I pull my face back, tucking my chin inward. This feels suspiciously like one of those messages you get on Facebook from a hacked account where they end up asking you for money. They always start with "Hi."

Do I write back? What would I even say? Such a strange thing to text someone. Just one word.

My phone beeps in my hand and I look down at the screen.

(480)555-1058: Sorry. This is Chase.

Okay, so if this is a hacker, they know a lot. I take the bait, just in case.

Maggie: Hi, Chase.

I sit on the edge of my bed as the three dots appear, each dot changing from light gray to dark in subsequent order as he types his reply.

(480)555-1058: How are you?

How … am … I? Crap. He's going to ask me for money, isn't he? I'm such an idiot.

Maggie: I'm doing okay

I type out "Do you need anything?" but then realize that I was just opening the door perfectly. So I delete it.

The dots appear again. I stare at my screen, wondering when the words will appear. After a while of watching the dots going away and then reappearing again, I put my phone down and go to my bathroom to finish getting ready so I'm not late for work.

So strange, Chase texting me out of the blue. It could be a hacker. I haven't really heard of that happening via text, but these days with thousands of hackers on the internet, it wouldn't surprise me.

Just as I've finished getting ready and am standing by my mom's jewelry box, putting my *k* necklace on, I hear my phone beep again.

I walk over to the bed and pick it up.

(480)555-1058: I was just hoping you're doing okay.

Okay. So maybe *not* a hacker trying to steal my money.

I guess that's kind of sweet. Still … a little creepy. But I did pour my heart out to this poor guy, unknowingly. I also complained about my period and went on and on about Dawson's butt, so I'm the real creeper in this scenario.

Still, I suppose I can see why he'd wonder how I was feeling.

Maggie: I'm hanging in there.

This is my standard answer. *I'm hanging in there.* Sometimes it's by a thick cord, and sometimes it's by silly

THE ACCIDENTAL TEXT

string. It just depends on the day. Or sometimes the moment.

> **(480)555-1058:** Good
>
> **Maggie:** Thanks for checking up on me.
>
> **(480)555-1058:** I guess I was wondering how long that awful feel-like-you-can't-get-a-good-breath part lasts.

I look at my phone, furrowing my brow. What's he talking about?

> **Maggie:** I'm … sorry?
>
> **(480)555-1058:** Sorry. My mom died three days ago. It was sudden.

My heart clenches. I sit back down on the edge of my bed. I know that awful feel-like-you-can't-get-a-good-breath part. I know it so well.

> **Maggie:** I'm so sorry
>
> **(480)555-1058:** Thanks. I'm sorry to text you like this. I feel kinda lost.
>
> **Maggie:** I get it

I run my tongue over my lips, looking down at my phone. I feel almost a responsibility right now, which is ridiculous. This is a complete stranger. But I know that desperation. I know exactly how he's feeling. All too well.

> **Maggie:** How old was she?

It was always helpful to talk about my mom after she died. When people who didn't know her wanted to know more, telling her story, or even just a tiny part of it, helped. It still does.

> **(480)555-1058:** 59

Only a year older than my mom. My heart does that clenching thing again. Too young. That's too young to die.

> **Maggie:** My mom was 58
>
> **(480)555-1058:** Gone too soon
>
> **Maggie:** Yes

The three dots are back.

> **(480)555-1058:** This is weird. I'm sorry. I feel out of my mind. I was thinking of the texts you sent, and I just had this thought to text you. This is probably not what you need right now. Thanks for writing me back.
>
> **(480)555-1058:** I won't bother you again.

I take a breath. I could let him go. I could just send him a heart emoji or something like that and just be done. I could do that …

> **Maggie:** A couple of weeks
>
> **(480)555-1058:** ??
>
> **Maggie:** It took me about two weeks to feel like I could really breathe again.
>
> **(480)555-1058:** Okay. Two weeks.

THE ACCIDENTAL TEXT

> **Maggie:** It's different for everyone, though.
>
> **(480)555-1058:** Not very helpful ;)

I smile at the winking emoji he added to the text. I like a person who can find humor, even in horrible, life-changing situations.

> **Maggie:** Would be nice if they could give you a magic pill to get you through the hard stuff.
>
> **(480)555-1058:** I can see why people turn to other stuff to cope.
>
> **Maggie:** Gotta be careful of that
>
> **(480)555-1058:** Right
>
> **Maggie:** What happened? If you don't mind me asking.
>
> **(480)555-1058:** Car accident

I don't know how to even respond to that. I know what I can't say. Things like: *She's in a better place*, or *It was God's time*, or *Everything happens for a reason*.

We heard so many clichéd comments after my mom passed. It became a running joke with me, Chelsea, and Devon. *Sorry for your loss … Her body is whole now … Sending hugs and prayers* and/or *thoughts*.

I get it. It's hard to know what to say. I still don't know what's right, to be honest. A simple "I'm sorry" seemed to do the trick for me.

I text that to Chase. And I am truly sorry. A car accident that takes your parent away suddenly sounds like such a terrible thing. I got a long goodbye with my mom. I got to tell her how much I loved her so many times before she died. I'm grateful for that.

> **(480)555-1058:** What about your mom?
>
> **Maggie:** Brain tumor. Fast acting. She was gone six months from diagnosis.
>
> **(480)555-1058:** Wow. I'm sorry.
>
> **Maggie:** Thank you
>
> **(480)555-1058:** I appreciate you texting me. I'll let you get back to whatever you're doing.
>
> **Maggie:** You're welcome
>
> **Maggie:** Have to go to work

I look down at my phone, chewing my bottom lip. Not sure if I should type next what I want to type.

> **Maggie:** If you ever need to talk, I'm here.

I hit send before I can overthink it. He'll probably never text me again. Maybe in a few weeks, I can check up on him. It's not like I'll forget his number. I'll probably never forget that number.

My phone beeps.

> **(480)555-1058:** Thanks

Chapter 8

"But is it going to be fun?" my dad asks as he sits at his big, ancient, oak work desk. "We need some fun."

It's Wednesday and Chelsea, Devon, and I are all standing around my dad's desk in his office at the shop, discussing the upcoming party we're having to celebrate the anniversary of Cooper's.

I've had a hard time getting Chase off my mind since we texted yesterday. I never heard from him again. There were quite a few times throughout the day that I found myself picking up my phone to text him back, but I stopped myself. It would be one thing if Chase were a long-lost friend of mine or even an acquaintance. But he's a stranger. A stranger who now has my mom's phone number. That's our only connection. That and now I guess the fact that we've both lost our moms.

My mind keeps going back to him, though. Back to his texts. It's hard to keep myself in the present.

But I need to because I can see that today my dad is antsy. He seems jittery ... possibly hopped up on caffeine? And Chelsea looks like her head might pop off at any minute.

Which means everything is going as expected.

My dad's office is just down the hall from mine. But, unlike mine, his has papers all over his desk and also a half-eaten sandwich wrapped in plastic that I'm pretty sure was from yesterday. Thank goodness there's plastic on it. This is Arizona, for crap's sake. Ants are a continuous problem.

My mom used to clean up his desk, stating how symbiotic they were. Dad, with his constant stream of thinking and the clutter that comes with it (he might be a tad ADHD), and Mom, with her organization and planning skills. Chelsea is like our mom, I'm a mix of the two, and we're not sure *what* Devon is.

It's been twenty-five years since Cooper's opened. My dad started the shop when Chelsea was four and I was barely a year old. It's been a part of my life since I can remember. I took my first steps in the front room of the small building my dad rented when he was getting things started.

As I grew up, so did the shop. We went from just my dad doing all of the work to a staff of thirty-five. Devon, Chelsea, and I run the day-to-day now, and my dad can just sit back and watch the well-oiled machine he built from the ground up do its thing.

If only that were the case.

Our dad is supposed to be traveling the world right now with Mom, visiting all the things they'd planned to see. Fulfilling so many lifelong wishes. But a large wrench was chucked into those plans when my mom got her diagnosis. They stopped looking toward the future and instead had to react to the present. Hospital visits, specialist calls, hours of research. There were lots of ups and downs and some promising outcomes that then turned out to not be promising. When they both realized that this was their future—and how little time was left—it became more about time, comfort, and long bouts of just being together.

Luckily, my dad had this totally organized business that stayed afloat during those times. Even Chelsea, Devon, and I were able to spend more time away from the shop and with our mom during the last part.

But now that our mom is gone, instead of finding a hobby or taking up golf, my dad has stuck his nose back into the shop.

He's a questioner, my dad. Lots and lots of questions. Even I, his most even-tempered kid, have felt my patience run thin with his questions.

"How can we make this party even better?" he asks, his head moving from me to Chelsea to Devon, and then back to Chelsea.

"We've got it all covered, Dad," Chelsea says, her face and voice indicating that she feels like this is a personal attack on her. Which, of course, it isn't. But Chelsea has headed up most of the decisions for this party, and Devon and I have let her because we know our roles. And also, neither of us wanted to do it.

"I know, Princess," my dad says, and Chelsea visibly relaxes, her shoulders falling just slightly. "I've just been looking forward to this."

"It's going to be great. I've rented the tent and ordered the food, and the DJ is scheduled. There will be an open bar and lots of opportunities to mingle."

All the employees are invited, as well as many of our clients. It's going to be quite the deal, with a big tent set up out in our parking lot. We've also asked some of our clients if they're willing to display some of their cars we've worked on around the outside of the tent. The Lamborghini that is my dad's pride and joy will be front and center. It's currently wrapped in a bright apple-green color with the shop's logo on both doors, the hood, and the trunk.

The ridiculous car was a "business investment." I believe those were the words my dad used when he had the harebrained idea to buy it. I think he just always wanted a car like that. He got a killer deal on a two-year-old Huracán. He's now had it for two years. He still sighs when he looks at it.

It does look great for the business, even if it's the most uncomfortable car I've ever been in. It was not designed for a woman like me, who needs space for her purse and also doesn't have the thigh muscles to get out of the thing without looking like a clumsy child just learning to walk. Let's just say a fairly tall girl of five foot eight plus heels is not a fit for a Lamborghini.

It's not like I use it. It's my dad's baby. Sometimes he'll let Devon take it out or let him race it when we do our charity race, Drives for Dreams, but it mostly stays at the shop, parked up in front of the store. We regularly change out the wrap for clients to see how easy it is and how safe it is on the paint.

"Sounds great," my dad says. "What about a comedian?"

We all look at him.

"You know," he says, looking at each of us in turn. "Someone who can make us laugh. Couldn't we all use a laugh?"

I look over at Chelsea and see her throat bob.

"I thought we were just going to keep it casual," she says.

"Yeah, Dad," Devon pipes in. "It's just supposed to be relaxed. No agenda. No big speeches or anything."

"What about a juggler or … maybe a clown?"

This time Chelsea gasps and covers her mouth with her hand. We're supposed to be dressed up for this party. Jugglers and clowns probably wouldn't fit into Chelsea's expectations.

I clear my throat. "I think we're running out of time for all that," I say. "It's in ten days."

"It's going to be great as we planned it, Dad. Don't worry," Devon offers.

My dad reaches up and swipes a hand down his face. "You're right. I was just … trying to amp it up a bit. But let's leave it how it is."

Chelsea lets go of the breath she was clearly holding.

"Are you bringing anyone to the party, Devon?" my dad asks.

"I thought we weren't bringing dates," Chelsea says.

My dad looks to Chelsea. "Mark will be there, won't he?"

"Well, I mean, yeah. But we're married. He swore in his vows that he would be my arm candy till death do us part. I meant I thought we weren't bringing people that won't understand that this isn't just a party—it's also a marketing event."

"Not for me," my dad says. "I plan on having some fun. We all need to have fun. Let's not get caught up in making this about sales."

"I'm sure I could find someone to bring," Devon pipes in, clearly getting on board with this idea.

"I was going to make Hannah come with me," I say.

Really, Hannah insisted that she come.

"Oh, good," Devon gives me a smirk. "Maybe I won't bring someone."

I reach over and grab the back of his arm and pinch him, hard.

Devon cusses, loudly, the words bouncing around the epoxy-finished cement floors of the office. He rubs the back of his arm and gives me a look that I know well. I better watch my back—revenge is coming.

"Devon," my dad says, his voice annoyed. My dad thinks there are better words than cusswords. Our mom, however, enjoyed dropping them freely, and especially for shock value. She was, by most definitions, the quintessential mom. Caring, nurturing, loving ... but with a potty mouth.

THE ACCIDENTAL TEXT

My dad takes a big breath, sitting back in his chair, he weaves his fingers together and places them in his lap. "I'm going to bring June," he announces.

Silence lands on the room. You could hear a pin drop. Or an ant scurry.

After a moment of staring at my dad, I turn my face to my left and right to see that both Chelsea's and Devon's eyes are wide and Devon's mouth is hanging open.

"You—you're bringing June?" I say after I can't take the silence anymore. "As your ... date?"

June, our neighbor? The widow?

My dad just looks at all of us. "As my friend," he says.

I feel the tension in the room take a big dramatic breather. I reach up and grab the *k* pendant and run it back and forth on the chain.

My dad takes another big inhale. "She's been very helpful with ... everything. She's been doing the widow thing for a while now. It's been nice to have someone to talk to. So as a thank you, I invited her to the party."

In my peripheral vision I see Devon's back go less rigid.

"Well, I think it's great," I say, trying to ease the tension that still hangs in the air. I'm not sure I feel all that great, to be honest.

Just the sheer fact that he's bringing someone to the party that's not our mom is weirding me out. I need to get over myself, though. My dad is a grown man. He can have friends. He just can't fall in love with said friends and then replace my mom and, oh my gosh, is the heat on in here?

"Yeah, Dad," Devon says, his voice void of inflection. "It's … great."

I look to Chelsea to see her nodding her head rapidly, like she's experiencing some sort of tremor.

We are clearly not okay with this.

"Thanks, kids," Dad says. "For all your hard work. I think it will be a great night."

We all say our goodbyes and file out of my dad's office.

I nod at my siblings as we walk down the hallway and, without words, we all go to my office for another sibling meeting.

Chapter 9

Maggie: How are you doing?

It took me twenty minutes of going back and forth to decide to text Chase. I kept buffering with a game on my phone. I'm not sure why I want to. It feels ... weird. But I do it anyway. His last texts still haunt me. I have this need to know how he is.

I'm sitting in my room the next Monday night, after sharing pizza with Hannah and then telling her I was going to go lie down after eating too much.

It wasn't a lie—I really did eat too much. But I also wanted to text Chase. And I had to do it in secret, because I know how Hannah is. She has to know everything. Anytime I'm texting someone in her presence, she asks who it is. She just needs to know. She can't help herself. I've even had to turn off my phone's lock screen text preview because of her snooping ways. It's also why I never texted my mom's phone in front of her. I'd usually escape to my room, like I am right now.

I would totally tell her about Chase, but I'd have to explain the story behind it, and I'm not ready to tell anyone.

I don't know if I ever will be. Every version I come up with in my head ends with me sounding like a crazy person.

The three dots show up on my phone and I feel my pulse pick up from the strangeness of this entire thing.

(480)555-1058: I've been better

So much context in that one message. I feel that ache in my heart again.

Maggie: I understand

(480)555-1058: The funeral was yesterday. Everything feels so final.

I nibble on my bottom lip, not sure what to say next.

My mom's funeral was a blur for me. I remember parts of it so strongly. Like some of the people that were there. And some of the things her friends told me about my mom, things that I didn't know but wanted to remember — to tuck away for a rainy day. My most vivid memory is my oldest niece, Alice, with her arms wrapped around her dad's legs, saying "No, Nana, no" with tears streaming down her face. I won't be able to forget that.

But most of it is bits and pieces put together in my mind. A fuzzy puzzle. The day, as a whole, felt like one big dream. Like I was having an out-of-body experience.

I text Chase back.

Maggie: How was the funeral?

(480)555-1058: It was sad but nice, I guess. Small. How she would have wanted it.

THE ACCIDENTAL TEXT

Tired of seeing my mom's number in my face, I click on the edit button and change the contact name to Chase's. It feels weird to do it since I don't know Chase, but it's better than seeing the number that used to belong to my mom.

I stare at my phone, wondering how I should respond. Or if I should. My phone beeps before I have a chance.

>**Chase:** How are you?
>
>**Maggie:** Pretty good
>
>**Chase:** That's what I like to hear. Pretty good. It means there's hope. I haven't felt any kind of good in nearly a week.

Do I tell him that I cried in the shower this morning? Better not.

>**Maggie:** It takes time
>
>**Chase:** How long would you say?
>
>**Maggie:** I'm on month four
>
>**Chase:** And how has month four been?

I look up from my phone, at my dresser with my mom's jewelry box sitting on it. How has month four been? I don't really know. I'm still getting over not texting my mom's phone anymore. That part's been hard. It was helping, more than I think I realized.

But if I look back to the first month and how difficult that was and compare it to now, I'm definitely better. I don't feel like myself still, and I'm starting to wonder if this is the new me. That thought scares me. I don't want to be this new anxious/chicken me. I miss my old self.

My phone beeps and I look down at my screen.

> **Chase:** That bad, huh?

I smile at my phone.

> **Maggie:** I'm definitely better. Less of the super tough moments. But I still don't feel like . . . me.
>
> **Chase:** I get that. What is it for you that makes you not feel like yourself?

I look up from my screen, wondering how to answer this. I don't want to go into details with this stranger. But also, what have I got to lose?

> **Maggie:** I guess I'm more anxious than I used to be.
>
> **Chase:** Like something else will go wrong.

I take in a quick breath. This is exactly how I feel. I keep wondering ... what could be next? What other piece of bad news will come my way? And this time, will I survive? Will it crush me into tiny bits until I'm just a pile of pebbles?

> **Maggie:** Yes! I can't shake it.
>
> **Chase:** I've been on edge myself, worried about that. So this is a long-term side effect, then. Good to know.
>
> **Maggie:** I'm pretty sure it's different for everyone.
>
> **Chase:** Pretty sure I'm not bouncing back from this anytime soon.

THE ACCIDENTAL TEXT

Now is the time to text back something cliché like, *Of course you'll bounce back*! Or *Time heals all wounds*, and then add a heart emoji for good measure. But those are the kind of answers someone who doesn't get what you're going through says.

I know. I know what he's experiencing. The what-ifs. The why-mes. The if-onlys. I know them all.

> **Maggie:** I'm starting to wonder if you ever fully do.
>
> **Chase:** But it does get better?
>
> **Maggie:** That's how it is for me. I feel … better. Not all the time, and not with everything. But I'm not huddled in the corner of my room anymore.
>
> **Chase:** How did you know that's where I am?
>
> **Chase:** Are you stalking me?

Chase's ability to make a joke, even this small one, surprises me. Like the funeral, the first week after my mom died is a blur. But unlike the funeral, I don't really remember much of anything. No bits and pieces to tie together. I remember the day it happened—everything about that day is clear in my head. But for the next week, I don't have much memory of it. Maybe I did make jokes. Maybe I did laugh. But I just don't remember.

I text him back.

> **Maggie:** You caught me
>
> **Chase:** You're a terrible stalker, then. Totally gave it away.

> **Maggie:** Is this your expertise?
>
> **Chase:** I've never tried. How does one start?
>
> **Maggie:** I can't give away my secrets.
>
> **Chase:** Damn

I smile at my phone. This was not what I was expecting or hoping for when I checked up on Chase. I didn't really have expectations. Just that I wanted to make sure he was okay.

My phone vibrates in my hand.

> **Chase:** Thanks for checking up on me. It made this day better.
>
> **Maggie:** You're welcome

I lay the phone down next to me and stare up at the ceiling again, feeling ... lighter. There's no real reason. No one thing I can pinpoint. Maybe it was just reaching out to Chase. I didn't set out to make his day better; I just wanted to check in on him.

My mom would sometimes tell us, when we were having a hard time with something, to look outside ourselves for answers. I never quite got what she meant until right now. Being there for someone else ... well, it sort of feels like a balm on my soul.

Is that what I've been missing? Have I been spending all this time worried about trying to find myself when I should have been looking outward?

It felt so good to check up on Chase, to do something for someone else. Maybe that's been my problem all along. I'm

THE ACCIDENTAL TEXT

having one of those moments where I feel like I've solved all the world's mysteries. Like I want to share it with everyone. I could write a book. I might be asked to do a TED talk.

Or ... maybe I shouldn't put the cart before the wagon. Or before the horse ... or is it the horse before the wagon? Whatever that saying is. I should probably test out this theory a little more.

I look at that heart on my ceiling. "You were right, Mom," I tell it.

I don't think that heart showed up only after my mom died. I'm not fanciful like that. I think it was there all along, but I was never compelled to look for it until she was gone. Maybe she wanted me to find it? Maybe she wanted me to see that she was still here, watching over me. Or maybe it's just from a texturizing gun and there's no significance whatsoever. But for now, I'm going to choose to think there's a reason, that it was on purpose, and that there are no coincidences.

Chapter 10

"Why do you look like you want to throw a rock through that window?" Chelsea says, snapping me out of my trance.

"Huh?" I shake my head a couple of times, trying to bring my brain back around.

"You look super pissed," she says.

"I'm fine. I was just thinking about something."

I was staring out the window, at Dawson and Robin walking together toward his car to go to lunch. I wish I could have snapped a picture for Hannah, since she doesn't believe me about them being together. I could have had the perfect proof. Robin saying something and Dawson laughing. A big ole guffaw kind of laugh. Head thrown back and everything. Then he put his arm around her and gave her a very cozy side hug. The kind where they rested their heads together.

And here I sit, watching the front desk, like a loser.

That's it. I'm firing Robin.

Except that I can't do that. Because it would be wrong. And Robin is really good at her job. I just wish she was a little bit ... not so attractive. Or funny. I mean, I haven't

THE ACCIDENTAL TEXT

actually heard her say anything funny, but clearly Dawson has.

Dang you, Robin, and your stupid humor and pretty face.

I even tested out my theory today, to look outside myself more. I was extra nice to her and told her how pretty she looked. It didn't make me feel any better. Not one bit. So I guess I'm done with that. Back to my regular inward-looking self.

"Is it June?"

"What?"

"Our neighbor? Coming to the party with Dad?" Chelsea furrows her brow at me, a mix of confusion and concern on her face.

"Yeah," I say, taking a split second to decide that this is the path I should go down. I don't want to explain this whole thing to Chelsea. She doesn't even know about my Dawson crush to begin with. Besides, it's a moot point.

And anyway, I *am* kind of annoyed by my dad bringing June to the party.

Chelsea turns so we're face-to-face over the high-top desk. She's got her I'm-the-big-sister face on. Oh, fun.

"Maggie, Dad is a grown man. We need to be okay with however he finds happiness." She gives me a closed-mouth smile and a quick dip of her chin.

I see right through it. "That was well rehearsed. Good job, you."

Chelsea lets her shoulders slouch. "I'm trying. I don't like it either."

"I know. But Dad said they were going as friends," I say confidently.

Chelsea eyes me wearily. "You fell for that?"

It's my turn to furrow my brow at her. "Well ... didn't you?"

"No," Chelsea says, her voice almost sounding shrill. "After some thought, I think that's Dad's way of gently letting us in on this thing."

"You're lying."

She just gives me a shrug of her shoulders in response.

"Who's lying?" Devon asks, walking up to us, the glass front door swinging behind him as he enters the lobby of the shop. He comes to stand by Chelsea, both of them now looking at me.

"Chelsea thinks Dad and June aren't just friends," I say, reaching up and tugging on the pendant on my necklace.

"Yeah," he says, like he can't believe I hadn't figured that out.

"You too?" I ask, my eyes wide.

"I think he's just trying to tell us in that Dad way like he always does," Devon says, and Chelsea turns her face toward him, giving him a nod of approval. Since when did these two bond? I'm supposed to be the glue that holds the two of them together. I'm the middle child; it's my job.

I feel my stomach sink as the realization settles on me. Dad ... and June?

"I don't like it either," Devon says in response to my scrunched-up facial expression. "I've caught him twice now texting on his phone and smiling at it." He shakes his head.

THE ACCIDENTAL TEXT

"Is that who you think he's been texting?" Chelsea asks, letting her jaw fall.

My mind flashes back to the jump—or the attempted jump—when I noticed my dad texting rapidly on his phone. At the time, I was doing my own rapid texting to my mom, so I didn't think much of it. But now that I think of it, there have been other times I've caught him doing the same. I just wrote it off as no big deal. Could he have been texting June? And that long ago?

"What do we do?" Chelsea asks.

Devon lifts his shoulders briefly. "Not much we can do."

"I'm suddenly feeling offended that he's been texting June so much, when all I ever get from him is one-word replies to my texts," Chelsea says. "I thought he was just bad at texting."

Of course Chelsea would make this about her.

"I think we're making a lot of assumptions here," I say.

"How can we find out?" Devon asks.

I twist my lips to the side. "Well ..."

"Well, what?" He squints his blue eyes at me.

"He's in the shop right now, trying to help your friend Chad learn how to wrap a door properly. No one seems to be able to teach him." I give my best look of disapproval to my brother.

Devon doesn't respond. He doesn't seem to care at all that Chad has probably cost us more money than he's made us.

"So what?" Chelsea says, her impatience starting to show.

Devon snaps his fingers and points at me. "His phone—"

"Is probably in the top drawer of his desk," I finish.

"Oh," Chelsea says, her eyes bright with understanding.

Without words, I set the main phone to go to voicemail and the three of us walk quietly to our dad's office, watching our backs as we go.

Sure enough, once we get there, there's no sign of our dad, and like the predictable man he is, the phone is sitting in his top drawer.

Chelsea is the one who grabs it. She holds it in her hand and looks at it like it's a foreign object she's never seen before. Then she holds the phone out to me.

"I don't think we should do this," she says.

"You mean you don't want to do this but you want me to," I say, giving her a knowing look.

"Yes," she says.

I take it from her and press the button on the older phone—the one we've been bothering our dad to upgrade—and watch the screen light up. No passcode, because passcodes are for people who can remember numbers, and our dad is not one of those people.

I go to the texting app and open it up, holding the phone out in front of me as we all gather around. Devon stands in a position so he can see the door in case Dad walks in and catches us.

This all seems so familiar. Like we've done this before. But I don't recall snooping on our parents like this. Not the three of us. What I do recall is me and Devon sneaking into

THE ACCIDENTAL TEXT

Chelsea's room and reading her diary, which was such a waste of snooping—it was so boring and *all* about boys.

I click on June's name, and there's definitely been some texting going on. The first few texts seem benign. Just chitchat, not a big deal. I feel my heart lighten a bit. Chelsea and Devon have it all wrong. Dad really is just friends with June.

Using my thumb, I scroll down, watching as older texts populate on the screen. I'm a mix of emotions—worry that we might get caught, anxiety about what we might find, and a dash of shame for snooping like this.

"Good hell, they use a lot of emojis," Devon says, pointing at the phone. He's right; it's mostly smiley faces and a few heart eyes sprinkled in. There's nothing of interest in actual wordage, though. Just June asking my dad to lunch and my dad sending back an emoji thumbs-up. Then my dad asking if her power went out, to which she sends back a thumbs-down emoji.

This is stupid. This is definitely like finding Chelsea's diary.

I scroll down again, watching some new texts populate.

My stomach does a little bobbing thing as these texts fill the screen. There's one with just a kissy-face emoji. And another text from my dad asking when she's coming over.

When I scroll down again, there's a text from June calling him "Babe," and then there's another one that's just the fire emoji, and next to it, it says "our song." To which my dad has sent back a fire emoji. There really are so many emojis going on here.

"*Our* song?" Chelsea reads the text out loud.

"What song is that?" Devon asks. "And why would they have a song?"

"Is there a fire song?" I ask, looking from Chelsea to Devon.

Chelsea pulls her phone from her back pocket and, pulling up her music app, does a search.

"There's a song called 'Fire,'" she says. "By ... the Pointer Sisters?"

"Play it," Devon says.

She hits play and then turns up the volume.

We all gather in tighter, listening to the song as it begins, the chords of an electric guitar playing a catchy rhythm with a strong bass line.

Chelsea lifts the phone up higher so we can hear it better through her tiny speaker. The singer starts out and we listen to the words, taking turns glancing at each other. I wonder if we got this right. Maybe June meant a different song.

The words are benign enough. Something about the car radio and someone's saying they're a liar. But then all of our eyes go wide as the opening verse moves to three-part harmony and suddenly they're singing about kissing and fire and, oh my gosh, this song is ... well, it's sexy and a little dirty and I kind of wish we never did this.

Chelsea, also looking a little green, stops the song and the three of us just stand there, staring at each other.

"What the hell?" Devon finally says.

I look down at the phone in my hand, my dad's phone. The screen has now timed out and gone black.

THE ACCIDENTAL TEXT

"Put it back," Chelsea says, almost in a panic. "Just, put it back now."

I do as she says, and then without words the three of us walk down the hall to my office.

"So this is bigger than we thought," I say as soon as the door is shut.

"What do we do?" Devon asks.

"What can we do?" says Chelsea.

We all look at each other.

You can tell when the answer hits all of us. There's nothing. We can do nothing.

Chelsea lets out a breath. "We could be supportive?"

"No," Devon says, shaking his head.

"Dev," she chides. "He's our dad. Don't we want him to be happy?"

"But what about the dog idea?" I offer.

She shakes her head at me. "If this is what Dad wants …"

"Aren't we getting ahead of ourselves?" Devon says. "This could just be dating. Or maybe … you know … other *stuff*."

"Gross!" I say loudly. Chelsea covers her mouth with her hand.

"No," I say after a few seconds of silence. "Devon is right. We're getting ahead of ourselves."

"But they have a song," Chelsea says. "That sounds more serious to me."

"That's true," I say.

Silence lands on the room again.

"I think it's crazy," Devon says. "Mom's only been gone four months."

"I know," Chelsea says, putting a hand on his arm. "But I read an article the other day that said widowed men who were in good relationships get remarried really fast. I didn't think it was true in our case, but now …"

"You guys, he's bringing a date to the party. Not a wife," I say. "And as far as we're supposed to know, she's only a friend."

We really are getting ahead of ourselves.

Devon runs his fingers through his thick brown hair. "I guess I don't even want him bringing a date."

We all nod solemnly at each other.

"I think we should just wait and see what happens," Chelsea says.

Chapter 11

Chase: When will I stop counting time in days?

I look down at my phone, scrunching my brow. I'm currently sitting on the couch watching television as I eat a bowl of pralines and cream ice cream for dinner. It's how I'm coping with my dad and June, and Robin and Dawson.

I need someone to talk to, but Hannah wasn't here when I got home and when I asked her when she'd be here, she just sent back that I shouldn't wait up. She's been working on a case that's kept her at the office late at night for the past week.

So I've been spending my night with ice cream and reruns of *Seinfeld*.

I text a question mark back to Chase.

> **Chase:** It's been ten days since my mom died. Tomorrow will be eleven.
>
> **Maggie:** Oh. Right. In my experience, it's days, then weeks, and then months. Then years ... I'm assuming. I haven't gotten to the year part yet.
>
> **Chase:** Is there anything else we count like this?
>
> **Maggie:** Babies? That's all I can think of.

Chase: So birth and death. Kind of interesting.

Maggie: I'd really never thought of that until right now.

Chase: I'm a thinker ... sometimes.

I smile at my phone.

Maggie: How is day ten?

Chase sends me back the poop emoji. Such a fitting response.

Maggie: Sounds about right

Chase: I'm tired of feeling sad

Maggie: It's not fun

Chase: I need to think about something else. Whatever happened to that guy with the nice butt?

My eyes go wide at my phone and I let out a little yelp. I'd somehow compartmentalized this whole thing. I'd put the stranger that had my mom's number, who read my texts for two weeks without telling me, in one box. And Chase, who's just lost his own mom, in another. I'd forgotten they were one and the same.

I send him back the dead emoji — the one with the x on both eyes.

Chase: Did I kill you?

Maggie: With embarrassment

Chase: Sorry. Didn't mean to embarrass you. So what happened to him?

THE ACCIDENTAL TEXT

I cover my eyes with one hand and try not to think about all the things that I told Chase. So many things. It was like he was reading my personal journal. Actually, that's exactly what it was.

> **Chase:** I'm waiting …
>
> **Maggie:** You're very pesky for someone I don't really know.
>
> **Chase:** What do you want to know?
>
> **Maggie:** Do you like Star Wars?
>
> **Chase:** Of course. But only the original three.

Ha! I was right about that. I wonder if I'm right about what he looks like. Lately I've been picturing him as a tall, lanky guy with brown hair. A bit like Benedict Cumberbatch. This could be my own manifestation of what I want him to look like, because I'm totally a Cumberbabe.

> **Chase:** My last name is Beckett. There, you can stalk me on Insta. But I have to warn you, I don't post a ton.
>
> **Chase:** I'll wait while you stalk me.

I smile at my phone again.

I open up Instagram and search for the name Chase Beckett. Ten names come up and I scroll through, wondering which one is him. I also feel a tingle of anxiousness travel down my spine. This whole situation is so unbelievably strange.

I scroll through the different profiles, narrowing down who I think the Chase Beckett I've been texting might be.

There are a couple of young kids that I rule out, a guy with a man bun that I do a silent prayer is not him. There's one guy standing with a yellow dog next to him. I can't really see much of that guy, since the profile pictures on Instagram are so small and this one is zoomed out pretty far.

> **Maggie:** Which one are you? There are like ten.
>
> **Chase:** There's a dog in my profile picture. A golden retriever.

I click on the Chase Beckett with the dog, and as it opens up I feel butterflies dance around in my stomach, almost not sure I want to look. I don't even know why I feel this way. It's just the reality of it all. I'm about to see what Chase looks like. I've had a picture in my head and I'm curious how he will match up.

"You really do suck at posting," I say out loud to my empty living room.

There are maybe a dozen posts, and only half of them are pictures. The rest are quotes or memes. I scan over them and find another one of him and the dog and click on it, watching as it fills up the screen.

The caption on the photo says: Me and Oscar.

Chase Beckett is a real person. I mean, of course I knew that. But that's him, on my screen. He has a dark-brown, thick head of hair. I can't really tell his eye color because of the lighting in the picture, but they look brown. He's got a good smile—a genuine-looking one. He's wearing a brown leather jacket over a white T-shirt and jeans. And he's handsome. Definitely not a Benedict Cumberbatch look-alike with those broad shoulders under that leather jacket. Also not Dawson handsome, because no one else could be *that* good looking, but by all definitions—at least my own definitions—Chase is handsome.

I'm not sure how I feel about this.

My phone beeps in my hand.

> **Chase:** You might be the slowest stalker ever.
>
> **Maggie:** You have a dog?
>
> **Chase:** Yep. Oscar. Best dog ever.

I click out of the picture of him and Oscar and scan over the other ones on his page, looking for more clues about him. I see one of a family and click on it. It's his family. It has to be—they all look like they're related. Same color hair, smiles that look like they go together.

I let my eyes focus on his mom. She looks so young for her age … if this was taken recently. She's beautiful, with shoulder-length brown hair, curled in waves. She's wearing a red sweater and jeans with knee-high black boots and standing next to a man that's probably what future Chase will look like—it's definitely his dad. Tall, like Chase, but lots of gray in that nice head of hair.

There's a woman standing next to Chase—his sister, I'm assuming. It's not hard to assume, they look so much alike.

> **Maggie:** Your mom is beautiful
>
> **Chase:** She is

> **Maggie:** How old are you in that picture?
>
> **Chase:** 28. We took it last year.
>
> **Maggie:** Your sister? Older or younger?
>
> **Chase:** Kenzie. She's older by two years. She's getting married next February.
>
> **Maggie:** Oh wow. How is she doing?
>
> **Chase:** About the same as me

He sends another poop emoji.

> **Maggie:** My last name is Cooper
>
> **Chase:** Let the REAL stalking begin!
>
> **Maggie:** I'm the one in the pink baseball hat.

In my profile picture I'm wearing a Cooper's hat, and it was my mom who took the photo. I'd just bought my Jeep and she snapped a picture of me through the open driver's side window. The future felt big and bright then, my smile full and wide. I found it on her phone after she died and made it my profile picture.

I go back to Instagram and pull up my page, feeling slightly nervous now about what he'll see on there. Not so nervous about the pictures of myself, because like all people my age, I tend to post only the best ones. I go minimal on the filters, but there are pictures in there that I took ten times (or more) before I got the one I felt was good enough to post.

I definitely post a lot more than Chase does, but not gratuitously. No pictures of my food or oversharing of my life. I post a lot about the shop, and pictures of my family and the things we do together, or *used* to do together. Going on jumps—so many pictures of that. But also zip-lining, bungee jumping, snorkeling. We did so many things together. My mom loved to try new experiences and would remind us constantly how lucky we were to be able to do all the things we did.

My heart does a little twisting thing when I think of those jumping pictures. It was my mom's favorite thing to do. She said she felt so free, so light up there. It still doesn't sound appealing to me. In fact, I don't much feel like doing any of the things we used to do together.

There are also a lot of pictures of my mom. Some of just her and me, some of the family, some with only her in them. I posted a lot about her after she died. It felt cathartic, in a way. I've hardly posted anything else since. It's all been her. Of course, it doesn't feel like much has happened since that November day. Nothing Instagram worthy, at least.

Except that right now a stranger I met because he has my mom's phone number is currently looking at my Instagram. That's not Instagram worthy, but it *is* therapist worthy.

My phone beeps.

> **Chase:** I like all the pictures of your mom. She's very pretty.
>
> **Maggie:** Thanks. I posted a lot. It was … therapeutic.
>
> **Chase:** I thought sending her texts was your therapy.

He adds a winking face. If we were in person, I would throw my well-worn flip-flop at his head.

Maggie: We shall never speak of that again.

Chase: Lips are sealed

Chase: Oh wow. Whose Lambo is that?

I pull Instagram back up and scroll down to see a picture of me sitting inside my dad's Lamborghini. This was from last year when we were doing Drives for Dreams. The car is wrapped in a bright-blue vinyl with our logo printed on it, similar to what you'd see on a race car. I'm in a racing suit, also covered in the Cooper's logo, and wearing a Cooper's baseball cap. I only sat in the car for the picture. I never race … we let Devon do that.

My smile in that photo looks pained to me now. I remember that day well. Mom was supposed to be there with us, but she wasn't feeling well, so she stayed home. That was two months before her diagnosis.

Sometimes I hate looking at these pictures.

Maggie: It's my dad's

Chase: Are you for real right now?

Maggie: It's for work

Chase: What does he do?

Maggie: We have a family business—Cooper's. We vinyl wrap cars.

Chase: That car … wow. So cool.

Maggie: It's not as cool as it looks

Chase: Stop trying to ruin my dreams

Maggie: That's what I've been called. A dream ruiner.

THE ACCIDENTAL TEXT

> **Chase:** I wouldn't have thought that about you. So sad.
>
> **Maggie:** Right?
>
> **Chase:** Who are the two little girls?

He must be looking at the picture of me with Alice and Avery. One of my favorite pictures of the girls and me. It was a month before my mom died. I needed a break from the hospital visits, so I volunteered to watch them while Chelsea ran some errands.

It was one of my better ideas. For a few hours I was able to put aside all the hard things and just play. In the picture, Avery has her little arms around my neck and Alice has a pout on her face. That's a normal look for Alice: pouting. I love her so much, my sassy little Alice. I love Avery too. She looks just like my mom did when she was her age, and she gives the best hugs, just like her nana used to.

> **Maggie:** My nieces
>
> **Chase:** Where do you land in the sibling order?
>
> **Maggie:** Middle. Chelsea is older, Devon is younger.
>
> **Chase:** Oh right. Chelsea is stubborn and bosses you around, and Devon is a player.

Oh, gosh. Did I write that to my mom? It sounds so crass coming from him.

> **Maggie:** Chelsea is a typical older sister, but she has her heart in the right place. And Devon … well, he's a player. But I love him. I feel bad that I wrote those things.

Chase: I'm not judging

Maggie: Thanks. I appreciate it.

Chase: So, how old are you?

Maggie: You never ask a woman that.

Chase: My bad. I'm a little rusty. Been a while.

Chase sends the sweating/smiling emoji.

Chase: My guess is you're in your thirties.

Maggie: I will cut you

Chase: Forties?

Maggie: I'm ending this text string and deleting you.

Chase: Kidding. My real guess is 25.

Maggie: Not bad. I'm 26.

Chase: But you don't look a day over 40.

Maggie: Don't make me find out where you live so I can slap you.

Chase: Tempe. There, I narrowed it down for you.

Maggie: I'm in Scottsdale

Chase: Of course you are

Maggie: What's that supposed to mean?

Chase: Snotsdale. That's what we call it where I live.

Maggie: Super original

Chase: Don't blame me. I didn't make it up.

Maggie: But I'm sure you say it

Chase: Of course

THE ACCIDENTAL TEXT

Scottsdale, where I grew up, has a reputation around here for being a little uppity. Or a lot uppity. I don't see it that way. It's just home for me. We've lived in this area since I was a baby.

> **Chase:** Okay, now that the stalking is out of the way. What about the guy with the butt?

I sigh at his text. What can I say about Dawson? I had a chance, blew it, and now he's with someone else?

> **Maggie:** Nothing is happening.
>
> **Chase:** I let you stalk me for that?

This time I laugh, out loud.

> **Chase:** I thought he was finally single.
>
> **Maggie:** I don't like that you have my texts memorized.
>
> **Chase:** Not all. Just parts.
>
> **Maggie:** I thought we made a deal that you'd delete them.
>
> **Chase:** I did. I promise. I just have a good memory.
>
> **Maggie:** Well, try to de-memorize them.
>
> **Chase:** I'll see what I can do. Have any hypnotizing skills?
>
> **Maggie:** I wish
>
> **Chase:** So there's nothing going on? This is not the distraction I was looking for.
>
> **Maggie:** Sorry to disappoint

Chase: VERY disappointing

Maggie: Well ... I mean, nothing's going on. He's dating my employee now. Fun times.

Chase: Well ... that's a bummer

Maggie: It's the story of my life

Chase: All the guys you've ever liked have ended up dating your employees?

That makes me snort laugh.

Maggie: No, just the guys I like always go for someone else.

Chase: Well, did you ever get to tell him you liked him?

Maggie: No, but I made it pretty obvious.

Chase: How obvious?

I think about this for a few seconds. I didn't outright tell him, but Dawson would have to be an idiot to not know. He's caught me staring at him more than once during our weekly staff meetings. I'm always all nervous and tongue-tied around him. I'm so obvious, I'm surprised Chelsea or Devon haven't caught on. They probably have and have kept it to themselves, a secret joke between them.

Maggie: Obvious enough

Chase: Want advice for next time? In case he's ever single again.

Maggie: Sure

Chase: Men are dumb

THE ACCIDENTAL TEXT

Maggie: Helpful

Chase: You have to spell things out for us.

Maggie: Like, actually spell things out? Should I have written him a note and asked him to check yes or no?

Chase: Pretty much

Chase: No, but you do have to be straight up.

Hannah is convinced that I've got this all wrong, that they aren't dating, so at the anniversary party this Saturday, she's going to play the role of my wingman. Or wingwoman, as she said she'd prefer to be called, before going off about the man-centric world we live in. She plans to check out the situation and find out what's really going on.

Then I have to do her laundry for a week if she's right. Joke's on her. I do her laundry anyway. Doesn't she wonder how her underwear is always clean? A magical fairy?

Chase: Too bad, though, about the girlfriend.

Maggie: Yeah

Chase: Unless all those pictures you posted on Insta are photoshopped, I'd say he's a fool.

I feel my cheeks heat up instantly from the compliment. I've never thought I was unattractive, but I've also never thought of myself as super attractive. Just … cute. Like girl-next-door cute.

There were a lot of implications in that last text from Chase.

My phone beeps and I look down at the screen.

Chase: Too far?

I smile and shake my head.

Maggie: No ... just processing. Also, thank you.

Chase: Well, save all this advice for the next guy. It's worth gold.

Maggie: And then if I try and fail miserably, I have you to blame.

Chase: Win-win

Maggie: I have only myself to blame with Dawson.

Chase: Right, Dawson. Forgot his name.

Maggie: Like you're supposed to. Good job. Forget all the things.

Chase sends back one of those emojis with the head exploding.

Chase: Why are you to blame?

Maggie: I should have just been blunt. I should have asked him out. But I've become a chicken since my mom died.

Chase: A chicken? You didn't tell me about this side effect. So month ... what is it?

Maggie: Month 4

Chase: Okay, so month 4, I'm going to turn into a chicken. I'll put that on my calendar.

THE ACCIDENTAL TEXT

> **Maggie:** I think it's been going on for longer than that, but I haven't had a chance to test it out until recently. Let's hope you don't get this one.
>
> **Chase:** I'm guessing it's an anxiety thing, and I've been feeling that already.
>
> **Maggie:** Right. That "what else could go wrong" feeling.
>
> **Chase:** Yeah, that one
>
> **Maggie:** It could be an extension of that. Never thought of it that way.
>
> **Chase:** Who needs therapy when you've got me?
>
> **Maggie:** Not sure I should be getting therapy from a stranger over text.

Or from someone who recently lost his mom. I don't think that's necessary to say, though.

> **Chase:** We're not strangers anymore.
>
> **Maggie:** True. You know too much already. I, however, don't know all that much about you.
>
> **Chase:** I don't know anything. I've un-remembered it.
>
> **Maggie:** Liar

Chase sends a smiling emoji.

> **Chase:** Thanks for this. For chatting with me. It helped. I've got some stuff I need to do, and I guess I should let you get back to whatever you were doing.

I look down at the tattered pajama shorts and cotton tank I'm wearing and then over to the now completely melted ice cream that I was drowning my frustrations with before Chase texted me.

I felt heavy tonight when I sat down to watch my shows and eat my junk food. But now I feel lighter. Interesting.

Maggie: Happy to help, and thanks for the tips.

Chase: Have a good night

Chapter 12

"I'm sorry, Maggie, but Halmoni wants me to tell you that you look too tan and that too much sun is bad for your skin."

Hannah turns toward me, giving the back of her head to her grandma, and mouths "sorry" while rolling her eyes.

"It's self-tanner," I say, nodding my head at the both of them.

Hannah tells her grandma this in Korean.

Halmoni says something back and then looks at me and shakes her head slowly, disappointment on her face.

"She doesn't believe you. She thinks you're going to tanning beds."

"I'm not! I promise."

Hannah closes her eyes and puffs air out of her cheeks. She says something to her grandma, her voice elevated, and Halmoni raises her voice back. They are basically now fighting over my fake tan.

This doesn't happen every time I'm here, but it happens often enough that I'm used to it and don't worry about it. I appreciate Halmoni's lecturing through Hannah. It's nice to know she cares. If Hannah's mom were here, she'd probably break it up, but I see her so rarely nowadays. She's always working. Hannah too. It sometimes worries me, seeing Hannah work so much.

I get back to the *jjajangmyeon* Hannah's grandma made us for dinner, while the two of them hash it out. I'm on my second bowl of the noodle dish; it's one of my favorite things that Halmoni makes, even if Hannah doesn't appreciate it as much. She says it's like a Korean version of mac and cheese. Which makes me wonder, who doesn't like mac and cheese? I'll even eat the boxed version, *on purpose*.

I feel my phone vibrate in my back pocket and pull it out to see I have a text from Chase.

> **Chase:** I listened to sad country music today.
>
> **Maggie:** Rookie mistake. I should have warned you.
>
> **Chase:** It was more painful than I thought it would be.
>
> **Maggie:** I can say that part does get better. I don't cry over any old song now. They have to be ones that mean something.
>
> **Chase:** She loved country music
>
> **Maggie:** My mom did too
>
> **Chase:** What are you up to?
>
> **Maggie:** Eating dinner at my friend's mom's house.
>
> **Chase:** Is this the one with the grandma who lectures you?

How does he know that? I do a search in my messaging app for Hannah's name and see this one I sent to my mom:

THE ACCIDENTAL TEXT

Maggie: We went to dinner at Hannah's tonight and her grandma made us those noodles you loved. I think she's made it her job to see that I'm fed. She also lectured me—through Hannah—about how my shirts are too old and I look like a slob. I just threw on an old T-shirt and some sweats to go over there. I probably did look like a slob. At least you can rest easy knowing I'm still being mommed. Miss you.

I go back to Chase's messages.

Maggie: You're not forgetting my texts, and you promised you would.

Chase: Right. Sorry. Will work harder.

Chase: How about I tell you something so we're even?

Maggie: I mean, you should probably tell me ten things. Even that won't come close.

Chase: Okay. Let me think about it. I'll get back to you.

Maggie: They have to be bad things. None of this "I save puppies in my spare time" junk. I mean, that would be cool if you did. I just need stuff to hold over your head.

Chase: Got it. I'll get you some real juicy stuff. Promise.

Chase: What have you been up to?

Maggie: Just getting ready for a big work party.

Chelsea has had me doing a lot of things this week for the party. Checking on little details, on RSVPs, making sure we have enough seating for everyone. It's taken up most of my week.

Chase: Oh yes, the anniversary party.

Maggie: Did I tell you about it?

I search my brain, trying to remember if I told him when we were texting yesterday. Chase sends back one of those sheepish-looking emojis.

Maggie: Oh my hell

Chase: I'm sorry. You were complaining about how much Chelsea was making you do, and wishing your mom could be there to celebrate. It's an easy one to remember.

I'm starting to wonder if Chase has a photographic memory or something. I mean, I can't even remember what I ate for breakfast this morning. Wait, yes I can. It was overnight oats with honey and cinnamon. My favorite. But still, his ability to remember the things I texted to him is a little frightening. Especially since I need him to forget it all.

Maggie: I want that list. Stat.

Chase: I'll work on it, promise.

"Who's Chase?" Hannah asks, and I jolt at the sound of her voice.

I was so caught up in the texting between Chase and me that I didn't realize the arguing had ended.

Now Hannah is standing over me, her eyes on my phone. Halmoni is cleaning up the kitchen, the argument she was having with Hannah resolved or forgotten.

Crap.

THE ACCIDENTAL TEXT

"Who's Chase, and why are you smiling at your phone like a weirdo?" she says, accusation in her tone.

"I haven't been smiling at my phone," I say, pulling my brows inward.

"Yes, you have. Like a weirdo. Now … who is Chase? And why have I never heard of this guy?"

"He's just … someone I met." I reach up and play with my necklace.

Hannah sits back down at the table. She now looks appalled. "And you didn't tell me about him?"

"You've been busy." This is true; however, it's also *not* the reason I withheld this information from her.

"Okay," she says, placing her forearms on the table and intertwining her fingers. I know this look. I'm about to be interrogated.

"Let us look at the facts," she starts.

"I didn't break any laws."

"I'll be the judge of that. And you did break the friendship code. While not illegal, it's offensive." She looks and sounds very lawyerly right now as she starts her interrogation.

"It's not what you think."

"That's what all guilty people say," she points out.

I slump in my seat and Halmoni tsks at me from the kitchen where she's currently cleaning dishes.

I sit up straight. "It's kind of a long story."

"I've got all night," Hannah says, looking me directly in the eyes.

"No, you don't. You have to go back to work."

"Fine," she says, annoyed. "I've got thirty minutes. Now, spill."

I let out a breath. "Fine," I say, my tone matching her annoyance.

Am I really going to tell her this? I guess I should tell someone. And if it has to be someone, Hannah is my safest space. She probably won't have me committed. I hope.

"Okay, so remember how I asked my dad to keep my mom's phone number? Just for a little while?"

"Uh-huh," she says, giving me a confused look.

"Well, he didn't."

"What?" She pulls her chin inward, her face scrunched. "How could he?"

"Right?"

"Well, okay. I mean, I didn't really get why you wanted to keep it, but I know Katherine Cooper's phone meant something to you, so I didn't question."

"I can't really explain it. It was like an extension of her. I know it was dumb."

"Not dumb. You have to do whatever to cope," Hannah says.

"Remember you said that, okay?"

Now Hannah looks concerned. "Tell me."

"So … I didn't know that my dad had turned off her number, and I knew no one was looking at her phone. So I started texting her."

"You were … texting your mom."

"Yes. And it became sort of a journal thing. Or a venting thing. I texted a lot of feelings."

THE ACCIDENTAL TEXT

"You were texting your recently deceased mother's phone about your feelings."

"Yes."

"Right."

"I know, it sounds a little crazy."

"I love you, but it sounds *a lot* crazy."

"I didn't mean for it to happen—it just did."

"Weren't you worried about your dad or someone seeing them?"

"Of course. But as time went on and no one did, I just got more confident," I say with a shrug.

"Right. So … I'm still not understanding how this is about this Chase person."

I will her with my eyes to see where this is going without me having to say it.

"My mom's number is no longer hers."

"I know," she says.

"It belongs to someone else now," I say, nodding my head slowly as if to nudge her along.

Hannah looks confused, but I decide I'm just going to let her lawyerly brain put the puzzle pieces together.

I see the moment she realizes. Her eyes practically bug out of her head. "The texts you were sending to your mom were going to this Chase guy?"

"Yes," I say, feeling suddenly relieved that this secret is no longer mine alone. It's almost like a weight I didn't realize was there has been lifted off my shoulders.

"What in the … the entire time?" I'm not sure her eyebrows can go any higher at this point.

"No, only for the last two weeks of it. It took him that long to tell me. I think he thought they would just go away, and when they didn't ... he finally texted me back to tell me."

"And now you're what? Texting buddies?" Her voice gets more shrill with every question.

"Sort of?"

Hannah stares at me. Her facial expressions vacillate between confusion and concern. She stands up and starts pacing the dining room, back and forth, and back and forth.

She finally stops in front of me.

"So you've been texting a stranger? Like, how often?"

I take in a breath. "Here's where it gets weird."

Her eyebrows shoot up again. "It gets *more* weird than this?"

"So he told me he had my mom's number, and that was that. I stopped texting my mom, obviously, and deleted the number off her contact page."

"Right," Hannah says, sitting back down at the table.

"And one night a few weeks later, Chase texted me."

"Creeper!" Hannah yells, and Halmoni says something to her from the kitchen.

"Mind your own business, woman!" she yells back at her.

"Go on," she says to me.

"I was initially concerned about him contacting me ... but he reached out because it turns out his mom died in a car accident."

THE ACCIDENTAL TEXT

"Oh," Hannah says, sitting back in her chair. "That's so sad."

"I know, and my heart just—"

"Wait, how do you know his mom died? How do you know he's not catfishing you?"

"He's not."

"But how do you know? Have you seen pictures of him?"

"I'm getting to that," I say, letting the impatience show in my tone.

"Oh my gosh, he sent you pictures? Please don't tell me they were of his junk. Were they of his junk? The world is full of pervs. I just saw a case where this woman was catfished by this old dude and he stole a bunch of money from her. Has he asked for money? Please tell me you didn't give him money. As your lawyer, I advise you against ever speaking to this guy again."

"Are you done?" I say, holding up a hand to stop her rant.

"I have more to say."

"Please hold your objections until the witness has finished."

The corner of her mouth lifts up slightly. "Well played with the attempt at lawyer speak," she says.

"He has not sent me pictures of his junk. I've only seen his Instagram page."

Hannah lets out a breath.

"If he was going to ask for money, it would be an elaborate scheme, and it's not like I'm some billionaire to make all the effort worth it. I've seen pictures of him, his family, and I even saw his mom's obituary in the newspaper."

After ending our texting yesterday, I did a bit more stalking. I found his sister's Instagram page and she had posted the obituary. It wasn't because I didn't believe Chase; I just wanted to know more.

"Well, that makes me feel a little better, I guess." She twists her mouth to the side. "But still ... why would he text you like that?"

I shrug. "I guess he needed someone to talk to. Made sense since he knows that I'd just gone through the same thing."

"Because of your texts to your mom."

"Yes. Exactly. I know it's ... weird."

She's silent for a few seconds, looking around the room as she thinks. "Yes. I maintain that this whole thing is weird. I mean, I wouldn't do that."

"But you're also heartless and dead on the inside."

She points a finger at me. "Correct."

This is Hannah's MO. But the truth is, she's a big softy. I just let her believe she's cold and hardened, even though it's not true.

"So now you're like, what? Friends with this guy?"

"Not really; I hardly know him. It's been nice to talk to him, though."

"What does he look like?"

THE ACCIDENTAL TEXT

"I can show you," I say, grabbing my phone from the table and pulling up the Instagram app. I type in his name and pull up his page.

Hannah takes my phone away and studies his picture. She moves the phone to the side and looks at me for a second, a questioning glare, and then brings the phone back to her face. I watch as she clicks out of the picture and studies the other ones in his feed.

"So"—she hands the phone back to me—"you should have started with 'I've been texting this random hot guy.' I would have had no problems with that."

I laugh. "Liar. What about the catfishing?"

"That's real, and you have to be careful. But like, that guy is super hot."

"Well, I mean, he's no Dawson," I say.

"Does he have a girlfriend? That Chase guy?"

"I believe he's single."

"How do you know? What if he's married?"

"Did you see anything in his Instagram feed that would make you think that? And besides, so what if he is? It's not like something is happening between him and me. He's actually been giving me advice about Dawson."

Hannah pulls her face back, looking confused. "How would he know about Dawson?"

Crap. I didn't mean to go there. "I ... may have been texting my mom about Dawson."

Hannah swipes a hand down her face. "So, to recap. You've been texting your life issues to Katherine Cooper's phone, only her number is now owned by some dude named Chase, who also lost his mom, and now the two of you are like besties and he's giving you men advice?"

"When you put it like that …"

She lets out a breath, slowly, through her nose. "Mags, this whole thing is above my pay grade."

"I know."

"Okay, I'll bite. What did he say about Dawson?"

I smile. "He said that men are dumb."

"He gets points for that."

"And that I have to spell it out for him … if I ever get another opportunity."

"Right," Hannah says. "He's right. I'm gonna get the scoop on Saturday; I'm ready to be your wingwoman."

"Well, it will probably be pointless."

"Or I'll be right and I get to rub it in your face."

"We'll see."

We sit there in silence, doused in the warm yellow hue from the light hanging over the dining room table. I pick at my nails while Hannah twists her faux-diamond earring around in her ear.

"I just want to know," she says after a bit. "Just for my own personal knowledge."

"Yeah?"

"Did you … was I not …" She takes a breath. "Was I not there for you enough? Is that why you were texting your mom's phone?"

I feel my stomach fall. "Han, no," I say, reaching over and touching her arm. "I just … I was feeling so many things, and there really wasn't anyone I could talk to about it, you know? Not even my family."

"I guess," she says. "I just want you to know that I'm here, any time you need to talk. I may be cold and heartless, but not when it comes to you."

"I know that," I say, rubbing her arm. "I love that about you."

She gives me a small smile. "Come on. Let's go raid my mom's closet."

I feel my stomach fill with warmth. As different as my life has become, some things never change.

Chapter 13

Chase: Distract me

It's Friday evening and I'm sitting in my office; most of the staff has gone home already. Only one day until the big party, and I've spent most of it being ordered around by Chelsea. Long story short, she's about to have a panic attack.

It's because she wants the whole thing to be perfect. Our dad has high expectations, and rather than just realizing that those expectations can never be met—which is how I think of it—she's doing everything in her power to meet them. The thing is, no one actually knows what my dad's hoping for; he's only said he wants it to be fun. And that maybe we should have a clown. That part is definitely not happening—Chelsea has her limits.

I also think the three of us are a little on edge because June is coming. It's adding a big dose of awkward to the whole experience.

Maggie: Distract how?

THE ACCIDENTAL TEXT

Chase: I have no idea. I was just considering distracting myself with some alcohol and thought I would text my old friend Maggie instead.

Maggie: Old friend?

Chase: Well, early 40s is kinda old.

Maggie: Goodbye

Chase: Wait! I'm kidding. Don't leave.

He sends me a GIF of a dog with sad eyes.

Maggie: We've moved to GIFS now?

Chase: I got desperate

Chase: Tell me what you're doing.

Maggie: Finishing stuff up for the party tomorrow.

Chase: How's that going?

Maggie: Well, Chelsea is freaking out.

Chase: And Devon is probably doing nothing.

I stare at my phone. What did I text my mom to make him think that? I mean, he's not wrong. Chelsea has been running around like her hair is on fire, and I've been doing her bidding while Devon has contributed a big pile of nothing.

He did come into my office earlier and tell me that he's not bringing anyone. Which means I'll also be on babysitting duty tomorrow, to keep him away from Robin. Hannah can fend for herself.

Although, if I let Devon go after Robin, then maybe whatever is going on with Dawson ... Nope. No. I can't do that.

> **Chase:** Crap. Supposed to be not remembering.
>
> **Maggie:** That's right. Curious, though, how did you figure that out? What did I say?

The thing about thought dumping is it's just that: thought dumps. There's no rhyme or reason to them. I said things that I would say in a journal, never expecting anyone to read it. I don't recall all the things I texted to my mom. Or how many times I wrote to her. I couldn't remember unless I went and looked back through the texts ... and I don't like doing that. It brings up too many feelings, too many memories. It's a hard thing for me to do.

> **Chase:** Wasn't those exact words.
>
> **Maggie:** What was it, then?
>
> **Chase:** I feel like I'm in trouble.
>
> **Maggie:** You are.
>
> **Maggie:** Fine. It's not your fault you happen to own the number I was sending texts to as a form of therapy.
>
> **Chase:** Now that I'm on the other side ... I get it.
>
> **Maggie:** Do you?
>
> **Chase:** It's not something I'd do ... but it makes sense to me now.
>
> **Maggie:** So what did I say about Devon?

THE ACCIDENTAL TEXT

> **Chase:** It was a combo of things you wrote, I guess. I just picked up on it. You said something about a Chad that he hired and then didn't bother training.
>
> **Maggie:** Are you sure you deleted my texts?
>
> **Chase:** I did. Scout's honor.
>
> **Maggie:** Are you a scout?
>
> **Chase:** No

I snort laugh at my phone, shaking my head.

> **Maggie:** You still owe me some gossip about you. I feel like you know all this stuff about me and I still don't know much about you.
>
> **Chase:** I'm working on it. I will get you some dirty stuff.
>
> **Maggie:** Please don't make it dirty.

I send him a gagging emoji.

> **Maggie:** How about we start with some basics. Where do you work?
>
> **Chase:** How do you know I have a job?
>
> **Maggie:** I don't. That's why I'm asking.
>
> **Chase:** I'm in the FBI
>
> **Maggie:** I don't believe you
>
> **Chase:** CIA?
>
> **Maggie:** Try again
>
> **Chase:** I work for SurveyWave

I've heard of that company. Kind of a big deal around here. They have a lot of employees. A few of my friends from college went on to work there.

> **Maggie:** And what does SurveyWave do?
>
> **Chase:** Online survey tools
>
> **Maggie:** Right. I mean, I should have gathered that from the name.
>
> **Chase:** Ever taken a survey online? Or when you were at school?
>
> **Maggie:** Of course
>
> **Chase:** We design and implement those. Where did you go to college?
>
> **Maggie:** ASU
>
> **Chase:** Chances are you used our surveys.
>
> **Maggie:** What do you do there?
>
> **Chase:** Sales. Just got promoted, actually.
>
> **Maggie:** Congrats!

I send him one of those confetti emojis. And then feel stupid for sending it.

> **Chase:** Thanks. Not as cool as your job.
>
> **Maggie:** My job sounds cooler than it is.
>
> **Chase:** I don't know … all those fancy cars?
>
> **Maggie:** I'm not into cars all that much.
>
> **Chase:** You should just keep that to yourself. Especially at the party tomorrow.

THE ACCIDENTAL TEXT

Maggie: Yes, I'm fully prepared to talk about torque, camber, horsepower, and all that other car mumbo jumbo.

Chase: I am so turned on right now.

Maggie: Shut up

I laugh out loud, then look up and realize where I am, seeing the epoxy floors of my office, and the walls filled with pictures of my family and some of the adventures we've had. It's weird when I'm texting Chase. It's like I'm transferred to another place.

My phone beeps and I look down at it. But then I hear a sort of choking, strangled noise, and I look up to find a raging Chelsea standing in the doorway of my office.

"ARE YOU FOR REAL RIGHT NOW?"

The messy bun on top of her head has flopped over to the side, and her face looks as if it could catch on fire at any moment. Very Miss Trunchbull.

The panic attack has officially begun.

"I was just texting Hannah," I say. I set my phone on my desk, feeling like I'm about to be put in the Chokey.

I'm not about to tell her who I'm really texting. I don't think I'll ever tell her about Chase and how that all came to be.

She inhales slowly and calculatedly, her face reddening even more. "I can't do this; it's too much. I have mom brain, and I'm so tired, and no one is helping me, and nothing is working out. And once this is done, I still have Drives for Dreams, and I can't do it all." This comes out through gritted teeth. My ears appreciate the lower decibel, but it feels a bit more sinister.

"Chels, it's going to be fine," I say, trying to calm her.

At those words, Chelsea bursts into tears.

I walk over to her and guide her into my office, shutting the door behind her so anyone that might still be here can't hear the breakdown happening right now. I walk her over to my chair and help her sit down.

"It's not fine," she says through her tears. "It's a big dumpster fire."

"What's going on?"

She takes a few moments to gather herself, the tears streaming down her face. "The caterer we hired had to change one of the sandwich orders from beef to chicken."

This sets off more tears. She's basically now blubbering in my office chair, her face in her hands, her shoulders shaking.

I know it's not the chicken that's the problem. The sandwiches are just the finger food that surpassed Chelsea's limit. This is a new thing, and I'm assuming a side effect from losing our mom. While high strung, Chelsea was always a champ with knowing where her limits lie. Since our mom died, I think she forgot where to draw the line.

I rub the upper part of her back in slow circles. "Chels, I think you need to go home and get some rest."

The crying stops instantly and she pulls her face away from her hands and looks at me. "Are you on drugs? I can't rest—I have so much to do!"

THE ACCIDENTAL TEXT

That was clearly not the right thing to say. I'm for sure getting put in the Chokey.

"Okay," I say softly, like I'm trying to calm a raging monster. "What's left to do?"

"I don't even know," she says, starting up the blubbering again.

"Is there a list or something? What needs to be done?"

She sniffs. "Can we find another caterer to do the beef sandwiches?"

"Probably not," I say.

I see the moment when she resigns herself to it. She does a full-body slouch in my black faux-leather office chair.

She sniffs again. "Maybe I *should* go to bed."

"I think so," I say.

"Wait—I need to mark where the cars will park tomorrow."

"I can do that," I say.

"But—"

"I've got this, Chels."

She has a detailed map of where everything will go, so I'm pretty sure I can figure it all out.

"Okay," she says so quietly I barely hear her.

"Okay?"

"Yeah." She reaches up and wipes her eyes. "I'll go home."

After a few minutes of arguing over whether she's actually capable of driving home, I pile Chelsea into her car and send her home with the strict rule that she go straight to bed, and then I text Mark for backup. I also text Chase and tell him why I haven't written him back.

With no response from him, I go to the back of the shop in search of the black tape to mark the parking lot with.

As I open the door, I see that there's a spotlight directed at a Mustang getting a full bright-red matte wrap. Dawson is at the front of the car, working on the hood, a belt around the waist of his coveralls with all his tools in it.

"Hi," I say, giving him a little wave when he looks my way. It's strange to see him in here by himself. Usually the room is bustling with people, lots of chatter and laughter as they work. It's quiet in here, except for the faint sounds of music coming from a portable speaker near where Dawson is working.

He gives me one of those irresistible smiles of his, and my heart does this little pitter-patter thing. *He's taken, Maggie. You utter fool.*

"What are you still doing here?" he asks.

"Just doing some last-minute stuff. Gotta mark where the cars on display are parking tomorrow."

"Gotcha."

"Is the tape—" I cut off, pointing over to the shelves on the left side of the shop where we keep most of the supplies.

"Yeah," he says, then joins me over by the wall, showing me where it is.

I grab a roll and hold it in my hands. "Thanks."

"Not a problem."

"I'll just," I say, pointing to the door, indicating where I plan to exit. Like a moron.

THE ACCIDENTAL TEXT

Then I realize we're alone. In the shop. Probably in the entire building.

"Why are you still working on that car?" I ask.

He looks at the Mustang and then back at me. "Chad," he says.

I nod. "Right," I say. "We probably should consider letting him go."

"I'd have to agree," he says, reaching up and running a hand through his thick dark-blond hair.

If we get rid of Chad, will we have anything to talk about?

"Ready for the party tomorrow?" I ask.

"Yep," he says, giving me a small smile. "I'll be there."

"Great," I say. "Are you bringing Robin with you?"

Did I really just ask that? It's like my mouth didn't even communicate with my brain.

Dawson tilts his head to the side, the corners of his eyes doing a sort of crinkling thing.

"Uh ... no," he says. "I'll see her there, I'm assuming."

"Oh ... right ... I just thought ..."

"We're just friends."

My mouth goes dry and I swallow. They're friends? Really? How did I get that so wrong?

"Right. Gotcha. Good ... to know."

He gives me a tight-lipped smile. "I'll see you tomorrow?"

Now's your chance, Maggie. Say something flirty. Be bold. Be brave.

"I'll be there," I say. Then I wave at him, with the tape (why? Why? WHY?), and walk out of the shop.

Way to chicken out, Maggie.

Chapter 14

To keep up with my chicken theme, I've also put all my eggs in one basket.

"I'm *so* sorry, babe," Hannah says.

We're on the phone, Hannah is at work, and I'm in the apartment with curls pinned up on my head, my makeup half-done.

"But … Dawson is single. I need you," I whine. "How can you ditch me at a time like this?"

I wasn't going to tell her; I was just going to let her find out at the party so I didn't have to listen to her go on and on about how right she was and how wrong I was. But she didn't even get a chance to gloat. She's been so busy at work.

"I'm not ditching you — I just don't know when I can get there. This case is taking all my time, and my boss is a real witch."

"She's your mom."

"Exactly," she says.

I breathe out my nose. "Fine. I'll try and not make a fool of myself."

I can try all I want, but a fool I will be. Look at my track record.

I don't know why I want Hannah there so badly—it's not like she's going to give me some superpower and I'll be magically less of a coward. But I just want her there. By my side. Making me laugh and telling me to get over myself.

I feel like a moron, going by myself now. I guess I'll have to hang out with Devon and try to keep his paws off all the single ladies. Or I could hang out with my dad and June. I do a very hard swallow at that thought.

"I'm so sorry. I'll hurry, I promise," she says. It sounds as if she's walking quickly somewhere. "I have to go—the boss just caught me on the phone."

"She's your *mom*," I say again.

"Exactly," she says again and hangs up.

I go back to the bathroom to finish my makeup. I chose to go only a little extra with my look, but not too extra.

While pulling the pins out of my hair my phone beeps, and I look down to where it's sitting on the laminate counter of my bathroom and see I have a text from Chase.

> **Chase:** You ready to party?
>
> **Maggie:** Not really
>
> **Chase:** Why?
>
> **Maggie:** I have no wingwoman.
>
> **Chase:** Wingwoman?
>
> **Maggie:** Hannah
>
> **Chase:** What do you need a wingwoman for? Isn't this a work party?

THE ACCIDENTAL TEXT

Maggie: Yes. But as it turns out, Dawson is single. Got the story wrong. And now my wingwoman has ditched me.

Chase: Ah … the plot thickens.

Maggie: Yes

I send him a crying emoji.

Chase: You know what? You don't need a wingman. You've got this.

Maggie: I feel like I need a wingman.

Chase: What about Devon?

I send him a laughing emoji. The one with the tears coming out of its eyes. I'm not really laughing, but that comment was ridiculous.

Maggie: Devon would be the worst wingman ever.

Chase: I'm assuming Chelsea is out too.

Maggie: Yep. No help at all.

There's also the issue that I've never said anything to them about it.

I take a breath and look in the mirror. I need to give myself a pep talk. I can be my own wingman. I will just walk myself over to Dawson, look him in the eye, and … what? What will I do? I'll probably choke, that's what I'll do. I'll walk up to him, look him in the eye, and say something about Chad. Because that's what we do.

Chase: Your dad?

Maggie: And June?

Chase: Who's June?

I send him off a text about June and how we think that there's something going on between them and that she's coming to the party.

Chase: That's ... wow.

Maggie: Yep

Chase: I don't think my dad will ever date anyone.

Maggie: That's what mine said.

Chase: My dad was pretty serious about it.

Maggie: So was mine

Chase: I don't like this conversation.

Maggie: I don't like it either.

Chase: Back to the party. I've got nothing going on tonight. I'll be your wingman.

I look down at my phone. Chase ... my wingman? Is he saying he'd come to the party with me? I'd meet Chase ... in person?

I have no idea how I feel about this. So many thoughts going through my head at once. I'm not so sure I want to meet him in person. I've never thought of this going beyond what it already is. I've never once pictured in my mind seeing Chase in real life. It was never on my radar.

THE ACCIDENTAL TEXT

I look around my bathroom, all the thoughts coming at me in rapid succession. Me ... and Chase ... meeting. Would that be a bad thing?

My phone beeps, and I look down at it.

> **Chase:** I mean on the phone. I'm not inviting myself to your work party. I just meant I'll be on hand to help.

My heart slows down when I see this. I hadn't even realized it had picked up. I also feel a range of emotions. From relief to ... something like disappointment, maybe? Like for a few seconds, I'd started to entertain the thought of having Chase at the party, meeting him in person. Seeing that smile of his in real life.

My phone beeps again.

> **Chase:** Did I scare you off?

I stare at my phone, chewing on my bottom lip. I'm not scared ... just contemplative. Okay, I was initially a little freaked out, I'll admit. But now the thought has entered my head and feels like it's on replay. Like a skipping record. *Meeting Chase. Meeting Chase. Meeting Chase.*

Do I want to see Chase for real? We haven't even talked on the phone. I don't even know what his voice sounds like. It seems like there are a lot of steps to take before meeting in person. But nowadays people meet online all the time. On some sites you meet someone in the morning and are hooking up by the evening. I've never been interested in anything like that. That's also not what Chase and I have. We have more than that. A shared bond.

I look at myself in the mirror. Taking in my green eyes and my brown hair in big wavy curls over my shoulders. I can see my chest rising and falling in my reflection.

I nod at myself in the mirror. And then pick up my phone.

> **Maggie:** Do you have a suit?
>
> **Chase:** ??
>
> **Maggie:** You know, a suit. Like one you'd wear to church.
>
> **Chase:** I know what a suit is. Yes, I have a few of those.
>
> **Maggie:** Want to put one on and meet me at a party?

I watch as the three dots appear and then disappear and then appear again. Was this a dumb idea? I feel like I may have acted on an impulse and now I'm second-guessing myself. I threw it out there without thinking that Chase might have the same thoughts I was having. Maybe he never wanted to meet me in person.

After a few eternal seconds and the persistent thought that I should figure out a way to take it back, to rewind my words, my phone beeps.

> **Chase:** Do I get to sit in the Lambo?

I laugh. One of those nervous ones. Breathy and not all that joyful sounding. I text back.

> **Maggie:** Of course

THE ACCIDENTAL TEXT

I watch as the three dots do their thing again. On and off. On and off.

> **Chase:** I'm in. Send me the address.

Before I can take it back, before my mind convinces me I should do otherwise, I send him a text with the address to the shop and then I let out a squeal. It's a nervous one, and I feel almost like I've dived out of a plane as I realize what I've just done.

My phone beeps and I look down at it.

> **Chase:** Does this seem as weird to you as it does to me?
>
> **Maggie:** Super weird.
>
> **Chase:** Glad we're on the same page.
>
> **Maggie:** I mean, don't come unless you want to.

I throw that out there for him—a lifeline. It gives him an excuse. He's got a good one. He's still in the heaviest part of the grieving process. He could easily say that, on second thought, he's not sure he's up for it, and I would fully understand. It's a good excuse.

> **Chase:** Are you trying to uninvite me?
>
> **Maggie:** No! I just don't want you to feel obligated or something.
>
> **Chase:** I'm up for it. I'm an excellent wingman, by the way.

I expel a big breath, slowly, through my lips.

Maggie: See you at 7.

I look in the mirror again, my eyes wide this time. I then set down my phone, pick up my blow dryer, put the setting on cool, and use it to dry my armpits.

Chapter 15

I'm a bundle of nerves. Jittery, like I just drank a bunch of caffeine.

I'm currently trying to tape a sign to the shop front door that says: "Restrooms Inside." But my fingers are fumbling, and the tape keeps getting stuck together before I can apply it. I've said a lot of cusswords under my breath.

Behind me, the catering company is moving around the tent getting everything into place, like busy worker bees. The DJ is setting up to the left, a wood dance floor laid out in front of him, taking over that entire corner of the tent.

There are high-top tables by the bar, and larger lower tables covered with tablecloths surrounded by chairs in matching fabric covers. Twinkle lights hang from the top of the tent, giving the space an ethereal feeling.

Chelsea is back to being Chelsea. No more freaking out, just calm and cool and making everything happen. She's in her element now, directing everyone in her pale-pink dress with a tulle skirt and beaded bodice. Gone is the Chelsea from yesterday with the red eyes and the look of panic on her face. It's amazing what a night of sleep can do.

I take in a breath after finally taping the sign to the door. So much anxiety moving through me right now. I also feel a bit first-day-of-school uncomfortable, like there's so much to anticipate, so many unknowns, and did I even pick the right outfit? I look down at my black cocktail dress. It's strapless and fitted, landing just above my knees. I have a jacket to put over it if I get cold, since we're still in the season when it's not over one hundred degrees for twenty-four hours of the day. According to the forecast, it could get down to the low sixties tonight, which is cold for Arizonans. Chelsea has placed tall patio heaters around the tent, just in case.

I don't think I'll need the jacket, with my body reacting the way it is. All antsy, with sweaty palms and pits.

"I don't have time for you to freak out," Chelsea says as she walks up to me where I'm still standing by the door I was assigned to put a sign on. Chelsea looks at the sign, eyeing it from different angles. She ends up taking it off and then putting it back on how she wants it. This is the story of my life. I'm surprised she didn't redo the spots I marked for the cars on display tonight. She may have while I wasn't here. I wouldn't know; I'm not as meticulous as she is.

"I'm not freaking out," I say, reaching up and running my fingers over the *k* pendant hanging from the chain around my neck.

"You look like you are," she says. She puts a hand on my shoulder. "Don't let June overwhelm you."

I wrinkle my nose. I'd completely forgotten June was going to be here. Inviting Chase and him agreeing to come superseded anything else I was worried about tonight. I don't want to tell her any of this, though. It's too long of a conversation, and Chelsea would probably worry that somehow Chase would ruin her perfectly put together party. She probably won't even notice he's here once everything gets started. That's why I texted him back and told him to come at seven thirty—so he'd show up a little after everything was in swing. That way his arrival will be more inconspicuous.

"You're right," I say, blaming June. Poor June. I've used her twice now. She doesn't deserve this.

"Remember, we aren't supposed to know that she's here as anything but a friend to Dad."

"I know," I say.

"Just pretend," Chelsea says, stepping back and looking me over, taking in my outfit. She reaches up and moves some of my hair around. Then she gives me a nod of approval and walks away.

Pretending is actually good life advice for me right now. I'm going to pretend that I invited my long-lost friend Chase out tonight, and not a stranger I met because he has my mom's phone number.

Forty-five minutes later, the party is just getting started. A lot of people are here—all of the Cooper's employees and many of our clients. I've been walking around talking to some of our regulars. One of my favorite clients, Andy Lawrence, is here with his wife, Nicki. She looks stunning in a plum-colored dress, her red hair half-pulled back. They are couple goals as I watch the way he looks at her while we're talking. Like she's the only person in the room. The only person his eyes want to see.

No one is dancing yet—the music is more background at this point. I suspect it will take more drinking to get people onto the dance floor. I'll definitely need some liquid courage myself. I worry that some of our employees might get a little carried away tonight. Okay, it's Chad. I'm mostly worried about Chad. I've already told Devon he has to keep an eye on him.

Dawson approached me when he first got here, telling me how pretty I looked tonight. I told him he looked pretty too. Those were my actual words: "You look pretty too, Dawson." It wasn't a lie. He's more than pretty in his charcoal-gray suit. He's straight off a modeling runway, with that light-blue shirt underneath the jacket, making his crystal-blue eyes pop. The collar is unbuttoned and no tie. It's sexy, is what it is.

There are so many adjectives I could have used. Handsome, gorgeous ... I could have kicked off this night of flirting I'd planned with the word *attractive*, even. Instead, I said *pretty*. Then I asked him something about Chad.

Yes. I sure did. I'm so predictable.

I blame Chase. His coming tonight has upped my anxiety game by a million. What was I thinking when I asked him? What's done is done. I should probably stay away from Dawson until Chase gets here. Until I've gotten my nerves in order. If that's possible.

THE ACCIDENTAL TEXT

I work my way around the party, saying hello to everyone. I see my dad and June standing by the bar, so I walk over to them. Might as well get this over with.

"Hi, Dad," I say as I approach.

"Magpie," he says, extra brightly. He gives me a hug and kisses me on the cheek. Then he holds on to my hands and takes a step back so we're at arm's length. "Well, don't you look fantastic tonight."

"Thanks, Dad. So do you." He's in a black suit and he looks ... relaxed. And happy. With his eyes doing that little crinkling thing in the corner that they do. I feel like I haven't seen that look on him in a while. Like his smiles have been empty as of late. But this feels like a genuine Nick Cooper smile.

He looks around the tent. "Everything turned out great," he says, letting go of my hands. "Happy twenty-five years." He grabs his drink from the bar, holds it out, and does an air toast.

"Happy twenty-five years, Dad. You made this happen." I smile at him, then add, "Make sure you tell Chelsea how great it is."

"Already did," he says. He winks at me.

He gestures over to June, who's standing next to him with a drink in her hand. She's in a pantsuit, the jacket sequined. Her dyed-blonde hair goes just past her shoulders. "You remember June."

I look to June, who gives me a grand smile. And then looks at my dad and shakes her head.

"Does she remember me? Are you serious, Nick? Come here, sweetie, give this old lady a hug."

She pulls me into a hug, and as much as I didn't want her to be here, or like the fact that she and my dad have a song, hugging her feels … nice. And familiar. It's a warm, tight hug, even if she's a few inches shorter than me.

I stand back after the hug and take in the two of them together. My dad with his graying hair, looking extra debonair tonight. June hardly looks her age, with her beautiful fair skin. She has a classic look with a pointy chin and petite nose. My dad looks happy. I can admit that. And they look good together.

My gut does a clenching thing at that thought. If things hadn't gone the way they had, it would be my mom standing here with my dad. She'd be fussing with my hair—kind of like Chelsea did—and she'd have a hand on me like she always did when she stood close. On my back or my arm. To comfort me and give me strength.

I blink my eyes a few times, feeling the heat burn behind them. I can't cry right now. That would be bad on so many levels.

Pretend, Maggie. Pretend.

"You here by yourself?" my dad asks, his lips pulled up into a small smile, his eyes twinkling in the colorful lights coming from the DJ table.

"Hannah is meeting me here later," I say, even though I doubt she'll show up. But I don't want my dad thinking I'm alone and then inviting me to stay with him and June. Plus, I have someone else coming. My stomach clenches again.

THE ACCIDENTAL TEXT

"You look gorgeous," June says.

"Thank you," I say, rubbing my sweaty hands on the sides of my thighs.

Telling them that I need to go find Chelsea, I excuse myself from June and my dad and walk over to the other side of the tent. I look out at the cars on display. They range from a Mustang to an Aston Martin. My dad's Lamborghini sits parked partially underneath the tent on the other side of the dance floor.

I think Chelsea and Devon were right. I think that whole "friend" pitch my dad gave us was just that: a pitch. I guess I knew that from their flirty texts, but I may have been holding out hope. Like it was a fluke or just an inside joke or something.

I blink back some more tears and take a big breath. Then I look at my watch and see that I have one minute until Chase is due to arrive. The teary feeling is now replaced by a big sack of rocks at the bottom of my gut.

I'm about to meet Chase.

I don't even know if he's the type of person to be early or late. Maybe he's already here? Will I even recognize him when I see him? I didn't even tell him what I was wearing so he could find me. Was this the craziest idea I've ever had? I invited the man who now has my mom's phone number to a party—a work party. This might be top on the list of craziest things I've done. And I've swam with sharks. In a tank, of course, but still.

"Maggie?" a rich-sounding deep voice says from behind me, interrupting my crazy train of thoughts.

I feel my pulse skip and jump. I take a steadying breath before turning around.

Chapter 16

"Chase?" I say as I turn and see a man standing there, wearing a black suit with a white shirt and skinny black tie. His brown hair is messy in a way that looks purposeful. He's taller and broader than I imagined him.

But it's him. It's definitely him.

Chase's mouth spreads into a huge smile, and before I can say anything else, he closes the few steps between us and pulls me into a hug. It's a bone-crushing one, and I'm fully wrapped in his embrace. So much that my feet come off the ground for a second as he leans back, taking me with him. He feels warm and smells of a cologne I recognize but can't remember by name.

"You made it," I say, after we pull away from each other.

"I made it," he says, the corner of his lips pulling up on one side.

Then we just stand there, looking at each other.

"Do you want—" I start, at the same time he says, "How's it been—"

We smile at each other and both do one of those nervous laughs.

"You go," he says, gesturing to me.

"Um, do you want a drink?" I say, with a backward tilt of my head toward the bar behind me. I look quickly over my shoulder to see if Dad and June have moved away from the bar and feel relieved when I see they've gone.

"Love one," he says.

We walk over to the bar and I order a Coke—not wanting alcohol just yet—and Chase orders a beer. We take them over to an empty high top and set our drinks down, claiming the table.

"So," he says, that half-smile back on his lips. It's a nice one, the side of his mouth pulled up with just a peek of straight white teeth.

"So," I echo.

"It's nice to officially meet you."

"Same."

"I wasn't sure what to expect."

I let out a breath. "Neither was I."

"I didn't even know how to find you; we didn't set anything up."

"But you found me," I say.

"I found you."

"You look ... great," I say, pointing toward his suit.

"Thanks." He looks down at himself. "Got this for the funeral."

"Ah," I say. It's easy to forget that Chase's mom died not that long ago. He seems so normal standing here in front of me. So casual. Of course, maybe this *is* Chase in pain. How would I know? He looks in better shape than I was at this point in my grief.

THE ACCIDENTAL TEXT

"Sorry, didn't meant to dampen the conversation."

"You didn't." I give him a reassuring smile.

Chase looks down at his hand resting on the table, holding his beer, his thumb running across the corner of the label.

He looks back at me. "You look great too," he says with a head bob toward me.

"Thanks."

"I like the dress."

"This old thing?"

We both laugh at my dumb joke, still with the same underlying tones of nervousness.

"So," he says.

"So," I reply. I realize that in order for this to go anywhere, we have to move past this awkward meeting stage that we seem to be stuck in. I've never done anything like this before. It would seem—with the silly smiling glances that we keep giving each other—that Chase hasn't either.

"What do we do now?" I ask him.

"Hi, Mags." Devon sidles up to the table before Chase can answer. He's got a cocktail in one hand. "You said Hannah was coming," he says to me, not even noticing Chase standing there.

With Devon's eyes focused out on the crowd of people gathered around, I sneak a look at Chase, who gives me a sly grin and then mouths, "Devon." I give him a quick nod.

"She's not here yet," I say. "Had to work late."

"Bummer," Devon says, and then takes a sip of his drink, still keeping his focus on the party. He turns just slightly to the side, sees Chase standing there, and does a double take. "Sorry, man." He reaches out a hand to shake Chase's. "Didn't see you there."

"Not a problem," Chase says. His eyes dart to me and we give each other knowing smiles like we have some sort of inside joke going on. I suppose we do.

"Sorry," I say. "Devon, this is Chase Beckett. He's interested in having his car wrapped."

I'm not sure where those words came from, but they roll off my tongue easily. It was a split-second decision on my part. Telling Devon that Chase was a friend would bring up too many questions. Like where did we meet? Why did I bring this "friend" with me without telling anyone first? My family is too smart and *way* too nosy. They'd never just accept that he was a friend that I'd never mentioned before and leave it at that. They'd need details.

"Excellent," Devon says. "We'd love to hook you up. What kind of car you got?"

Chase looks to me; I see his eyes widen briefly before turning back to Devon. "A Honda Accord?"

Devon's brows pull inward at this. Chase is clearly not as smooth of a storyteller as I am.

"But he's buying a Lexus LC five hundred," I add quickly. It was the first car I thought of. We had one come through the shop not that long ago.

"Solid," Devon says, sounding impressed. "The touring or the sports package?"

THE ACCIDENTAL TEXT

"Uh ... sports," Chase says, his answer coming out more in the form of a question. He looks to me, and I give him a small nod.

"Good choice," Devon says. He reaches into the inside pocket of his navy tailored jacket, pulls out a business card, and hands it to Devon. "Give me a call when you're ready for a wrap."

"I'll do that." Chase takes the card from him.

Devon looks at me. "Tell Hannah to find me when she gets here." He gives me a wink and a smirk before walking away.

"Don't worry, I won't," I say loudly, calling after him.

"Devon and Hannah, huh?" Chase asks, with a double eyebrow raise after Devon is out of earshot.

"Over my dead body," I say. "It's the chase. He knows she's off-limits."

"And what does Hannah think?"

"She thinks he's a creeper."

Chase laughs at that.

Chase holds the business card up, the black lettering of Devon's name stark against the white background. "I guess I have to buy a car now. How much will the LC five hundred set me back?"

"Ninety K," I say, and give him a sheepish grin.

"Yikes." Chase's eyes go wide. "Better get a second job."

I snort laugh. "Sorry. I didn't want Devon asking questions. He would have. Protective brother and all that."

"I guess I didn't realize that you didn't tell your family about me having your mom's number."

My eyes go wide. "I haven't told anyone. No one even knows about all the texting I did to my mom. They would probably think I need to be put away."

"Really?"

"I honestly don't know what they'd do, but I don't want to find out."

"Got it," Chase says. "So that's my cover story tonight?"

"Sure, why not?"

"I probably need to google the car, then," he says. "So I don't sound like an idiot."

I laugh again. "Don't worry about it—I've got you covered."

"I believe you," he says. "I bet all the guys like your car knowledge."

I think about that for a second. It hasn't really helped me all that much. "I don't know about that."

"Well, I'm impressed."

I smile at him and he gives me that same side smile again. I know I just met him in person, but so far, it's my favorite thing about him. There's something so warm and accepting wrapped up in that half-grin.

I look around the room and spot Dawson standing by the dance floor. I clear my throat. "So how does this work?" I ask.

"How does what work?"

"The wingman thing," I say.

"Right," Chase says, and then takes a quick pull from his beer. "Let's go find Dawson."

THE ACCIDENTAL TEXT

I pull my head back, my lips pulling into a frown. "And then what?"

"You talk to him," he says.

"Um … that's not what I thought a wingman did."

"Well, I mean, normally I'd introduce you to him: 'Have you met my girl, Maggie?'" he says, holding his hand out toward me, pretending to introduce me to a fake Dawson. "But since Dawson already knows you and has no idea who I am, that won't go so well."

"Right," I say, and then nibble on my bottom lip.

"How about you bring me over and introduce me as a client? Then we'll go from there."

"Okay," I say. "Let's go find him."

Chase holds out a finger. "Hold up. Let me try to find him by your description." He starts looking around the room, and I crinkle my nose trying to remember how I described Dawson to my mom. I spy Dawson still standing off to the side of the dance floor, now talking to Chad, his hand on Chad's shoulder.

"Hmm," Chase says, resting his chin in his hand. He takes a breath through his teeth. "I don't know; there are a lot of great butts out there tonight."

"Shut up," I say, through a laugh. "He's standing by the dance floor, near the DJ table."

"The guy in the gray suit?"

"Yes."

"Ah, yes," Chase says after he spots him, nodding his head. "Good-looking guy. I would've never recognized him from the front, though."

"Oh my gosh," I say, laughing again. "Why couldn't my mom's number have gone to an old senile woman?"

Chase shrugs. "Someone named Gertrude?"

"She'd totally be a Gertrude."

"But what kind of wingman would Gertrude even be? No way would she be better than this." He drags a hand down his torso.

"I haven't exactly seen your skills yet, have I? Plus, Gertrude wouldn't remember all my texts."

"I can't apologize for my genius brain," he says, tapping the side of his head.

"I'm not sure that makes you a genius."

"It does," he says. "Trust me."

Chase sets his beer down deliberately and then stands up straight and says, "Let's do this."

He walks around to my side of the table, grabs me by the hand, and starts dragging me toward the area where Dawson is standing.

"You can't … what are … would you …" I sputter as I try to keep up with Chase. I wasn't ready. I have questions. I was supposed to drink something to loosen myself up, and I haven't done that yet.

But before I can get any of that out of my head, we're standing next to Dawson, who's still talking to Chad. He looks over at me, gives me a relieved look, and then, giving Chad a tap on the back with his hand, excuses himself and walks over to me and Chase.

THE ACCIDENTAL TEXT

"Maggie," he says as he approaches. "You saved me. Chad was getting pretty sentimental there. I think he's had too much to drink already."

"Great," is all I say. I do add an eye roll for emphasis, but that's it. I'm choking already. I can feel it. KFC, here I come.

Chase puts a hand on my back and very subtly pushes me forward. Right. I've got backup. I can do this.

Dawson's eyes move up to Chase standing just behind me and then back down to me.

"This is Chase Beckett," I say, taking a step to the side and gesturing toward him with my hand. "He's interested in having his car wrapped."

"Sweet," Dawson says, giving Chase a wide smile. "We'd love to hook you up."

Dawson is great at running the shop, but I bet he'd give Devon a run for his money with sales. He just oozes charm.

"I'll definitely be hitting you up," Chase says. "Maggie here has been giving me all the details."

Dawson looks at me appreciatively. "Couldn't run this place without her," he says, and then gives me a wink.

The music suddenly moves up a bunch of decibels, and the DJ gets on and announces that it's time to dance. He asks that the team at Cooper's get this party started and invites us all to the dance floor as he plays an upbeat Beyoncé song.

"I guess we're supposed to dance," Dawson says, his voice now loud so he can be heard over the speakers.

"You and Maggie should get out there," Chase says.

"Right," says Dawson. Then he holds out a hand to me and my heart speeds up as he says, "Shall we?"

Chase puts his hand on my lower back and nudges me toward Dawson, again. Apparently I was stuck in place.

I put my hand in Dawson's and pray that my sweaty palms aren't obvious, then follow him to the dance floor. He grabs my other hand in his and swings me out, pulls me in toward him, and then lets one hand go and swings me out again, spinning me as he brings me in once more.

My eyes widen and I smile. Dawson can dance. Not that I'm surprised by this. He looks like someone who's good at a lot of things. Like kissing. My stomach is instantly full of butterflies at the thought. I bet he's an amazing kisser. With just the right amount of tongue.

Focus on the dancing, Maggie. No stepping on toes.

I let myself indulge in the feeling of dancing with Dawson as he continues to lead me. It's so enchanting that I find myself laughing as I let him guide me around the floor. Dawson is laughing and smiling too.

Well done, Chase the wingman.

I look over Dawson's shoulder to see my dad and June joining everyone on the dance floor, my dad doing his best "dad" moves as June bops along with him. So many thoughts enter my mind at once, but I push them out and focus back on Dawson. I need to stay in the moment. And this is *the* moment. Or at least the start of the moment.

When the song ends and a jazzy slow number starts up, for a moment I wonder if I should ask him to dance, if I should make a move, but then Dawson gives me a look. His

THE ACCIDENTAL TEXT

blue eyes are bright, and it feels like there are so many words written in them. Without saying anything, I move in and I feel his hand on my waist, pulling me toward him. My heart skips a few beats as I go to put my hand on his shoulder. I feel drawn in by his eyes, which seem to be penetrating mine. This is turning out better than I'd hoped.

"BABE!" I hear a squeal to my left and I jerk back as ridiculous pink fake-fur arms wrap around Dawson's neck.

"Natasha," Dawson says as he attempts to untangle himself from her. He's not successful.

"Sorry I'm late," she says, pulling him toward her and planting a big lip-gloss kiss on his cheek. Under her massive pink fluffy jacket, she's wearing a white shirt and a skirt that barely covers her lady bits. She also has on over-the-top tall black stilettos. Her blonde hair is slick and straight, and there's so much contouring and highlighting going on with her flawless skin, she looks nearly plastic.

What in the hell? *Sorry she's late?* Did he invite her?

Dawson clears his throat, looking at a loss for words. With Natasha's arms still around his neck, he gestures to me. "You remember Maggie?"

She turns her face so now she and Dawson are cheek to cheek. Her eyes widen, like she had no idea I was standing there, about to dance with the man she has nearly in a headlock.

"Oh, hey, Maddie," she says.

"Maggie," Dawson corrects her.

"What?" she asks, looking at him and scrunching her perfect button nose. "I can't really hear you over the music."

Yep. I've been unceremoniously put in my place. That trollop. And here I thought Robin was going to be my competition tonight. Now there's a whole new wrench in the plans.

Natasha gives me a little shrug, as if she gave it her best effort. "I'm thirsty; let's go get a drink," she says to Dawson. She releases her arms from his neck and entangles her hand with his.

For Dawson's part, he looks a little pained. He gives me a thin smile. I give him one back. And then—looking almost resigned—he lets Natasha drag him off the dance floor, where I stand in the center, couples dancing around me.

What just happened?

·

Chapter 17

I kind of feel like laughing one of those maniacal laughs. Seriously, what just happened? I'm not sure where to start. This whole evening is so ridiculous, it borders on comical.

"Hey," Chase says. He's standing next to me and I have no idea how he got there—I never saw him approach.

I feel instant relief at his presence, so grateful to have him here. Even if he's part of the reason this night is so farcical. The fact that he's here, but also that he's suddenly become a life force tonight. A beacon.

Without words he faces me, grabbing my hand and placing it on his shoulder, and then he wraps his hand around my waist, pulling me toward him, our bodies pressed together. He grabs my other hand with his and lifts it up and then begins to move us in a circle.

"What happened?" he asks, leaning in so we're nearly cheek to cheek, his mouth right by my ear. He's tall, so he has to lean his head down to meet mine.

"Natasha happened," I say, spying my dad and June on the other side of the dance floor, dancing and smiling at each other.

"Ah, Natasha," Chase says.

I pull back so I can see his face. "Please tell me I didn't text my mom about Natasha." What a waste of words that would have been.

He gives me that slight smile and then leans in again. "Nah, I can just put two and two together."

"Right. Well, he invited her, apparently."

"Oh," is all he says, drawing out the word.

"Yeah," I say, leaning closer to him so we're nearly cheek to cheek again.

We move around in a circle; I let Chase guide me, feeling something like defeat settle over me.

I make eye contact with Chelsea, who's dancing not far from me, her arms wrapped around Mark. She gives me bright, questioning eyes. Insinuating eyes. I scrunch my face at her. My younger sister way of telling her to bug off. She won't, though. I will be questioned about this later.

"Whatever," I say to Chase, after nudging him so he turns us and I'm no longer facing my sister. "It's fine."

"Is it?"

"I mean, it felt like we had a moment."

"It looked like you had one," Chase says. "I wasn't creeping … just making sure I did my job."

I sigh. "This is not how I saw this night going."

"Me either. I mean, I was going to have crappy delivery pizza and watch a violent movie, and now I'm in a suit, dancing with a pretty woman."

I pull my head back so I can see his face again. He smiles at me.

"Sorry to waste your night."

THE ACCIDENTAL TEXT

His brow instantly furrows. "Totally not a waste," he says. "I'm having a great time."

"Well, you do have some mad wingman skills."

"Sorry it wasn't enough," he says as he puts his cheek close to mine again. "We can try another strategy?"

I look over toward the bar and see Natasha and Dawson, drinks in hand. Natasha has her arm weaved through his and they're standing close to each other. She whispers something in his ear, and he laughs.

"No," I say to Chase as the song ends. I pull away and hold him by the lapels of his suit jacket. "You're released from your duties."

A heavy bass rhythm that I can feel in my throat starts up, and I don't much feel like dancing to anything upbeat. Only sad, sappy songs for this gal. Perhaps the DJ could play "Everybody Hurts" by R.E.M. as I walk away with my head hanging. It feels like a proper soundtrack to my life.

I lead Chase off the dance floor. "Wanna grab a drink and go sit in the Lambo?" I say when we've gotten far enough away from the dance floor that we no longer have to scream or be cheek to cheek to communicate. Not that I minded being cheek to cheek with Chase. It was … comfortable.

Chase stops in his tracks and I turn to see him there with big wide eyes that remind me of the heart eyes emoji face.

He clears his throat and sniffs, now taking on an extra cool demeanor to counter the drooling he almost did. "You mean that lame car over there in the corner that I *have not* been looking at or dreaming about all night? Nah, I'm good."

I give him a sardonic smile. "Oh, okay, so you don't want to see it? That works."

"I mean"—Chase tilts his head to the side—"it's not a big deal, of course. But you *did* say we could, and I *did* get you on the dance floor with Dawson. I can't help that Fluffy Barbie showed up."

I laugh. That's a fantastic way to describe Natasha. I might steal that. "It's true, you did your job."

I grab him by the hand and drag him toward the bar, which is thankfully now free of Dawson and Natasha. We grab drinks—this time mine has alcohol in it—and we walk to the other side of the tent, over to my dad's fourth child.

Chase blows out a breath, his cheeks popping out as he does. There's almost a reverence about him as we approach the car.

Chase gets in the driver's side, and before I get into the passenger side, I open up the door, lean inside, and put my drink in the cup holder. I know from experience that it takes a lot of ab and thigh muscle to get into this low-riding car without flashing anyone. Especially in this tight dress and heels. It would have been helpful if Hannah and I had kept up the workout routine that we started at the beginning of the year. It only lasted a week.

After some maneuvering, I shut the door on my side and turn on the specialty LED cab lights my dad had installed. With one little click, blue lighting appears, giving the space a sort of otherworldly hue.

THE ACCIDENTAL TEXT

"Wow," Chase says, awestruck.

I feel cocooned in here, with all the noise of the party now dampened.

"Yep," I say.

"This is ... amazing," he says almost reverently. He flicks open the cover of the start button in the middle console, his expression reminding me of my niece Alice when she first found her feet.

"Want the specs?"

Chase lets out a breath. "I don't know if I can handle it."

I laugh, a real belly one. I reach up and touch the dash, running my hand over it. I clear my throat to give the spiel I've given so many times. "This here is a four-year-old Lamborghini Huracán," I start, using an overexaggerated presenter's voice. "It sports a mid-mounted five-point-two-liter V-ten engine. With six hundred and twenty horsepower, it can go from zero to sixty in two point nine seconds, with a top speed of two hundred and two miles per hour."

I look over at Chase who's now slack-jawed. "I think I might be in love."

"With me or the car?"

"Both," he says.

I smile and chuckle as I sit back in the bucket seat and watch him as he looks around the space. After a minute, Chase leans back, letting his head fall on his headrest. He turns to look at me.

"I know this isn't how you thought the night would go," he says.

I look out the front window of the car, which has a perfect view of the dance floor, and see Dawson and Natasha dancing together, their bodies practically fused they're so close.

I turn my head toward Chase. "It's not so bad. At least now I know he's back with Natasha and I can let this whole stupid crush go."

"Maybe he's not?"

We both turn our heads to see Natasha tip her face up and kiss Dawson, right smack on the lips. I feel a wave of nausea. Letting go of this crush may be harder than I thought.

"I'm gonna say he is," I say, turning my head back toward Chase.

"Well, if it's any consolation, this is the first fun thing I've done since my mom died."

I reach over and curl my fingers around the top of his hand, and he curls his fingers around mine. It feels like a good thing to do. A right thing to do. "I'm glad," I say.

He takes a breath and then exhales through his nose. "Is it ..."

"What?"

He starts and stops a few times before turning his head and looking at me. "I know it's weird how we met."

I snort. "So weird."

"But what's even more weird ... is that it doesn't feel all that weird anymore."

I squeeze his hand. "I know what you mean."

THE ACCIDENTAL TEXT

I do know what he means. I went from feeling so nervous that he was coming, to now sitting in this car, so grateful that he's here. It's not weird, and it probably should be.

We sit in silence, feeling the heavy bass of a fast song start, watching more people get on the dance floor.

"Can I ask you something?" Chase says.

"Sure."

"I know I'm supposed to forget your texts—"

"Guhhh," I say, cutting him off. "You know, you still owe me some secrets."

"I do. But first, there's something I've wanted to ask you about."

"Okay?" I ask skeptically.

"Are you really supposed to release your mom's ashes jumping out of a plane?"

I smile, looking down at my hands. "Those were her wishes."

He chuckles. "That's ... the craziest thing. My family ... we don't do any of that. We're so boring."

"Well, my mom was the ringleader. The rest of us were along for the ride. And now she's gone ..."

"And wants you to spread her ashes while diving out of a plane. Why?"

I tell him the story about the jumpers she saw spreading their friend's ashes that one time, how she told us afterward that's what she wanted.

"Wow," he says. "She sounds like someone I'd have liked to meet."

I feel a little dip in my stomach, wondering if she's somewhere out there and can see Chase and me sitting in Dad's ridiculous car, me talking to the man that has her phone number. She'd love this. It would be like an adventure to her.

"So, I have until May to get my crap together so we can honor those wishes."

"May?"

"That's the new date Chelsea's chosen. May fifteenth, my mom's birthday. A month and a half from now." My gut sinks at that realization.

"Don't you get a say?"

"No," I say, not intending the word to come out as indignant as it does. But it's my fate. Chelsea has spoken. And I can't let my dad down again. I know he said it was fine and hasn't said anything about it since, but there had to be some disappointment. I was disappointed in myself. This new anxiety that I've developed since my mom's death is affecting all of us.

"Right. Sounds like my sister," Chase says. "So what happened ... the last time?"

I turn my head toward him, lifting my shoulders just once. "I choked."

"Why?"

"I just ..." I let out a breath. "It feels unsafe. I've told you that I've become a chicken since my mom died."

Chase nods his head. "But you've done it before ... jumped out of a plane."

THE ACCIDENTAL TEXT

"Yes," I say. "Lots of times. But it feels too risky now. Like, what if someone got hurt?"

"You've already lost one person."

"Exactly." There's that connection again with Chase. He just gets this part of me. More than my family, more than Hannah.

"Is it unsafe to jump, though?" he asks. "I mean, it sounds a little scary to me."

"It's actually more dangerous to get behind the wheel of a car than it is to skydive," I say, echoing my mom's canned answer.

"But knowing that isn't enough."

"Yep. And my family doesn't get it. I don't even get it, honestly."

"Is it the chicken thing? The anxious feeling?"

"Yeah," I say. "The truth is, none of the stuff we used to do together sounds appealing. I've lost my desire to do any of it."

"Why?"

"Don't know."

"Does it make you … feel too much?" He asks this quietly, like he's tiptoeing toward me with his voice.

"I don't think so," I say, looking forward, out the window of the car. "I've just lost my zest for things, you know?"

"I do," he says.

I sigh. "But the jumping … there's real fear there. I don't know how to face it. I have to, though. I don't have long to do it. I don't like this new anxious me."

I turn my face toward Chase, and he turns toward me. We're both leaning back on our headrests, looking at each other.

"I was anxious about meeting you tonight," I say.

"I think that's normal anxiety. Anyone would feel that way."

"Did you?"

He gives me the tiniest of shrugs. "Yeah, of course."

"Anxious now?"

"Not even a bit."

"Me either," I say, and we both smile.

Once Chase has had his fill of the Lamborghini, we get out and return to the party. In truth, I had to bribe him to get out, promising that he could come back and see it during the day. I knew if I stayed in there any longer, Chelsea would get suspicious.

We enter back into the fray. Even more people are dancing now, and the volume of the music seems louder. I'm not sure if it's because the party is ramping up or if it's just such a contrast from the quiet of being in the car with Chase.

"Where have you been?" a voice I recognize says over the noise.

I look to my left, a few feet away toward the bar, to see a very annoyed Hannah. She's in a dark-purple pencil dress with spaghetti straps, one of the ones we stole from her mom's closet. She looks amazing. Devon is next to her and gives me a double eyebrow raise when I approach. He thinks he's one-upped me somehow. I roll my eyes at him.

THE ACCIDENTAL TEXT

I walk over to her and Devon, Chase trailing behind me.

"I was ..." what do I tell her? I decide to turn the question back on her. "When did you get here?"

"Like twenty minutes ago," she says, her lips puckering like she's sucked on something sour. She leans to the side a little to see Chase standing behind me. She makes eye contact with me and points a finger at him. "Um, who's this tall drink of hotness?"

It's at this point I realize that I never expected Hannah to show up tonight and so I never thought I'd have to explain anything to her. I would have told her tomorrow, of course. I wouldn't have been able to keep something this big from her. But I have nothing prepared to say to her right now. I also can't explain everything in front of Devon. He would *not* understand.

"I'm Chase," Chase says, coming out from behind me. He leans in toward her, holding out a hand to shake hers. "You must be Hannah."

Hannah side-eyes Chase while shaking his hand, her face oozing skepticism. I see the lawyer in her coming out, and that means the questions are about to begin. Which means I need to get her away from Devon as soon as possible.

Devon shoots Chase a quick wave. "Hey, man," he says.

Hannah looks to me and then looks to Chase and then back to me. I watch as the wheels in her head churn, until her eyebrows lift high on her head and I know that everything has clicked into place.

"You're ... you?" She points again at Chase. "And ... you!" She points at me, but it's more of an accusatory pointing.

I open my eyes wide and shake my head in tiny little movements. Devon can't find out who Chase really is.

"Who's who?" Devon asks. He's leaning his body against the bar, a glass of something in his hand.

"Nobody is who," I say, loudly. Giving Hannah another warning glare.

Devon pulls his brows inward.

Before Devon can ask another question, I grab Hannah by the hand and drag her away from Devon, who starts to protest my taking her away from him.

"Never going to happen, Devon," I say to him as we walk away.

Hannah lets me guide her inside the shop and to my office, Chase following us.

"What's going on?" Hannah asks once the door is shut.

I take a breath. "Stop freaking out. Everything's fine."

"I'll decide that once I get an explanation."

"You ditched me. And I needed a wingman." I decide to take a blaming approach. Even if it never works with Hannah. Neither does sympathy.

"So because of that, you invited the stranger who now has your mom's number? *That* seemed like a good idea?"

"Well, we're not *total* strangers," Chase interjects.

Hannah holds up a finger to Chase. "You don't get to talk right now."

THE ACCIDENTAL TEXT

Chase takes a large step backward, clasping his hands together in front of him, a sheepish look on his face. He turns around and looks at the wall of pictures I put up of my family doing adventurous things. I put it up after my mom died. It felt like therapy.

Hannah takes a large breath, her eyes on me. "Is he a creeper?"

"I'm right here," Chase says, his back to us now.

"No," I say, shaking my head at her. "He's been great."

"Well, he's a terrible wingman. I saw Dawson and some chick getting cozy in the back corner of the tent. Robin?"

"Natasha."

"Why is *she* here?"

I let my shoulders slump. "She was invited."

Chase turns back toward us. "But she didn't show up until after I got Maggie and Dawson on the dance floor."

"That's true. Chase is a good wingman. We just didn't know that Natasha was going to show."

"So you're not like a stalker or anything," Hannah says to Chase.

"I've never been accused of it." Chase holds out his hands as if to plead his innocence. "But also, I'd have to be a pretty awesome stalker to make it work out so Maggie would invite me tonight."

Hannah folds her arms. "That's a solid point." She breathes like a bull getting ready to charge, her lips puckered again. "You two do know how weird this is, right?"

"Totally," I say at the same time Chase says, "Super weird."

I give him a small smile, and he gives me one back. A secret smile. We just had this conversation in the Lambo. It is weird, but not for the reason Hannah thinks it is.

"Okay fine. I guess you better tell me about yourself, Chase," Hannah says.

"What do you want to know?"

"Are you married?"

He snort laughs. "Uh … no."

"Okay, then are you in a serious relationship?"

"No," he says. "I mean, I feel pretty serious about my dog, Oscar."

Normal people would say something like *how sweet* at that comment. But animals don't impress Hannah.

"Do you live in your parents' basement?"

He pulls his chin back. "I have my own place in Tempe."

This takes a chink out of Hannah's armor. Her shoulders fall a minuscule amount.

It's also something I didn't know about Chase, but I probably shouldn't call attention to that and give Hannah any extra fodder. There's still so much I don't know about him.

"Do you have a job?" She eyes him warily.

"I work at SurveyWave. In sales."

"I know that place," she says. "My friend Ally Hawkins works there."

THE ACCIDENTAL TEXT

Chase's brows shoot up. "I know Ally; I worked in her department up until I got a promotion last month. She's great."

"Her dad works at my mom's firm," she says to me when I give her questioning eyes.

Hannah pulls her phone out of the top of her dress. I hold back my lecture about how unsafe that is, but tuck it away for later. Right now is not the best time.

She texts something, her thumbs moving rapidly over her keyboard.

I scrunch my face at her. What's she doing?

"So, Chase in sales, how long have you worked for SurveyWave?" she asks once she's finished texting.

"Two years," he says.

"And do you plan on staying with them for a while?"

"Hannah, Chase is not on trial," I say.

"I plan on it," Chase answers her, and then gives me that signature half-smile of his. Like he doesn't mind this and can handle Hannah. "I'm still training. I'm going to London in May to train there for a while."

"You are?" I ask, feeling my brows pulling inward.

"Yeah, for like six months," he says.

Six months? My heart drops a little at this. I don't know why. It's just that … well, Chase and I only met officially tonight. I think I'd like to hang out with him more. There's an instant comfort with Chase that I haven't felt in a long time. It could be our shared bond of being motherless. But it feels like more than that. And now he's leaving?

Hannah's phone starts to ding in rapid succession and she looks down at it. Her eyes widen as she scrolls through the multiple texts she's just received.

"Well, Chase," Hannah says, "it appears you have a fan in Ally."

She shows the phone to me.

> **Ally:** I ADORE Chase!
>
> **Ally:** One of the best guys you'll meet!
>
> **Ally:** Tell him hi for me!
>
> **Ally:** Tell him that his old dept misses him!
>
> **Ally:** Give him a hug for me!

There are hearts and heart eyes all over the texts. I find it hard to believe that Hannah is friends with this person. If Hannah ever sent me heart eyes, I'd think her phone was stolen or she'd been kidnapped. Actually, I'd know it.

I read the texts aloud and then look over at Chase, who's now focused on the floor, his lips curled up just slightly, the tips of his ears turning pink. He's cute when he's embarrassed.

"I'm not hugging you," Hannah says.

"That works," says Chase.

"Well," Hannah says, "I guess we should get back to the party." Apparently, Ally's approval was enough for her.

"You're done? Don't you want to ask Chase his Social Security number? Grill him until he gives you the PIN code to his ATM card?" I ask, my tone sarcastic.

THE ACCIDENTAL TEXT

She turns to Chase, her back straight. "Thank you for being Maggie's wingman tonight," she says, her tone almost robotic. "Also, I'm very sorry about your mom."

Chase just gives her a taut smile and a head nod. He's so much stronger than I was at this point in my grief. For at least a month, anytime anyone told me how sorry they were, I'd immediately tear up. There's no sign of tears in Chase's eyes right now, not anything more than the stoic dip of his chin he just gave Hannah. I'm not judging him. If there's one thing I've learned from my mom's death, it's that everyone grieves differently.

With that, Hannah turns and walks out the door.

"She likes you," I say.

Chase exhales deeply. "She's scary."

"You're not the first person to say that."

Chapter 18

"Who was that guy you were getting cozy with at the party?"

I inwardly groan. I'd made it through the entire Drives for Dreams meeting without one word from Chelsea. She even made it to the doorway of my office before turning around to interrogate me.

I'd hoped maybe she didn't notice, maybe for once in my life she didn't pay attention. No such luck.

And now she has her judging face on.

"What?" I scrunch my face at her, like I have no idea what she's asking. Even though I know *exactly* what she's asking.

After Hannah grilled Chase, we went back to the party. We danced, drank, ate, and had fun. Real fun. More fun than I can remember having in a long time. I smiled and laughed so much, my cheeks hurt.

"The guy ... the one in the black suit. You were dancing with him. I saw him holding your hand." Her lip curls up.

"Oh, that guy," I say, reaching up and tugging on my *k* pendant.

THE ACCIDENTAL TEXT

I didn't think she'd caught the hand-holding. Especially since it was at an emotional part of the evening when my dad got on the microphone and gave a little speech, thanking everyone for a great twenty-five years. Then he choked up as he said he wished the person who'd had his back and been right by his side during nearly all of those twenty-five years could be there.

Chase had grabbed my hand, intertwining our fingers during that part. Tears were escaping my eyes, and I latched on to the comfort. It didn't even feel foreign for him to do it. I'd say that our texting thing has turned into a real, bona fide friendship. Or, at least, the beginning of one.

Chelsea stands in the doorway staring at me, awaiting an answer.

"Don't you have Drives for Dreams to work on?"

"I do, but I have a minute and this is what I'm choosing to do with my minute."

Of course. Fortunately, I have a story all made up in my head for this exact conversation that I knew I wouldn't be able to avoid. I got a lot of questioning stares from Chelsea that night at the party. I knew I'd get grilled later. Not for the hand-holding part, though. I should have known better.

"He's a potential client," I say. "Nice guy. We got to chatting after I gave him info about a wrap for his new car."

I pray that didn't sound as rehearsed to Chelsea as it did to me. I thought it was a great story and would also lead into everyone understanding why Chase and I would hang out in the future. For everyone but Hannah, it will look like we hit it off at the party and a friendship blossomed. That's sort of what happened. He did get invited to the party, and a friendship did blossom. I'll just be taking all the other stuff that led up to it to my grave. Especially where Chelsea is concerned.

She puts a hand on her hip. "Who invited him?"

"No idea," I say with a shrug.

This was also part of my story. I could have blamed Devon for inviting Chase, but she could easily ask him. I thought about blaming Chad but then didn't want Chase associated with him. So I went with having no idea. I texted all of this to Chase yesterday so he was on board. Not that I plan on parading him around my family anytime soon.

"Interesting," Chelsea says, and I look up to see her giving me her squinty eyes.

"Indeed." I nod my head. I will not give in. Chelsea will never know how Chase really ended up coming to the party.

Chelsea twists her lips to the side, thinking. "You don't think he was one of those creepy party crashers, do you?"

"No," I say, sounding offended. I feel like I need to defend Chase, which is silly. "He's genuinely interested in getting his car wrapped."

"Who wants his car wrapped?" Devon says, moving into my office doorway, next to Chelsea.

"Chase," I say.

"Oh, yeah. That guy," Devon says.

Thank goodness Devon showed up. He can vouch for Chase and then Chelsea can get off my back.

"You met him?" she asks.

"Yeah," he says. "Nice guy ... buying a Lexus."

"LC five hundred," I add.

"Right," he says, pointing at me. "Why are you asking?" He turns to Chelsea.

"I saw him holding Maggie's hand," Chelsea says, a very tattletale tone to her voice.

Devon pulls his chin inward and squints his eyes at me. "He held your hand?"

"He was just comforting me during Dad's speech."

"Oh." Devon nods, totally accepting this answer. Of course he would; he's a guy. Men know that holding hands is not as big of a deal to them as it is to women. Not that I read anything into Chase holding my hand the way he did. It was comfort. A gesture of understanding.

"Also, his mom passed away not that long ago. So ... he gets it."

"Oh," Chelsea says, her facial expression changing to a more sympathetic one. Maybe I should have led with this.

"That sucks," says Devon.

"Yeah," I agree.

Silence lands on the room. I recognize the empathetic look on Devon's and Chelsea's faces.

"How are we all feeling about June?" I finally say, hoping to change the subject, but also wanting to know. My dad hasn't come in yet today, so I feel comfortable speaking freely.

Devon shrugs. "It's ... whatever."

"I don't love it," Chelsea says.

"Me neither."

There's a knock on the wall behind Chelsea's head. Devon turns. "Dawson," he says with that bro voice of his.

"Just came to talk to Maggie," Dawson says. I can barely see his face over the top of Chelsea's shoulder.

Devon and Chelsea excuse themselves, and Chelsea gives me a look that says, *We aren't done talking about this* before leaving.

"Hey," I say as Dawson walks into my office. He's back in his coveralls. I miss that charcoal-gray suit he wore to the party. It was a sight to behold. He looks good in his work attire too. It just leaves a lot more to the imagination than that suit did.

The image of Natasha's arms wrapped around him pops up in my head. They left together at the end of the party. I guess they must be back together. Surprisingly, I didn't get that sinking feeling in my gut when I saw them walking hand in hand toward the parking lot.

That's not true. My stomach did a full plummet. But then Chase made a joke about Fluffy Barbie and I got over it.

Today, I feel almost a sense of relief as he walks into my office. I'm relieved because first, he saved me from more grilling by Chelsea, and second, I no longer have to waste my time and energy on making my feelings known to him. I'll just get over them and let those butterflies I get in my stomach whenever he's around fly away into the sky.

That may take some time. Right now the butterflies are fighting for space. I take a breath.

"What can I do for you?" I ask.

"Got a question for you." He takes a seat in one of the guest chairs in front of my desk.

"Is it about Chad?"

"It ... is," he says, with a thin smile. "It's an HR question, actually."

"Oh, great. What's our dear friend Chad done now?"

"Well, he thought it would be funny to wrap all my tools in vinyl."

I nod my head. I mean ... that *is* kind of funny.

"Right," I say, mirroring his unamused grimace, holding in my smile. "Well, didn't we decide it was time to let him go?"

"I asked Devon," he says.

"What did he say?"

"He asked me to keep him around a little longer."

"I mean, it's technically your call, not Devon's."

He gives me a nod. "Okay, that's what I thought. I just wanted to make sure with you before I do anything."

I furrow my brow, looking down at my desk. Is it just me, or does this conversation feel ... contrived? There was no real reason for us to have this talk since we already sort of did, the night before the party. And it's about Chad. Of course.

"It was fun ..."

I look up at him. "Fun?"

He smiles, apologetically. Like he didn't mean for the words to escape his mouth. "Yeah ... the party. It was fun."

"It was," I say. I want to add *no thanks to you* but decide that's probably not my best move. Chase was the real reason I had fun at the party.

"I'm sorry we didn't get to dance more."

Oh. That's not what I thought he was going to say. I didn't really have a notion of what he was going to say, but it definitely wasn't *that*.

"Me too," I say. "But, you had Natasha."

"Yeah," he says. "I didn't …" He stops himself again, holding out his hand, palm up. "I didn't invite her, just so you know."

I shake my head. "We said you could bring a guest."

"Well, I hadn't planned on it. She'd called me that day and I told her about the party … and she just showed up."

And then you walked off hand in hand as you left.

"Well," I say. "It was … fine for her to be there. Glad you had fun."

"I did. You?"

"I … did too," I say. I want to throw out *and so did Chad* because it feels so natural to bring him back into a conversation with Dawson. But Chad had to be sent home in a taxi—he got so drunk he could barely walk. I mean, maybe that's fun for Chad. I prefer to remember my parties.

"You seemed to spend a lot of time with that guy, Chase," he says.

So he noticed that. I thought I'd caught him glancing my way a couple of times.

"Yeah," I say. "We have a lot in common, it turns out."

"Oh?"

THE ACCIDENTAL TEXT

"Uh ... his mom also died recently."

"Oh," Dawson says, giving me a sad smile.

"So we had a lot to talk about."

"Right," he says.

"Well, I guess you and Natasha are ..." I let that sentence trail off because why would I even say that? And because I don't think I want to know the answer. Apparently, my subconscious did.

Dawson doesn't seem that taken aback by it. "It's complicated."

Ah, yes. The old "it's complicated" line.

"I hope it gets ... un ... complicated." Oh, wow. I should just bring the conversation back to Chad. Right now.

He places his hands on the tops of his thighs and stands up from the chair. "See you later, Maggie," he says.

My phone beeps as I lie in my bed later that night, staring at the heart shape on the ceiling, thinking about so many things. The party, the conversation with Dawson ... Chase.

I pat around the side of the bed where I'm pretty sure I set my phone and pull it up to my face once I find it. I see Chase's name and I smile.

> **Chase:** I have an idea
>
> **Maggie:** Should I be scared?
>
> **Chase:** Maybe

Maggie: Let's hear it

Chase: Well, I'm texting you right now, so you'll have to read it.

Maggie: You're an idiot

Chase: Okay, so … you need to jump out of a plane in May, yes?

Maggie: Correct. The 15th.

Chase: And I'm leaving for London on the 14th.

I send him a sad face.

Chase: Yeah. I've already pushed off the date. They wanted me to go last month but postponed so I could have more time with my family after my mom …

It occurs to me that I would have never met Chase if my mom hadn't died. And we wouldn't have gotten to know each other if his mom hadn't. In fact, he would be in London right now, training. And I'd just be living my life here in Scottsdale. Never to even know who he was. Life is strange.

Chase: So … I want to jump out of a plane.

Maggie: ??

Chase: I want to do something daring.

Maggie: ??

Chase: I've never done anything adventurous. And I just feel like … I should.

Maggie: Okay …

THE ACCIDENTAL TEXT

Chase's number pops up on my screen and suddenly my phone is vibrating in my hand.

"Hello?" I say.

"Hi," he says.

"No one talks on the phone anymore."

"It was too long to text. I figured since we met in person already, it wouldn't be that weird to talk on the phone."

"You couldn't Marco Polo me like everyone else?"

"Do you hate the phone that much? Fine," he says. "I'll send you a Polo."

"I'm kidding. But really, only old people talk on the phone."

"I'm an old soul."

"So … you want to jump out of a plane?"

"Yes," he says. "I've been thinking since I saw those pictures on your office wall. I haven't done anything all that adventurous in my life."

"Well, then jump out of a plane."

"Yes, but my plan helps us both."

"How's that?"

"I don't want to just jump out of a plane. I want to try other things too. Maybe start small and lead up to that."

"Okay," I say, dragging out the word.

"And you need to jump out of a plane in May."

I take a breath. I'm resigned to do it. It has to happen or Chelsea will probably wring my neck. *Not* probably—definitely.

"I'm not following what this has to do with me."

"I want to do some other stuff before I take a big jump like that. And I think we should do it together. It might help you get your mojo back. Maybe you'll remember your zest for it all. And then it might be easier to do the jump with your family."

"What do you want to do?"

"I don't know ... I thought you might have some ideas," Chase says. "Aren't you the adventure expert?"

"I mean ... I did hike Machu Picchu."

"You're so cool."

"I am," I say. "Actually, it was the shortened version of the hike. But still."

"Aw, why did you have to tell me that? You just lost some cool points."

I laugh. I picture Chase talking to me while sitting on a couch in his place, his dog Oscar lying in his lap. I wonder what kind of home he has. Is it like a bachelor pad with sparse décor? No edible food in the refrigerator?

"I don't have time to hike Machu Picchu. Anything we can do locally?" he asks.

"I mean, there's plenty to do around here. I'm just not sure how this benefits us both."

"I told you: you need a reminder of all the fun you used to have. And you get to help me have some fun in the process."

Fun. That's a novel idea.

"You still there?" Chase asks.

"I'm here. I'm just thinking."

THE ACCIDENTAL TEXT

"Well, how about this: at the very least, you could come with me. It'll give you something else to do besides work and … whatever else you do."

"I work and I text you. That's pretty much it."

He chuckles. "That's sad. I've only been talking to you for a couple of weeks. What did you do before that?"

"Work, I guess."

"Thank goodness I came along."

"It's true."

"So what do you say?"

"I don't know."

"How about you just do it for me?"

I take a breath. "Okay, fine. I'm in."

Chase whoops on the other end and I have to hold my phone back so it doesn't blast my ear out.

"This will be good," he says.

"Maybe," I say. "What should we do first?"

"I don't know?"

"Well, how about you figure that out and let me know."

"Okay, I can do that. Just be prepared to do something adventurous on Saturday. With me."

Chase asks about work, and I tell him about Chelsea grilling me about him, and then what Dawson said about Natasha.

"Does he usually talk to you about Natasha?" he asks after I finish telling him what happened.

"Never."

"Yeah, that's … interesting. Are they together?"

"He said, and I quote, 'It's complicated.'"

"Yikes," Chase says. "I hate that status."

"Me too." I yawn into the phone.

"Well, I'll let you go to bed. I'm going to watch a movie."

"When do you work?" I ask him, wondering how we've gotten this far into our friendship and I have yet to hear about him going to work. Does he work from home? So many things I still don't know about Chase.

"I ... haven't been. I go back next Monday," he says. "They gave me an extended bereavement period because I was supposed to be in London and they don't have all that much for me to do here until I've been trained," he says.

"Oh, right."

"But I'm doing some virtual training on Monday. It'll be good to get back to it. Something to keep my mind on ... other than ..."

He doesn't need to finish that sentence. It sounds nice on paper that the company he works for gave him so much time, but that much time without the normal daily grind might have made that first part even harder for me. We were all back at work a week after my mom passed. None of us wanted to sit home with our thoughts. It occurs to me that maybe this whole adventure thing might be Chase's way of coping with that. It makes me want to do it even more. For him.

I yawn again and Chase tells me to get some sleep. We hang up and I turn over on my side, now staring at the white wall in front of me.

"Miss you, Mom," I say. I wonder if she can hear me. I hope she can.

Chapter 19

On Saturday, Chase picks me up midmorning in his black Honda Accord for our first adventure. He did a bunch of research this week and made a decision. I told him to surprise me. The only hint I got was to wear jeans and a T-shirt I didn't mind getting dirty.

I had a lot of ideas about what it would be, but driving an ATV around the Sonoran Desert wasn't one of them. Bonus is, I've never done this before. I've ridden in ATVs, but more of the buggy-style ones that seat more than one person and come with roofs. My dad or Devon always did the driving.

But on this tour, I get to drive myself since we're on single-person ATVs. They look more like a fat motorbike, with a bigger seat and four smaller, wider wheels. They don't call it a quad for nothing. That's what the tour guide, Gary, says. He's had a lot of dad jokes up his sleeve.

First thing we do is get all our equipment, then we are taught how to drive the ATVs and all the safety mumbo jumbo. Then we practice for a bit on a large flat dirt area, which is full of tire tracks from all the other people who've practiced here before. After that, it is time for some off-roading.

Before we leave on our tour, I tell Chase about my mom's tradition before we did something adventurous. She'd say, "Kiss for good luck?" and then give us a kiss. When we were little it was a kiss on the mouth, but as we got older it became a kiss on the cheek. And when Devon was a teen and thought he was too cool for school, she had to give him a kiss on the top of his head. But he never turned her down. None of us did.

"A kiss for good luck? I remember you saying that in your texts," Chase says after I finish explaining. He's sitting on his ATV, holding his helmet in his hands, wearing a pair of dark faded jeans and a gray T-shirt.

I put my hand on my hip and give him my best death stare. "You're not supposed to remember my texts."

His lips pull into that little knowing smile he does. "I know. I can't help my memory. I think we'll have to bleach my brain."

"That can be arranged."

The other side of his lip pulls upward, his straight white teeth in full view.

"How about that kiss?" he says, and then gives me a wink.

"It's on the cheek, creeper."

"I'd expect nothing more."

He turns his cheek and leans toward me, and I kiss him. Right on the apple of his cheek, where facial hair doesn't grow. His skin is soft and warm under my skin, and for a second I think about leaning in and kissing him again. Just because it wasn't what I was expecting. But I hold myself back.

The sunlight feels nice on my back as we travel through the Bradshaw Mountains, sagebrush and saguaro cacti on both sides of us. Flash floods have carved out most of the canyons in these mountains (another tidbit from Gary). We go slower through the most rugged parts but are able to go faster on the flatter parts of the trail.

Chase is in front of me and he whoops and hollers when we pick up speed; he's loving every second of this. I'm enjoying myself too. This would have been right up my mom's alley. She would have loved driving herself, feeling the wind on her body, with no reason to have her phone out. Well, I've had mine out to take pictures and videos of Chase acting like he's never been allowed to go outside in his life. To use against him later, of course.

We stop at an overlook so our group of seven can get off and rest for a few minutes. I walk over to Chase, who's just getting off his ATV. We're both covered in dirt, except for our faces, which have been protected by our helmets and goggles.

"You seem like you hate this," I say as I take off my helmet. Chase has already taken his off.

"Oh yeah, this is really roughing it." He does that partial smile thing as he takes in the view around us.

The sky is a dreamy shade of blue, not a cloud to be seen. It makes a perfect backdrop behind the mountain peaks.

"My mom would have loved this," I say.

"Yeah?"

"Totally. I wish she could have experienced it." I turn around in my spot, taking in a three-sixty of our surroundings. "Would your mom have liked something like this?"

Chase's smile drops and he lifts a shoulder. "She never wanted to do stuff like this."

"Did she ever try it?"

"Nah," he says, shaking his head. "Hey, look over there." He points over to the hills across from us. "I see deer," he says. He walks over to the edge to get a better look.

A prickle of something moves its way into my gut. That's the third time he's changed the subject when I bring up his mom. I can understand having periods of not wanting to talk about it—heaven knows I've had my own moments of needing a break from it all. But, thinking back, I don't know if Chase has spoken about his mom at all. Not since I saw her picture on Instagram. I only know her name because I stalked him and found her obituary. Heidi Beckett. That was her. She has lighter hair than Chase, but those same dark-brown eyes.

Gary tells us to get back on our vehicles, and off we go. Chase back to his whooping. His excitement is contagious and I feel myself letting go of worry. It won't do me any good up here anyway.

Later, as we drive back to Scottsdale after getting burgers off the Happy Valley Road exit, Chase's enthusiasm is still contagious. He's almost giddy—the adrenaline is flowing through him. I know that feeling. I remember it. I even feel a little of it myself. Maybe this idea of Chase's will help me somehow. I just don't know exactly how that will be.

"Thanks for going with me," he says, a toothpick hanging out the side of his mouth. I don't know if I've ever known anyone who actually uses toothpicks. With his aviator sunglasses on, he looks like a throwback to another time.

"You're welcome. Glad I went; it was nice to think about other things for a bit."

"For sure," he says.

I clear my throat after a few beats of silence. "It's time," I say. I reach up and turn down the top forty music station we've been listening to.

"Time?" he asks, a quick glance over at me before his eyes go back to the road.

"Yes, you promised me a list."

"Oh, that."

"You know too much about me. It's time for you to talk."

"What do you want to know?"

I contemplate asking him something about his mom to test my theory and see if he'd change the subject, but then realize that I don't want to be a buzzkill. It's none of my business, really. I guess I just find it odd. I want to talk about my mom pretty much all the time. Sure, there were times when I needed a break from talking about her or thinking about her being gone, but for the most part, talking about my mom has been part of my grieving process.

"Do you have any friends?"

He snort laughs. "Yeah, I have friends."

I fold my arms and stare at him.

"What?" he says, quickly looking over and seeing my glare.

"Tell me about them."

He moves the toothpick over to the other side of his mouth with his tongue. It's captivating to watch the toothpick nestled between his lips. Chase has lovely lips. Full bottom, thinner top.

"So, my closest friend is Xavier. But he goes by Z. I've known him since we were kids. We met in the sixth grade."

"I got you beat. I've known Hannah since we were six."

"That's cool," he says, doing a little head bob thing.

"It is. And now I have to keep her around forever. She knows too much."

"Like me? Do you plan on keeping me around?" That half-smile is back as he darts another look in my direction.

I smirk. "The jury is still out. Right now I'm just trying to make things more fair. So spill."

"What else is there to tell?"

I curl my lip. Did he really think that telling me his best friend's name and how long they've known each other is good information about him?

"Men are so bad at this," I say, shaking my head.

"Bad at what?"

"Sharing things."

He lets his jaw drop, the toothpick miraculously staying in his mouth. "That's generalizing."

"Fine. *You're* bad at this."

"Ah, you got me figured out."

"Okay, fine. If I were to ask Z about you, what would he say?"

Chase thinks about this for a second. "That's an interesting question. I'm not sure. I guess he'd probably tell you about the mischief we got into in high school."

I rub my hands together. "Now we're onto something. Tell me about that."

He thinks about this for a minute. "I mean, nothing really stands out. We did a lot of stupid stuff. One time we put a goat in the lunchroom."

I smile. "Did you get in trouble?"

"Never got caught."

"Well done."

"I guess there's one thing that not a lot of people know about," Chase says after a few beats of silence.

"Give it to me."

"I wanted to ask Jennifer Hunt to homecoming, junior year. She was probably the prettiest girl in school. I was more gangly back then, but I had some game."

"Oh, I'm sure you had *so* much game," I say, teasing him.

He probably did. I imagine younger Chase, with that half-smile of his and his dark-brown hair. Gangly or not, the girls were probably into him. I wonder what I would have thought of him if we'd gone to the same high school.

One thing's for sure, gangly would not be a description used for Chase now. I look over at his extended arm, his hand on the steering wheel, the sleeve of his gray T-shirt pulled taut over his large bicep.

"Z knew where her locker was, so I put a big sign on it asking her and decorated it with balloons."

"Aren't you cute," I say.

"Well, my mom and sister helped."

Chase pauses, the toothpick stilling in his mouth. I'm quiet, moving my eyes to the dashboard of his car. I know these moments well—the realization that she's gone. It's so easy to forget sometimes. I'm nearly five months in and sometimes it still hits me.

I wonder if I should put a hand on him. Just on his arm, to let him know I'm here and I get it. But something holds me back. I get a feeling that might be too much for Chase. I just need to let him have his moment.

He clears his throat and swallows. "I … I didn't put Jennifer's name on it because it was her locker and I was going to pop out right after she saw it. My mom and sister didn't know her name, and when they asked me—or really, grilled me—I didn't offer much. It's embarrassing to talk about girls with your family when you're in high school."

Funny, that was not the case for me. Devon was rather open about the women in his life. He still is. I sort of wish he'd been a little more like Chase in that way.

"So," Chase continues, "the next day at school, Z and I hide near the locker and wait for her to show up. You can see where this is going, right?"

"Oh, yes … wrong locker."

"Yep."

THE ACCIDENTAL TEXT

"So whose was it?"

He takes in a breath. "Her name was Kelli."

"And what was Kelli like?"

"Kelli … well, at the time, no one knew much about her. She'd just moved to Phoenix from Denver. She had alopecia. Completely bald, no eyebrows."

"Ah, got it. So what happened?" I fist my hand, feeling my nails dig into my palm, worried what might come next. I asked him to share things with me, and he's doing that now … but what if what he tells me makes me change my opinion of him? It shouldn't, really; I know that. This was younger Chase. People change and grow.

"I took her to homecoming."

"Kelli?"

"Yep," he says. "And it was one of the better dances I went to. Kelli's hilarious. I'm still good friends with her."

I look over at him and smile.

"The only person who knew that Kelli wasn't the girl I meant to ask was Z. And I guess, now you."

"Well," I say, putting my hands on my heart. "I'm honored. However …"

"What?"

"That was a *good* story about you. Not a juicy one."

Chase chuckles. "I'm no saint. I thought of everything I could to get out of that dance. I even considered faking sick or something. I got made fun of by some of my so-called friends. Even Z told me I should ditch her. Up until the night of the dance, even when I was driving to her house to pick her up, I was still trying to get out of it. But then I just sucked it up and went."

"And look what you would have missed out on had you not gone."

"A really great person." He dips his chin once.

"What happened to her?"

"She lives in Boston. Married and has a kid. A boy."

We sit in silence, the low hum of the road beneath us the only sound.

"If you hadn't texted me, I'd have missed out on this too," Chase says after a bit.

This time I do reach over and give his arm a squeeze. "Strange how life works."

Chapter 20

The next Saturday, I'm waiting for Chase under a big tent.

It's Drives for Dreams day, and I look forward to it more than anything else we do at Cooper's. Sure, it's taxing, and when I finally roll into bed afterward, I feel like I've run a marathon. But it's one of the most fun, most rewarding things we do.

It was my mom's idea, but Chelsea made it happen. I have to give it to her—planning an anniversary party and Drives for Dreams in not only the same year but within weeks of each other might have given the average person heart palpitations. But not Chelsea. She somehow managed to make both happen and with only one *slight* meltdown.

"Wow," Chase says as he walks toward me. He looks good in cargo shorts and a dark-blue T-shirt. He's got those aviator sunglasses on again and a toothpick sticking out the corner of his mouth.

"Yep, pretty cool, huh?" I say. I'm wearing a white Cooper's polo, shorts, and a red baseball cap, ready to tackle the day. I put an arm around Chase's waist as soon as he's standing next to me, giving him a side hug. He reciprocates.

"So cool." He does that half-grin, but I can see the giddiness underneath.

There are tables set up underneath the tent, balloons and Drives for Dreams banners decorating the space. Near the front is a full buffet. Right now they're setting up for breakfast, and they'll switch to lunch later, as this a nearly all-day affair.

Beyond the tent, just over a large wire fence and under a beautiful blue cloudless sky, is a full racetrack one mile in length. We're set up off to the side of the grandstand seating, which will soon be full of people.

Each spring Cooper's puts on this event, and we donate the proceeds to various local charities. We've used the same track since we started — the owner donates the facility. Our high-profile clients can come out and race their own car, the entrance fee acting as a donation. We also sell tickets for onlookers to come and watch the fun.

All in all, it's been a very successful venture. Something to be proud of. I know I am, and Chelsea is usually happy with everything once the event is over and she can relax, when she declares that she will *never* do this again. But, somehow, she musters up the energy to do it again the next year. Thank goodness, because neither Devon nor I could.

"Are you ready?" I ask, looking up at Chase, who's still taking in everything. We're here early, with the Cooper's employees and vendors finishing up last-minute things.

THE ACCIDENTAL TEXT

As part of Chase's quest for adventure, I've arranged it so Devon will give him a ride around the track in the Lamborghini. Chase sent a GIF of someone fainting when I asked him if he wanted to do it.

It wasn't hard to set up—I just mentioned it to Devon, and being the salesman that he is, he thought it would be a great idea to give some extra attention to our "potential client." I feel a little sick about the dishonesty, but I'm already in too deep here.

So I told Chase to meet us here early, before all the festivities start.

"Let's go," I say, dropping my hand from around Chase's waist and gesturing for him to follow me. He ditches his toothpick in a trash bin on the way.

We walk over to the entrance to the track, where Devon is waiting, looking official in his Cooper's racing suit, the Lamborghini still wrapped in bright green with the company name all over it. We didn't have time to change out the wrap like Chelsea had requested. I had to talk her down after she found that out. The green works, even if it doesn't go perfectly with her color theme of red and charcoal gray.

"Hey, man," Devon says as we approach.

"Devon," Chase says. "Thanks for doing this."

"Not a problem. Mags gave you all the info, I'm assuming."

I nod my head.

"Then let's do this," he says.

I did give Chase the rundown: no breakfast beforehand in case he gets carsick, get a good night's sleep—all the stuff Devon told me to say. But I also needed to make sure Chase didn't somehow blurt out how we met. I might have repeated myself a lot. I don't need my family finding out that Chase is not a client but the current owner of our mom's old phone number.

Devon gives Chase a helmet and I walk him over to the passenger side. He stands by the door, helmet in hand, Devon already in the car waiting.

He gives me a mischievous grin and I eye him dubiously.

"Aren't you forgetting something?" he asks.

"I don't think so …"

He reaches up and taps on his cheek with a finger. "Where's my kiss for good luck?"

I shake my head as I approach him and give him the quickest of kisses on his cheek so as not to be caught by Devon. Not that he could see anything from his vantage point in the low-riding car.

Chase smiles, takes off his sunglasses, and puts on his helmet. He gets in the car and with a rev of the engine, they're off. Starting slow and then building up the pace. Devon is trained to drive my dad's car quite fast on this track. I have no idea how fast he'll go, but he does like to show off.

The sight of them driving off reminds me of my mom and how much she used to love speeding around the track. Sometimes she'd drive, and sometimes she'd let my dad or Devon—when he was old enough—drive her. I can still see her face afterward, bright and glowing, and hear her laughter, warm and full.

I watch as Devon and Chase go around the track, and then again, and I think I count ten times before I see the car start to slow down. As they get closer, it looks like the car is swerving a little. Is something wrong? I can barely see them through the angle of the windshield. I feel a tingle of panic travel down my back as the car pulls up to me and stops with a jerk. Did Chase say something to Devon? Not that you can do much talking in that car, the engine is so loud.

Chase's door opens and he practically crawls out. He makes a moaning sound as he throws off his helmet and proceeds to throw up all over the ground.

"Oh my gosh," I say as I run over to him. I cover my mouth and nose with both hands, not wanting to smell anything, as I consider myself a sympathetic barfer. Some people cry when other people cry. I do that too, but I also barf when other people barf. I've got a very healthy gag reflex.

"I thought you told him not to eat!" Devon says, irritated. He takes off his helmet and tosses it inside the car.

"I did!" I rub my hand up and down Chase's back, keeping my mouth and nose covered with my other hand and my eyes on anything but him as he continues to throw up pretty much anything and everything in his stomach.

Chase groans when he's finished. He sits back on his butt, on the asphalt of the track. He wipes his mouth with the back of his hand. My gag reflex struggles, and I choke back the feeling.

"Are you okay?" I ask.

He looks up at me, his eyes red and watering.

"Dude, you okay?" Devon asks, coming to stand near me.

Chase looks at us, and for a moment I wonder if he's going to yell. I can't tell by the look on his face what he's thinking right now. Then a slow smile spreads across his face, wide and broad. "That. Was. Awesome," Chase says, full body movements with each word. Then he starts to laugh. A big belly one.

I look to Devon, squinting my eyes at him. "What did you do to him?"

Devon scrunches his face at me. "What do you mean?"

"How fast did you go?"

"As fast as I've gone with any other client." Devon looks at Chase. "Do you get carsick, man?"

"Yeah? Sometimes," Chase says, not laughing anymore, looking a little pained, like the up might chuck again. He puts a hand on his stomach.

Devon turns to me. "Did you even ask him if he gets carsick?"

"I thought I did. I know I told him not to eat."

"No, you didn't," Chase says. "I grabbed something on the way over."

I reach up and cover my mouth. Could I have been so worried that somehow Chase would spill the beans on how we met that I forgot to tell him everything I was supposed to?

THE ACCIDENTAL TEXT

Devon gives me a look of frustration, his eyes sending daggers in my direction.

He turns to Chase, who's still on the ground. "I wouldn't have driven so fast had I known, man. So sorry," Devon says, clearly worried about losing the sale—a sale that was never going to happen. Maybe we could rent a luxury car and have it wrapped? Seems like a lot of work. I'm going to have to figure a way out of this and a way to let Devon know that it was nothing he did that caused Chase to not get his nonexistent car wrapped at Cooper's.

"You don't need to apologize," Chase says to Devon. "That's got to be a highlight of my life. Even with the puking."

Devon chuckles. "Glad to hear it."

Chase stands up from his spot, dusting the back of his shorts off. He still looks a little green, but he seems to be okay.

"I'm really sorry," I say to him, putting a hand on his back. "I didn't know you got carsick."

"It's been a long time since I have," Chase says.

"Go get him something to drink," Devon instructs. "I'll get someone to … hose this down."

"I could do it," Chase offers.

"No worries, man. Not your fault," says Devon. Then he darts me a look that indicates where he thinks the blame lies.

"Come on," I say, "let's go get you a drink."

After stopping by the bathroom so Chase can wash up, and more apologies from me, we go to the tent to find him a Sprite or something to help settle his stomach.

People are starting to arrive, getting plates of food and sitting down under the tent. Some of the clients, most dressed in racing gear, are gathered together, chatting. Cooper's employees are busy running around doing last-minute things, no doubt on orders from Chelsea, given through the walkie-talkies they're all carrying.

I spy my dad standing by the buffet and briefly wonder if we should take another route to the drinks, but think better of it. I might as well introduce Chase to my dad.

"Hey, Dad," I say as we approach.

"Magpie," he says when he sees me. He pulls me in for a hug, giving me a kiss on the top of my head. "Who you got here?"

"Right." I pull out of the hug. "This is Chase Beckett. Chase, this is my dad, Nick Cooper."

"Didn't I see you at the anniversary party?" Dad asks, reaching his hand out.

Chase nods and then shakes my dad's hand. I'm a little surprised that he remembered Chase being there. He's not all that observant; plus, June was with him. I thought he'd be too occupied to really notice. It wasn't like Chase and I were getting all close and personal, except for the hand-holding thing. But I know my dad didn't notice that. Only Chelsea is snoopy enough to notice that.

"Yes, sir," Chase says. "It was a great party."

"How did you get to know Maggie, here?" Dad asks, his fatherly voice in full effect.

"I'm ... interested in having my car wrapped," Chase says. I caught his beat of hesitance and feel a little tinge of guilt work its way down my spine.

I know I practically beat the story into Chase on the phone last night, so much so that I neglected to tell him all the things I was supposed to. But it feels extra wrong to lead my dad astray like this. Hence the reason I wanted to avoid him in the first place.

My dad's eyes widen. His demeanor changes from protective father to businessman in an instant. "Well, we'd be happy to help you with that," my dad says.

"Sorry, Dad," I say before he starts plying Chase with car questions, "you'll have to excuse us. I actually need to get Chase here a Sprite. Devon just took him around the track in the Lambo."

"Did he? What did you think?" The look of pride on my dad's face is unmistakable.

"It was ... amazing," Chase says, looking almost reverent.

"How about that horsepower?" My dad mirrors Chase's expression.

"Unbelievable," Chase says.

"Next time, you'll have to drive it," Dad says, reaching up and patting Chase on the shoulder just once.

Chase puts a hand to his heart. "I'd be honored."

I roll my eyes. I guess cars are cool and all, but not on the religious level I'm witnessing right now.

"Let this man drive the Lambo," Dad declares to me.

"Sounds good," I say. "First let me get him a Sprite."

"I've gotta say, I don't love all this lying to your family," Chase tells me as we walk away, leaning his head in toward me so he won't be heard.

"I know, I don't like it either."

We approach a large drink cooler and I open it and fish around for a Sprite. I try to wipe off some of the water from the can and then hand it to him.

"Can't we just tell them the truth?"

I pull my head backward, surely giving myself multiple chins. "Do you like having me around?"

Chase wrinkles his brow. "Well … yes."

"Then we can't tell them. We'll have to come up with another excuse. They'd probably have me committed."

Chase smacks his mouth at this. "No, they wouldn't. You have a great family. Plus, it's not all that crazy."

I tilt my head and press my lips into a thin line.

"Okay, it's a little crazy."

"I do have a great family," I say, reaching up and dusting a piece of lint off Chase's shirt. "I just think it's better that we not tell them."

"Okay," he says. "But we need to find a way out of this car wrapping business. Or I'll just have to buy an expensive car."

"Don't worry," I say. "I have a plan. We'll tell them you changed your mind on the car but now we're friends."

"Can we do it soon?"

"Yes," I say, and give him a nod.

"Are you Chase?" I hear a voice say from behind me and I widen my eyes. I turn to see Chelsea standing there, a clipboard in one hand, a walkie-talkie in the other.

Chase steps around me. "I am," he says. "You must be Chelsea." He gives her a little wave, since he can't exactly shake her full hands.

A look of confusion passes over Chelsea's face. "Are you here with Maggie?"

"Well … she invited me," Chase says.

"I've heard you're looking into getting your car wrapped." There's an accusation to her tone, like she's not buying any of this. Which is ridiculous. I've come up with a solid story.

Chase looks to me, a question in his eyes. Now is not the time to change our story. "Yes," I say, jumping in. "He's just got to buy the car."

"Which … I'm doing next week," Chase adds, not sounding convincing at all.

"That's right." I nod my head quickly and then stop myself. Methinks I doth protest too much.

Chelsea looks at us, her blue eyes moving back and forth between Chase and me. I see the moment when she realizes she doesn't have time for this crap.

She holds out the walkie-talkie to me. "You ready to get to work?" she asks. She's got her irritated, sarcastic voice on.

"Of course," I say, taking the device from her. She's acting as if I'm just here for the fun while she works her butt off. I know my assignment, and it doesn't start until the racing begins.

"Nice to meet you, Chase," Chelsea says, and then turns around and walks the other way, pulling another walkie-talkie off the waistband of her jeans and saying something into it.

"Guess you better work." Chase moves to stand in front of me, a nod at the device in my hands.

"I've got a little longer. I'm in charge of making sure everything on the track goes smoothly. Racing doesn't start for another hour."

Chase nods and then something over my shoulder catches his eye. He leans in. "Dawson, twelve o'clock."

"Oh, right," I say. I'd forgotten that I'd see him here.

I knew he'd be here, of course, since all Cooper's employees have to be. I just didn't think all that much about seeing him. I've hardly spoken to him since the last time he was in my office. Only one time that I can think of, when I was manning the desk for Robin and he was on his way out for lunch. He stopped to say hi and tell me that he'd decided to give Chad another chance. Of course he brought up Chad. Always Chad.

What's weird is that I didn't worry or agonize over seeing him today, like I normally do. I must have been so caught up in getting Chase his dream ride in the Lambo that I didn't have a chance to think about it. I didn't even bother wondering if Dawson and I would talk and what I'd say to him. Or *if* I could say something to him.

THE ACCIDENTAL TEXT

Maybe seeing him at that party with Natasha was the remedy I needed for this stupid crush.

"Should we go talk to him?" Chase pulls me from my thoughts with his question.

"Dusting off those wingman skills?" I lift my brow.

"I mean, I'm not just using you for the Lamborghini."

I laugh. "I'm not sure I believe you."

"So, what should we do?" he asks, his pointer finger tapping on his can of soda. "I could strike up a conversation and see what's really happening with Natasha."

I scrunch my face. "How would you do that?"

He lifts a shoulder and then lets it drop. "Dunno. You've seen my skills, though. I could make it happen."

"I don't doubt it." I look over my shoulder at Dawson and see him talking to Chad, then I turn back to Chase. "You know what?" I say. "I don't much feel like it today."

"No?"

"Nope. I think I'm just going to take a break from all that."

"All right, then," Chase says, giving me that slight smile of his. "I'll be ready with my wingman skills. Just say the word."

I smile up at him. "I appreciate that."

Chapter 21

"All in all, it was our best Drives for Dreams yet," my dad tells the team at our weekly meeting.

Devon starts clapping and the rest of us join in, with a couple adding whoops and cheers.

It's Monday, and we're all gathered in the back of the shop, where 90 percent of the work we do at Cooper's gets done. The whole company is here, all thirty-five of us. Behind the gathering sits a half-wrapped Corvette Stingray. The room smells of plastic from the vinyl and the faint hint of gasoline. Also, a distinct cheap cologne scent from someone standing not too far from me. My money is on Chad.

"Let's give a round of applause to the person who made this all happen," my dad says after the clapping dies down. "Chelsea, come up here." He waves Chelsea over from where she's standing toward the side of the room.

She walks up to the front and my dad puts an arm around her while we all clap. You can see the pride in his face as he looks at her, and Chelsea, although giving us her best trying-to-be-humble look, is loving every minute of this.

THE ACCIDENTAL TEXT

"Chelsea worked so hard and I couldn't be more proud of her." He beams. One of those big fatherly smiles. "Drives for Dreams wouldn't have happened if it weren't for you."

I'm halfway waiting for him to call her Chelsy-bells like he did when we were younger. Devon was Devonion. I'm the only one he still calls by a nickname—Magpie—on a fairly regular basis.

"Yeah, Chelsea!" one of the shopworkers yells from the back of the room.

"Stay up here for a second," my dad says. "Actually, Devon and Maggie, come up here too." Devon and I go to stand by our dad.

I make eye contact with Dawson, who's leaning up against the wall where all the shelving is. He smiles at me. It's a dazzling smile … one that doesn't make my heart skip quite as many beats as it used to. It's like I can appreciate it without obsessing over it.

My dad takes a breath. "We usually give the proceeds to a variety of charities, but this year I thought we'd do just one." He turns and looks at us with a wobbly smile, and I feel my heart do a little dipping thing.

He doesn't even have to say it; I know what's coming. I can feel the emotions building, tears pooling in my bottom lids, and that tickling sensation at the top of my nose as I try to fight it.

I wrap an arm around Devon, who's standing next to me, and can tell he's also fighting back tears. He reciprocates, putting his arm around me. He's got his other arm around Chelsea.

"It's a place that means a lot to us," Dad continues, choking just a little bit on the words. "This year's Drives for Dreams donation is going to the Holly Brain Tumor Center."

I'm unable to fight the emotion and the tears come hot and fast. I feel so much in this moment. Like my heart is breaking but also bursting with joy. All at the same time.

The clapping starts up again, the whoops and cheers even louder as we all stand there, crying and smiling at everyone.

After the meeting ends and I'm back in my office, still choking up when I think of my dad making that announcement, I hear a knock on the wall outside my door.

"Hey," Dawson says. "You got a minute?"

"Sure," I say on a breath. His presence still does weird things to me, but they feel dampened today. When I told Chase on Saturday that I was taking a break from my crush on Dawson, I didn't think my body would listen. It usually acts of its own accord around him. But today it seems sort of numb to it all. Maybe it's all the emotions I felt earlier and am still feeling.

Dawson walks into my office, wearing those charcoal-gray coveralls again, Converse on his feet. He takes a seat in the black mesh guest chair opposite me. He leans back, weaving his fingers together and placing his hands in his lap.

"I know you can probably guess why I'm here," he says.

Please don't say Chad, please don't say Chad.

THE ACCIDENTAL TEXT

"Chad," he says. He chuckles. Maybe he realizes that's all we talk about too? Or maybe he's just laughing at the fact that he has to keep constantly talking to me about the guy.

"What did he do now?" Perhaps Dawson noticed Chad's offensive cologne smell too.

He looks down at his hands and then back up at me. "I'm letting him go … today," he says.

I give him a nod. "Okay, well, you're the boss."

"I guess I'll need all the paperwork and formal stuff from you."

"Right," I say. "I'll get on that."

I should say something funny right now like, *What will we have to talk about now?* Or, *Let's not let Devon hire any more friends, mmkay?* But I'm not really in a joking mood.

I think he's going to leave — at least it feels like this is the point in the conversation when it would seem appropriate for him to make his departure — but he just sits there. Half of a grin on his face. It's kind of like Chase's half-grin. But I like Chase's way more.

He opens his mouth to talk and then stops himself. And then does it again. Open and close. "I saw that Chase guy at Drives for Dreams," he says, finally. "The one from the party?"

So he noticed that. Interesting. "Yeah," I say. "Uh … Devon gave him a ride in the Lamborghini."

"Right," Dawson says, nodding his head. "I heard he threw up."

I picture poor Chase on the asphalt of the track, releasing everything he'd eaten before he got there. I feel bad that word got around about that, though I doubt he would care. "Yeah, he did."

Dawson reaches up and rubs his jaw, chuckling. He looks to the side, toward the wall with all my pictures of my family. The one that semi-inspired Chase to follow his adventurous dreams.

"I saw Natasha," I say.

She showed up toward the end. This time in a short jean skirt, a tight tube top, and platform sandals. She looked like she was going clubbing rather than hanging out at a racetrack. She kept taking selfies with all the cars, doing this pout thing with her lips.

"Yeah," says Dawson.

"That must have been ... fun." It's so hard for me to fake it when it comes to her.

He takes a deep breath in through his teeth. "Yeah, you won't be seeing much of her anymore."

"No?"

"We're officially done."

"Oh," I say. "I'm sorry?"

He smiles, and I think it's because I said that in the form of a question. "Thanks," he says. Then he stands up. "Well, I guess I should get to it."

"Good luck," I say.

I watch as he walks away. I may be feeling a little numb toward him, but I can't help a quick glance at his retreating form. Just before he goes out my office door, he looks back over his shoulder at me and smiles.

THE ACCIDENTAL TEXT

"Oh, sister, he wanted you to know that," Hannah says, pointing her chopsticks at me.

We're back at Hannah's childhood home, eating food made by Halmoni, and I've just told her all about my day. Halmoni made my favorite noodles tonight. She also lectured me—through Hannah—about my split ends. I really am overdue for a trim.

"Chase said the same thing."

Hannah freezes, noodles dangling in front of her mouth. "You told Chase before me?"

"You didn't answer your phone," I say defensively. The truth is that I told Chase first, on purpose, without even thinking about it, but she doesn't need to know this.

"This annoys me."

"Sorry. You know I love you best."

"I'm starting to wonder."

I ignore her and focus on my noodles.

After a quiet bit while we eat and Halmoni can be heard cleaning in the kitchen, I say, "Is it weird that I'm kind of *meh* about it ... about Dawson?"

"A little," she says, after taking a bite. "But maybe you're like hormonal or something. Or just emotionally spent."

I raise an eyebrow at her. "What would you know about being emotionally spent?"

She lifts one shoulder and lets it drop. "I read about it somewhere."

We smile at each other, both knowing that Hannah is a lot more emotional than she lets on. I love that we can have full conversations with just a smile.

"So what are you going to do with this information?"

I reach up and tug on my necklace. "I think I'll just wait."

"Wait?"

"Maybe I'm just tired today. Maybe I'll feel different tomorrow."

"You aren't going all KFC on me again, are you?"

"No," I protest. "At least … I don't think I am."

"Well, don't wait too long."

"I know, I know."

After dinner, I walk down to my dad's house and use my key to let myself in through the front door. I thought I'd pop over and see how he's doing. His announcement about where the money from Drives for Dreams was going affected me throughout the day. And if I felt a bit drained from it, I know he did too.

There's not a lot of light in the house as I enter, but I can see a dim one coming from the living room, and hear soft music playing. So I walk toward it, not calling for my dad in case he's asleep on the couch in front of the television. I don't want to scare him. I've done that before.

I hear low, mumbling chatter as I approach, the soft music getting more distinct. I can make out my dad's voice for sure. So maybe not asleep. Is he on the phone? But then I hear June's distinct laugh. I could pick it out from any crowd. It's higher pitched, with notes of warmth. This time, though, there's a definite hint of flirtation. I stop in my tracks, right at the entrance to the living room.

The lights are dimmed, the sounds of Michael Bublé crooning in the background. My dad and June, ever so close on the couch.

I should back out. I should just go as softly as I can, and then I can go home and pretend I never saw this … this intimacy. This perfect picture of two people who are clearly into each other. Which would not be a big deal if one of them wasn't my recently widowed father. Well, it's been five months. Is that considered recent?

I start to leave but end up turning more swiftly than I intended, and the keys I'd tucked in my pocket fall out and hit the floor with a loud clank.

"Hello?" I hear my dad say.

The light in the room gets brighter—I'd forgotten that he'd recently converted the house to a smart home and all the lighting and everything was now run by remote control.

"Maggie?" he says, when I finally stand up and turn around so he can see me. I'd briefly thought I could grab my keys and just crawl away.

"Dad," I say. Then I turn my head. "June."

"Hello, my dear," June says. She's calm and has a serene smile on her face as she sits back on the couch, a wineglass in her hand.

My dad, on the other hand, looks as if he's a teenager that's just been caught doing naughty things on the couch with his girlfriend.

My, how the tables have turned. I believe my dad caught Devon doing some naughty things with a girl on this very couch he's been snuggling up to June on.

Actually, no. My parents sold that couch not long after. Smart move.

"What are you doing here?" my dad asks, his face vacillating between shock and confusion.

He might be mirroring my facial expressions. But, in truth, I'm not as shocked as I should be. While this is disturbing for sure, it's not wholly unexpected. I've seen the texts. I know there's something more going on here than my dad is letting on.

"I just stopped by to say hi. I was eating dinner at Hannah's."

"Right," my dad says. "Well, come have a seat." He gestures toward the sofa.

"Yes," June says. "Come and sit."

I look at June and then at my dad. He's got a sort of sheepish grin on his face. Like he can't decide how he should be reacting. There's a lot of nostril flaring going on.

I hold up a hand. "I don't want to interrupt anything."

"No," June says, patting the spot next to her.

"You are definitely not interrupting," my dad says, his voice sounding very over the top and not at all convincing.

"Well, I can only stay for a minute."

I walk into the large open living room and my dad takes a seat on the sofa across from June, as if to say, *See? Nothing is happening here.* I decide that I'll just take a seat in one of the leather contemporary armchairs rather than sit next to either of them.

"So," my dad says, his hand fidgeting with the smart home remote.

"So," I say.

"What did Young-Hee make for dinner?" asks June.

I look at June and for a split second I forget that Young-Hee is Halmoni's actual name. But of course June would know that, since we've all lived in the same neighborhood for decades.

"She made my favorite noodles," I say.

"I love her cooking."

Silence lands on the already-stilted conversation. Michael Bublé sings about feeling good, and my dad is still messing with the remote control.

"How was work today?" June asks, obviously feeling like she needs to keep up the conversation.

"It was pretty good," I say.

"Your dad told me about the charity he picked." She smiles warmly.

I will myself not to think of it, because every time I picture him, with tears in his eyes, making that announcement, I get choked up.

One thing, though, is clear: my dad talks to June about my mom. I don't know why, but I'd wondered if he did. Or if it was like a past relationship that you don't bring up with your new relationship — if that's what's even happening here. Is this a relationship? I'm not ready to ask.

"Well," I say leaning forward in my chair. "I guess I better get going. I probably should head home."

"Are you sure, Magpie?" my dad asks, finally piping in. It's one of those questions you ask someone as a formality. I don't get the idea that he'd like me to stay. Not necessarily because I've interrupted something, but because he's not ready to be open about this. If he were, we'd all already know.

"Yeah," I say as I stand up. "It was good to see you, June." I walk over to my dad, who's getting up from his chair, and give him a hug.

"Love you, Magpie," he says in my ear, with his arms tightly around me. "So much."

Chapter 22

Things may never happen with Dawson, but at least I'll have Oscar—Chase's dog—to fall back on as a companion.

"I think my dog likes you more than me," Chase says, a slightly annoyed expression on his face.

After a long day we ended up back at Chase's house, which is a three-bedroom townhome near Tempe Town Lake. It's more modern looking than I would've thought Chase would pick. I guess I never gave much thought to Chase's style, but now that I'm here, it fits. I like the straight lines and stainless steel detailing. It's definitely got that bachelor pad feel.

There's almost a sterile feeling to his place—a lack of decor. If this were my house, there would be art on the walls and pictures of my family and *way* more color. It's mostly blacks and grays throughout. Not much personality, not a lot of personal touches. Except for one framed family picture, a five by seven, sitting on the kitchen counter.

It's the perfect location for a dog, though, with all the trails and the lake nearby. I can picture Chase and Oscar making good use of all the amenities.

I'm currently sitting at one end of a black leather sectional couch, Chase on the other end, his legs sprawled out, with a very fluffy golden retriever's head in my lap. Oscar's tongue hangs out the side of his mouth as I rub his head. He's been next to me since the minute Chase introduced us.

"Well, if he wants to come home with me, I'm okay with that." Oscar's eyes open and I start scratching under his chin. "Do you want to live with me, Oscar? Do you?" I say, using that voice everyone uses when talking to dogs.

Chase scowls at me. "He may have fallen in love with you, but he's not going anywhere. Sorry, boy."

"What can I say? I just have this effect on all men." I bat my eyelashes at Chase. "It's a curse."

"I believe it," he says, giving me that signature half-smile of his.

I look down at the scrape on my arm as I scratch behind Oscar's ears. It's a good three inches and looks like long thin tire tracks. All in the name of adventure.

Chase notices me looking at it. "We should probably put something on that," he says.

I feel like a mess right now, dusty and tired and crampy. There are muscles aching on my body that I didn't even know I had. The scratch doesn't even hurt; or if it does, I have too many other aches and pains to realize it. I lean my head back on the couch, thinking about the day.

Chase got me up early this morning and we drove nearly two hours to Oracle, where we tried our hand at zip-lining.

THE ACCIDENTAL TEXT

Well, this was Chase's first time. It was never top of my parents' list for adventure, but I've done it a few times.

There were five different zip lines, so we worked our way up to the longest one, which was around fifteen hundred feet. It was a beautiful day, the wind whipping through my hair as we rode. The sky was a bright shade of blue and the desert below us seemed to go on forever.

Chase loved it. He hollered and yelled every time, full of energy and adrenaline that kept him pepped up all the way home.

Even knowing that this wasn't my mom's favorite thing to do, adventure-wise, I couldn't help but picture her acting much like Chase, whooping and laughing, her hair whipping out from under her helmet, a big smile on her face.

Before we left, we found this cave nearby that you can explore without a tour guide. I'd been spelunking before, but Chase never had.

We had to rent headlamps from an older man at a sporting goods store in the small town of Oracle. He was wearing a fishing hat and a pair of worn-out tan coveralls that were nothing like the ones that Dawson wears to work. Or maybe he just didn't wear the coveralls like Dawson does. He warned us many times about the dangers of the cave. Claustrophobia being the biggest one. Also, there's no cell reception inside the cave, so we couldn't call anyone to save us if we ran into trouble.

After reading comments and reviews online, it seemed that the store owner might have been exaggerating. There were no horror stories that we could find, and according to posts, there was plenty of signage to get us through the cave.

We found the entrance, got about a quarter of a mile in, and then hit a spot where you basically had to shimmy down into a very small crevice. It was at that point that both Chase and I realized we'd had enough adventure for the day, so we went back the way we came. It was just as we were getting to the end, where we could see daylight coming through the small entrance of the cave, that I took a dive, tripping over something and scratched up my arm. That kiss for good luck before we entered apparently only worked for Chase, who made it out without a scratch.

The drive was my favorite part. I learned a lot about Chase on the way up and back. I got to ask the questions, since we're still not even. I stayed away from too many about his mom. I think I've known him long enough to understand that he doesn't want to talk about her all that much. Definitely not about her death or the funeral. He's at least been able to tell me some stories with her in them without having a sad moment. They're mostly funny stories. Heidi Beckett was a funny woman, it would seem. That's where Chase gets it, I'd bet. He doesn't tell all that many stories about his dad, who seems more stoic, more serious. He was definitely the disciplinarian in the family.

But we never get to feelings. Or even recent stories. People mourn differently; I know that. Chelsea, Devon, and I have all experienced different reactions to losing our mom. I'm sure Chase is dealing with it in his own way. Maybe all of this adventuring is helping.

But even avoiding that topic, I still learned that Chase hates baseball (I almost made him pull the car over and let me out over this), studied business marketing in college (he went to ASU, too, but was a couple of years ahead of me), is a morning person, and likes all kinds of food but hates cilantro (prompting my second request to pull over and let me out).

We talked about past relationships; his dating history is fairly similar to mine, except his longest relationship was two years with a woman named Amelia, and they went their separate ways when they both decided they wanted different things. Amelia wanted to settle down and have a family. Chase, not so much.

"You don't want a family?" I asked as we were driving along the 10, the sun just starting to set.

"I do," he said. "I just didn't want one then. And if I'm being honest, I don't think I wanted one with Amelia. We had different ideals about family. She came from a broken home—which isn't a problem for me, but for her, it was. It affected her."

"Gotcha," I said. "Well, I've never made it past sixth months in a relationship."

"How come?"

"There were only two guys that I considered boyfriends. There was Brian. We dated for nearly six months until things just … fizzled out. It was during college and we were both young … and dumb. After college, I dated a guy named Jace for four months. I thought there might be a future with him, but then I realized that I was trying to make something work there that just wasn't. So I broke up with him."

Chase glanced over at me and then back at the road. "Don't take this wrong, but is there something wrong with you?"

I reached over and whacked him on the arm. "How am I not supposed to take that wrong?"

"Like a weird hobby? Or stinky feet?"

"You tell me. I took my shoes off as soon as we got in the car."

"Is that what I smell?"

"Shut up."

I looked over at Chase and he's doing that little smile of his. "What I'm saying is, you're ... very pretty."

"I fifty percent forgive you for saying that."

He chuckled. "You're attractive, and you're kind of funny." That got him another whack. "And you ... how do I say this? You—"

"Have a pathetic dating life," I interjected.

"Your words, not mine," he said. "It ... confuses me."

"You and me both," I said. I looked out the window, watching the sagebrush and the cacti zoom by. "Maybe there is something wrong with me." This came out quietly and mostly for my own ears.

"I don't think so," he said.

THE ACCIDENTAL TEXT

I looked over at him. "See, and you're the person who should be able to tell me what's wrong with me. You read those texts—you saw some of my innermost thoughts."

"I forgot them."

"Lies."

We sat in silence for a bit, just the low volume of a rock station making background noise.

"I guess that's why I'm confused," Chase finally said. "I read things that you never meant to be read. Your innermost thoughts, or whatever. And—" He stopped and took a breath. "It just ... doesn't add up."

I felt the tips of my ears warm at his words. "You're now eighty-five percent forgiven."

Now, sitting here on Chase's couch, feeling drowsy from the day's events as I snuggle with my new best friend, Oscar, I feel ... peaceful. I can't remember when I've felt like this. Not in the past five months, that's for sure. And definitely not for the six months before that. I don't know if it's all the fun we've been having or the fact that I just really like Chase. He makes me laugh. And I feel like ... me around him.

I feel like me.

Chapter 23

> **Maggie:** I will give you all my worldly possessions if you come to my parents' house and save me from this.

I send this text to Chase, my phone partially hidden under the large dining room table where Devon, Chelsea and her family, and I are having dinner with my dad ... and June.

There are pictures of my mom and our family hanging all over the walls of this room. Her touch is everywhere, from the drapes, to the large contemporary shelving on the south side of the room, to the floors, which were updated a couple of years ago. This room is all her. This house is all her.

My dad is sitting in his normal seat at the head of the table, and on his right sits June. Their adjoined hands resting on the top of the table.

"June and I are dating," my dad says, grinning at all of us. He looks over at June and they give each other a smile. It's one of those intimate ones, full of meaning.

He didn't just start with that. There was a lot of pomp and circumstance leading up to this announcement. First the invitation, which we all got late last night via text. It's not rare for us to all have Sunday dinner as a family, but we haven't done it in a while. It didn't seem like a big deal until the second text came in.

> **Dad:** I'd like to talk to you all about something.

That's when we switched over to our sibling WhatsApp group.

> **Chelsea:** What do you think Dad's going to tell us?
> **Maggie:** My gut is on June.
> **Devon:** Gross.

Turns out my gut was right. Stupid gut.

Chelsea got there first, and then Devon and I somehow showed up at the same time not long after her. Chelsea nodded her head toward the kitchen when Devon and I entered the house, and we walked over to find June there, helping my dad with the finishing touches on dinner. He made roasted chicken and potatoes, one of our favorite family dinners growing up. My dad and June smiled at each other and laughed as they worked together.

It was different than the two of them sitting in a dim room listening to music and drinking wine. Under normal circumstances, I might have thought this whole kitchen routine was cute; instead it felt foreign and odd.

I think I'm the least taken aback, because of what I caught the other night. But I never shared it with Chelsea and Devon—it somehow didn't feel right to. I was still processing it myself. In hindsight, I probably should have told them — maybe this would have felt less awkward.

When we entered the dining room, the table was set nicer than it usually is. June's doing, I'd guess. My dad was never one to set the table formally. We were using Mom's fine china and silver that we'd usually only bring out at Christmas. My heart did a little wrenching thing when I saw it. I took some steadying breaths.

Then when we went to seat ourselves and June took the spot where our mom used to sit, I felt a weight land in my gut, like I had swallowed a massive rock. Roasted chicken may no longer be my favorite dinner. It might always be associated with this feeling.

"That's ... great." Mark, Chelsea's husband, is the first to speak. I think he couldn't take the awkward silence that landed on the room after our dad's announcement.

"Yeah," I say, my voice coming out breathy.

"Yeah, great," Chelsea says, using her extra cheerful fake-sounding voice. Avery is on her lap, playing with the white cloth napkin, putting it on her face and giggling.

Devon just sits there, his arms folded, an angry look on his face.

"I know this might be strange for all of you," June says. "I promise, this is not what we were expecting." She looks at my dad again.

"June has been wonderful, helping me work through my grief. She's been a rock for me."

Devon snorts and it sounds sarcastic.

THE ACCIDENTAL TEXT

"Are you going to get married, Papa?" Alice asks, sitting in the seat next to me. She's a very astute four-year-old—she picks up on things that a normal child her age probably wouldn't. But she's smart like that. She already knows her ABCs.

She also has an obsession with Disney princesses, as evidenced by the Elsa dress she's chosen to wear to dinner. She's holding a butter knife—a silver one from my mom's collection—and has it pointed at my dad and June. Chelsea reaches over and snatches the knife out of her hand. I give Alice my phone to keep her occupied.

My dad does a nervous laugh. "Not yet, Alice in Wonderland," he says, using the nickname he gave her at birth.

Not ... *yet*?

I need my phone back. I need to text Chase for help. He's got to use his wingman skills and get me out of here. But Elsa, a.k.a. Alice, has my phone.

"Mommy, what does C-H-A-S-E spell?" Alice asks, holding my phone up to show Chelsea.

"Chase," Chelsea says. She looks at my phone and then at me. Her brow pinched. "You're getting texts from him?"

I grab the phone from Alice, seeing Chase's name on the lock screen. "We're friends. I told you."

"No one can replace her," Devon says, his voice elevated.

Chelsea and I look over at the other side of the table where my dad and June are still sitting, still holding hands, and Devon is staring at them, red faced.

I just missed something. What did I miss?

"I'm not looking to replace your mom." My dad's face is starting to turn a matching shade of red.

I swivel my head back to Chelsea, who gives me wide eyes and a quick shake of her head. We need to intervene. But I'm not sure how to do it.

"Couldn't you, like, get a dog or something?" Devon asks, his voice getting louder.

"This isn't about being lonely," Dad says.

"Sex, then?" Devon asks.

"Devon!" Chelsea says, the pitch of her voice bordering on shrill.

"That's not your business, son," my dad says, his voice loud and booming.

"What is sex?" Alice asks the room.

June is now the color of a beet, and it feels like the temperature in the room has gone up a hundred degrees.

Everyone starts talking over each other—words are being said between Devon and my dad that are going to be hard to take back. June looks like she might cry.

I glance at Chelsea and see a look of desperation on her face. We make eye contact and her eyes plead with me. I know my job. I've always been the peacemaker of the family. It's the plight of the middle child. How do I fix this? What can I say?

I look down at the phone in my lap. And then my head jerks up.

"CHASE HAS MOM'S PHONE NUMBER!"

THE ACCIDENTAL TEXT

The words come out super loud, like they just exploded from my mouth.

The room goes silent. All heads turn toward me. Avery starts to whine in Chelsea's lap, and Mark gets up and lifts her into his arms. He coaxes Alice from the table with promises of candy and the three of them exit the room. Lucky.

"What?" Chelsea asks as her family leaves, confusion on her face.

"Who's Chase?" Dad asks.

"Mom's phone?" says Devon.

I swallow. That was a real knee-jerk reaction. I could have yelled fire ... that might have been better.

I take a breath. "You all know Chase. He was at the party and then at Drives for Dreams."

My dad nods his head slowly, remembering. He looks to June, who gives him questioning eyes.

"Devon gave him a ride in the Lambo?" my dad asks.

I nod my head. "Yes. He's ... he's not a client or a potential client. His name is Chase Beckett. And he has Mom's phone number," I say.

"What?" Devon says, his ire now directed at me. *Good, good* ... that was the point of my outburst. Even if I have so many regrets already.

"I don't understand," says Chelsea.

I close my eyes and take a steadying breath before opening them. "I was texting Mom's phone. After she died. It was kind of like therapy," I add, after seeing the confused/concerned look on my dad's face. "It felt like therapy, at least."

"Maggie," Chelsea says, and I look to see her watery eyes.

I blink rapidly, looking away from her. I can't cry right now. "So then I found out that Dad had turned off Mom's phone."

"I'm so sorry, Magpie," my dad says, his voice quiet. "Had I known—"

"It's okay, Dad." I cut him off. "I understand." I give him a closed-mouth smile. "It turns out that my texts started going to someone."

Chelsea's eyes go wide. "Chase?"

"Yes," I say. "Chase."

"Wait … the guy that wants to bring his car to the shop?" Devon asks. He's still not grasping this. "The one I gave a ride in the Lamborghini?"

"Wait … why was he at both events?" Chelsea asks.

"I … invited him." I nibble on my bottom lip after this declaration. It's weird to begin with, but inviting him to that party and then to Drives for Dreams makes it ten times crazier.

"I don't understand, Magpie," Dad says.

I swallow, looking at him and then to June. She gives me a comforting smile, dipping her chin as if to urge me on. I'm suddenly grateful for her steadying presence.

"Chase wrote me back after he started getting my texts that were meant for Mom, and we sort of … started texting."

THE ACCIDENTAL TEXT

"What?" Devon says. He's got triple chins now, the way he's pulled his face so far inward. His lips are pulled downward.

"Catch up, Devon," Chelsea says. "Our sister has been texting a stranger, thinking it was Mom's phone, and then invited him to our family business work events."

I shoot her an annoyed look. There's an accusatory tone to her voice. She's not wrong, but it's so much more than that.

"So he doesn't want his car wrapped?" Devon asks.

I shake my head.

"No Lexus LC five hundred?"

"He really does drive a Honda Accord."

Devon makes a sour face at this bit of info.

"Wait ... so that story was totally made up. Did his mom really die?" Chelsea asks.

"She did," I say.

"Before Mom?"

I shake my head. It feels wrong to share this part of Chase. Like it's not my story to tell. "In March," is all I offer.

I'm not sure if my family can put two and two together with this information.

"That's ... how sad," June says, her head tilted to the side, her soft eyes on me.

"So are you like, what? Are you with this guy or something?" Devon asks.

"No." I shake my head. "We're friends."

June makes a little smacking noise with her mouth and I look back at her. She has her hand resting on her heart. "I think that's just lovely," she says. "What a way to meet someone."

"A creepy way," Chelsea says.

I squint my eyes at Chelsea, annoyed with her reaction. I should be more understanding. Chase has become more to me than just someone I've been texting. *So* much more. But it's hard to convey that when the way we met is just so freaking weird.

"I'm sorry I lied to you," I say, looking around the room at my family. The family who will probably have another meeting without me, this time to discuss my sanity. I'm now fragile with a side of insane.

"Well," my dad says after a few beats of silence. He looks around the room. "Who wants some pie?"

Devon raises his hand. "I'll take some."

"Me too," Chelsea says.

And just like that, my job is done. Peace once again restored. At least for now.

I feel Chase's chuckle more than I hear it. We're lying on my bed and I'm turned toward him, my face buried into his shoulder, his arm around me.

"You said you would take it to the grave," Chase says.

"I know," I say, the words coming out muffled with my face against his shirt.

THE ACCIDENTAL TEXT

He smells of that same cologne—the one I still can't name—mixed with the scent of fabric softener from the black fitted tee he's wearing.

I lift my face up and give him a defeated look. Then I lie back, using his bicep as a pillow. He pulls me toward him, resting his hand on my arm. He gives it a squeeze.

I texted Chase before I left my dad's house, asking if he could come over. Hannah has been working all weekend on the same case, the one that's been taking all her time for the past month.

I needed to vent, and who better to vent to than the reason for my need to vent? Sort of. He's more like an innocent bystander.

When Chase got here I gave him a tour of our small apartment, and then we took a seat on my bed and I started telling him what happened. As we talked, he kicked off his flip-flops, scooted back on my full-size bed, and laid his head on my pillow, patting the spot he'd left next to him. That's how we ended up here, lying on my bed, looking up at the dormant ceiling fan.

"Well, the cat's out of the bag," he says.

"I hate that saying. Who puts a cat in a bag?"

"Fine, the pig is in the poke?"

"Try again."

He lets out a breath. "You can't take it back. It's out there."

"I could find a witch and have her cast a spell?"

"Excellent idea."

I sigh. "I swear my dad looked at me differently afterward."

I caught my dad giving me sad smiles while we were eating pie. Or maybe I was just being overly sensitive about it. Devon was okay with it, or at least he seemed to be. After having taken so long to put the pieces together, I thought for sure he'd be annoyed with me, especially for lying to him like I did. But he seemed fine.

Later, when we were cleaning up and Chelsea pried me with more questions, Devon even came to my rescue, telling her it wasn't a big deal and to leave me alone. I doubt that will keep Chelsea away. If only.

"Why do you think he looked at you differently?"

"He probably thinks I need therapy."

Chase chuckles again. "At least he cares. I've barely said two words to my dad since the funeral."

I turn my head to the side and tilt it upward to see him looking at my ceiling. It's the first time he's said much of anything about his dad.

"Why do you think that is?" I ask.

I feel his shrug. "He's not really been talking to me or Kenzie. Not more than one- or two-word sentences."

"That … must be hard. How is Kenzie handling everything?"

"I haven't talked to her in a few days. She's busy planning a wedding."

"Right," I say. "How's that going?"

"It's going," he says.

THE ACCIDENTAL TEXT

We fall into silence, only the sound of the cars on the street below my open window filling the quiet. I leave the conversation open for Chase to say more, wanting him to talk to me more about how he's feeling. He seems so open when we talk about other things, but shuts down when we talk about his family.

"There's a heart on your ceiling," Chase says, pointing toward the spot near my fan.

"You see that?"

"Totally. It's a perfect-shaped one. A rare find on a ceiling," he says. "I've found a pretty good Batman shape in my room."

I turn my head toward him again, feeling so much kinship with this man lying on my bed, his hand now rubbing lazy patterns on my arm. It's a dumb thing, really. How many millions of people look for shapes in clouds? Certainly a ceiling with accidental patterns from a texture gun is not much different.

"There's two-thirds of a shamrock on my bathroom wall," I say.

Another chuckle. "I'm pretty sure I can see my grandpa's profile in my kitchen. I sometimes say hi to it."

This time it's my turn to giggle. "I think I might miss you when you go to London."

He gives my arm a squeeze. "Might?" he says.

"Well, I'll for sure miss Oscar."

"He'll miss you," Chase says. "And I'll probably miss you. Maybe."

"What's going on in here?"

We both look over to see Hannah standing just inside the door of my room, taking in the sight of Chase and me on my bed. His arm around me, my body semi-snuggled up to his. We probably *do* look a little cozy.

"Hey, Han," I say, using a very casual tone as if to say, *Do not read into this.*

She's apparently too tired to care, because she suddenly drops her purse on the floor, in dramatic Hannah fashion, and then comes over to the bed. "Scoot," she instructs.

Chase and I comply, and now I'm in between the two of them. It's odd how right this feels. Like we've been doing this for years.

"How's work?" Chase asks.

Hannah lets out a grunt. "Let's not talk about it."

"Mags told her family about me tonight," Chase says.

"Chase," I say, my voice a reprimand. I reach over and pinch his arm, and he wiggles it away from me.

"Wait, what?" Hannah asks. "You told them what about Chase?"

"The whole thing," Chase says.

"I can speak for myself, you noob," I say.

"No way. What happened? Why did you tell them?"

"Well, my dad and June are dating," I say.

"So you thought to up the ante by telling them the truth about your texting lover?"

I pinch her arm this time. "Not lovers," I say.

"Yeah," Chase says. "Bummer."

THE ACCIDENTAL TEXT

I look over at him and see a smile on his face, his eyes on the ceiling. He's teasing, obviously. So why do I feel a warm sensation starting to swirl in my belly?

"Shut up," I say, to him *and* my stomach.

I turn my head toward Hannah and give her most of the details but not everything, my need to vent gone now that I already did that with Chase.

"Wow," she says. "That wasn't well thought out, was it?"

Chase laughs. "No, it wasn't."

"Stop ganging up on me."

"It's really easy to fix this," says Hannah.

"Really?" I turn my head toward her.

"Just do something even crazier … like rob a bank or something."

"Helpful," I say.

"If there's one thing I know," she says, after yawning loudly, "it's that the Coopers get over stuff. It's one of your talents. I wish that was a thing with my family. Halmoni still lectures me about the one time I came home past curfew when I was seventeen."

I snort laugh and Chase chuckles next to me.

We're silent for a bit and I stare up at the heart on my ceiling, feeling so grateful for it right now.

Chapter 24

The following Monday I'm in my office, working on some new hire paperwork. Chad has officially been replaced. I guess Dawson and I will have to find something new to talk about. Like the weather. Or even worse, politics. Gross.

Chad's replacement was interviewed and hired last week, and today is his first day. I have a lovely stack of papers for him to fill out. Cooper's is still old school when it comes to employee paperwork. Someday we'll get with the times.

The new hire's name is Mateo, and he's got very dreamy eyes. I obviously didn't tell him that when I interviewed him, because that wouldn't be very HR of me. But I thought it in my head. They're the darkest brown, like chocolate. And his eyelashes are every girl's fantasy—for themselves, of course. It's such a shame when men have beautiful, lush eyelashes. They don't even appreciate them.

I'm feeling a little tired today since I spent the entire weekend with Chase. On Saturday we went indoor skydiving to help Chase prep for his big jump. That's what he said anyway. I warned him that it's not really like jumping out of a plane. Like, hardly at all. He didn't seem to care. He loved it and it was another check mark on his adventure list.

Sunday, Chase invited me over to spend the afternoon at the park with my new boyfriend, Oscar. He didn't actually call Oscar my boyfriend, and he did get slightly irritated when he threw out a Frisbee for Oscar to catch and Oscar kept bringing it back to me.

I so badly want to take him while Chase is in London, but his sister, Kenzie, has already volunteered for the job. My third-story apartment wouldn't be all that fun for a big dog anyway.

"Mags," I hear someone say from the doorway, and look up to see Chelsea standing there. She looks a little haggard—not like someone who just got back from vacation. If you can call visiting her in-laws in Fresno with two young children in tow a vacation.

"Hey, Chels," I say, and give her a smile.

We haven't talked—not since the Sunday before, when I told everyone who Chase really was. I'd thought maybe since she was leaving the next day that she'd take a week to forget or at least get over it.

But by the look on her face, I can tell she's anxious to talk to me. Which means none of that happened. What probably *did* happen is that she thought about it a lot, got worked up, and is now here to lecture me. Can't wait.

"How was your trip?" I ask, deciding that stalling is my best tactic.

"It was ... okay," she says. She walks into my office and takes a seat in the black mesh chair across from me.

"That fun, huh?" I say.

"Well, you know. It's ... Fresno."

I chuckle. "Right."

"How was your week?"

"It was good," I say. "We hired someone to replace Chad."

"Finally," she says. "Do you know that he tried to wrap my car?"

"What?"

"Yeah, one time Dawson told him to go get the next car from the lot and start on the door, and when Dawson came back my minivan was in the shop, and the driver's side door was wrapped in hot pink."

I snort laugh at that. It's possible I might end up missing dear old Chad. At least he gave me something to laugh about—and something to talk with Dawson about.

She gets a serious look on her face. "Listen, Maggie, I've been thinking a lot this past week while I was gone and realized something." She pauses to take a deep breath. "I don't think I've been here for you enough. Since ... since Mom died."

My face falls. "Chels—"

She holds up a hand. "I was caught up in my own life, in my own grief, and I feel like I neglected you."

"No way," I say shaking my head. "Chelsea, making sure I'm fine is *not* your job." Typical oldest sibling.

THE ACCIDENTAL TEXT

"I know that. I guess I just thought that since you felt the need to send those texts to Mom's phone, maybe ... I could have been more supportive. I wasn't here for you enough, and I'm sorry."

I'm at a loss for words. This wasn't what I was expecting at all when she came in here. I was expecting a lecture or some sort of nudge toward therapy.

"Chels, I've never felt like you weren't here for me," I say. I let out a breath before continuing ... before explaining. "Texting Mom's phone was my thing. It wasn't some outlet because I wasn't getting what I needed from you or Dad or Devon. It was just ... me working through my feelings. That's all it was."

She looks to the side, toward my wall of pictures. "Just so you know, I'm here. You can talk or text or whatever you need."

I pull my lips upward. "I never once thought I couldn't."

She takes a big inhale and then gives me a few quick nods of her head. "Okay," she says. "That makes me feel better. I just kept thinking about everything and I was ... worried about you."

I smile. "And I love you for it. I'm sorry if it ruined your trip."

"No." She waves my words away with her hand. "Mark's mom had that job."

"That bad?"

She blows air out of her cheeks and lets her head hang down slightly. "Worse than bad."

"Tell me," I say.

"I can't right now, but I promise I will later. I have so much work to catch up on," she says, standing up from the chair.

She says goodbye, looking much lighter than she did when she first came in, and walks out the door.

Thirty seconds later there's a knock on the wall outside my door and I lift my head up, expecting to see Chelsea back again. But then I remember Chelsea never knocks.

Instead, Dawson is in my doorway, in black coveralls, his dark-blond hair styled just perfectly. He looks rather delicious, even if my heart doesn't speed up all that much in his presence. My pits seem completely dry right now too. My palms are slightly sweaty, though. I may never *not* have a reaction to him.

"Hey there," I say, feeling the words roll off my tongue. I haven't felt tongue-tied around Dawson in a while. Maybe it's because I haven't even tried to make a move in a long time. It doesn't feel like something I want to do right now. I'm not saying it's off the table completely, but I've set that thought on the back burner.

"Hey," he says in response. "You got that paperwork for Mateo?"

"Yep, right here," I say, tapping on the neat stack of papers on my desk. I grab a manila folder from the bottom drawer and place the paperwork inside of it.

"May I?" he asks, gesturing toward the folder.

It's funny, now that I'm not so caught up in making my feelings known to him, I'm noticing new things about Dawson. Like how sort of shy he is. Especially around me.

THE ACCIDENTAL TEXT

His cheeks turn a light shade of pink, just on the apples, nearly every time we have a conversation. I don't know if this is a new development or I'm just noticing now because I can take note of such things without the distraction of my erratically beating heart and my sweaty palms and pits.

I give him a nod and he walks up to grab the paperwork. I push the folder toward the other side of my desk to make it easy for him to grab, and maybe I pushed too far, or Dawson didn't get a good hold on the folder, because somehow it ends up falling off my desk and all of the papers fall out and fly around, landing in all directions on the floor.

Dawson swears under his breath.

"So sorry," I say, and stand up from my chair. I move around to the other side of my desk where Dawson is already on hands and knees trying to gather up all the paperwork. I get down on the ground and help him.

"No, I'm the one that's sorry," he says as he's trying to gather everything. There are probably only about twenty sheets, but they're spread out around us and hard to pick up off the epoxy flooring. There's no give between the paper and the floor, making it hard to get a finger underneath.

We end up sort of brushing them into a pile with our hands, which makes it easier to pick up. We're also laughing at the ridiculousness of the whole thing: both of us on the floor, trying like mad to pick up all these papers.

Once we get it all somewhat together, we're both still chuckling, and we sit back on our heels, so close that I can feel his shoulder touching mine. I turn my head to find Dawson watching me, and something shifts in his expression. He's not smiling anymore and his eyes have taken on a more serious look — almost like he's determined to do something. Before I can think of what that might be, he leans his face in and presses his lips against mine.

His lips are warm and full, and my eyes flutter shut at the contact. The kiss probably only lasts a few seconds before he pulls away. I keep my eyes closed, feeling so many things right now. So many thoughts running through my mind. When I open my eyes he's looking at me, his cheeks red, his eyes curious.

I touch my fingers to my lips, not entirely sure what just transpired.

"Was that ... did I ..." he says, not completing a sentence.

My body, working on its own, stands up from the floor. It's an instinctive response, like a fight-or-flight thing.

Dawson jumps up to his feet as well. He swipes a hand down his face. "I'm ... so sorry, Maggie. Did I ... did I get that wrong?"

"What?"

He closes his eyes for just a second and then opens them. "It seemed like ... I thought that ..." he stops himself, looking frustrated by his inability to form a full sentence.

I let out a breath. "You didn't get that wrong, Dawson," I say, and he does a whole upper-body sagging thing, in relief.

THE ACCIDENTAL TEXT

He then stands up straight and walks toward me, this time with a more definitive expression. A man on a mission.

I hold out a hand to stop him. "You didn't get that wrong, but ... I'm not sure how I feel about it."

"Oh," he says, his face falling a little.

"It's not that ... I just ..." I let out a breath, not sure what to say or how to say it. Maybe I should just go with the truth. If only I could pinpoint exactly what that is.

"Is it that Chase guy?" Dawson asks.

"What?" I feel my eyes widen. "No ... Chase ... I—"

"Sorry," he interrupts. "It just seemed like maybe something could be happening between you."

I look to the ground, my brain firing off again. Is my change in feelings toward Dawson because of ... Chase? I try the thought on for a second but end up feeling even more confused.

"So then ... what?" he asks.

I let out a breath. "If you had done that like ... two weeks ago?" I say. "I would have been so thrilled. Like, jumping for joy, thrilled."

"Ah, okay. But ... not now."

"Now," I say, and then nibble on my bottom lip while I think. "Now, I'm just ... not sure."

"Got it. I missed my chance." He rubs a hand down his face again.

"No," I say. "Maybe. I don't know."

"Right," he says. "So maybe think on it?"

I smile. "I can do that."

"Okay." He echoes my smile. "Then I can wait."

He comes closer to me and leans in, and for a second, I wonder if he understands the concept of waiting. But all he does is brush his lips on my cheek. And then, with a soft smile, he walks out of my office.

Chapter 25

"Has any of this been helping you?" Chase asks as we walk along the Bell Trail, the heat in the low nineties. We're about two hours north of Tempe, not all that far from Sedona. It's beautiful outside and the trail follows along a creek, which is pretty on its own, with trees lining each side of the slowly flowing water. There's a distinct scent of dirt and brush as we walk.

Today's adventure includes a three-and-a-half-mile hike toward a watering hole called the Crack. That's the actual name, and every time I say it, Chase snickers. We're apparently trying out cliff diving. There's not a lot of that around here, so this is the best we can do. I've been told—by Chase, of course—that the Crack boasts cliff dives as high as thirty feet, which isn't too shabby. I did a fifty-foot one in Hawaii one time on vacation, and I don't think I would go that high again.

It's not really a hike—at least not this first part. It's more like a walk. The dirt trail is wide and mostly flat and sprawling. But it supposedly gets a little more difficult closer to the watering hole. Chase instructed me to wear sneakers and, of course, my bathing suit, which I'm wearing underneath some light-gray running shorts — that I've never actually used for running — and a light-blue tank top.

Chase has on some board shorts with a blue Hawaiian pattern and a white T-shirt. Also those aviator glasses that I find so endearing. He's carrying a backpack with towels, water, and some lunch for us. He's quite prepared. I like that about Chase. He's always thoughtful about what I might want or need.

It feels nice to be out here after being in the shop all week, to feel the light breeze on my face and the hot sun overhead.

"Helping me how?" I ask.

"You know ... to get your mojo back?"

I think about that. It's the first of May, so that means only two weeks until jump time. I'd love to say that all this adventuring with Chase has caused some awakening in me and the jump sounds like something I could do in my sleep ... like the old me. But the thought of it — going up in that tiny plane, so high up, all of us jumping, sending my mom's ashes into the sky — still causes tendrils of anxiety to run through me.

"I don't know," I say.

"But you think you can jump," he says.

"I mean, I have to," I say. I'm resigned to do it. I don't think I'll choke, because I can't let myself have the option.

"What about you?"

"I think I'm becoming an adrenaline junkie."

THE ACCIDENTAL TEXT

I snicker. "That could become an issue," I say. "Has it … helped you with things?"

I skirt over what I really want to talk about, knowing he'll understand me, hoping maybe he'll open up about how he's feeling. Even if just a little. He's only given me tiny tidbits here and there. And even those might just be things I've picked up on, not things he's actually said. Like a look I've seen on his face a few times, or his eyes going unfocused for a moment.

He lifts a shoulder and lets it drop. "It's helping."

That's it? I will him with my brain to tell me more. *Come on, Chase, open up.*

"Not sure I'll be able to keep this up in London," he says, and my heart does a little dropping thing at his immediate change of subject.

"Sure you can; plenty of things to do there."

"Have you been?"

"No," I say.

He does that slight smile. "Well, whatever I do find, it won't be half as fun without you there." He bumps my side with his as we walk on the path.

"Please. You'll find some cute British bird to keep you company," I say. And then feel a little drop in my stomach at the thought. I don't want Chase to find someone else to hang out with. It's a ridiculous thought, really. How selfish of me.

"Hardly," he says. "I'll be working a lot."

I'm bummed that he's leaving. I've become so used to having him around, I think it'll feel a little like withdrawal when he's gone. At least we already have a texting thing going, so we'll still have that. But with the time difference and his work, I know it will be different. Gone will be the days that I text him and get an almost immediate response. And I've come to rely on Chase a lot for my sanity.

"And how was Cooper's yesterday? Get any new cars in that I can come sit in?" Chase asks this as we get to a sign that says we're at the halfway point. There's a split in the trail and I follow him when he takes the one to the left, past a sign that says Coconino National Forest.

"Oh yes, we got a new Ferrari F-eight Spider in yesterday," I say.

Chase lets out a whistle. "How much would that put me back?"

"About two hundred and fifty k."

He waves a hand at that. "That cheap?"

"So cheap."

"And Dawson?" he asks. He sounds almost like it was hard to get the words out.

"He's ... good, I think," I say.

I haven't told Chase about the Dawson kiss yet. I was planning to today. But ... I kind of don't want to. I don't know why. Maybe it's because I haven't decided what I think about it.

For Dawson's part, he's been pretty darn cute. Coming by my office just to say hi or going out of his way just to talk to me. We've had some actual conversations now that Chad is gone. Or maybe because we've moved past something now. Some invisible barrier that was there, but is gone now that our feelings are out. Well, I'm pretty sure I know what his feelings are. I'm just not so sure about my own. Am I one of those girls that once she gets what she wants, no longer wants it? Is it just the chase for me? I don't think that's the case, since my feelings for Dawson had started to wane even before that kiss.

I talked to Hannah about it, of course. We stayed up late the other night discussing. I thought if anyone could help me figure out how I'm feeling, it would be her. Instead, I was more confused. She didn't seem all that excited, like I thought she would be. I thought she'd be cheering and telling me to *Get on that right now!* But she didn't. Her conclusion was that maybe it just wasn't our time. Not very helpful.

"How was work for you?" I ask Chase as we walk along the trail. The landscape is starting to change from flat and sprawling to redder and rockier as we walk. It reminds me of Sedona, with the beautiful red rocks and the green trees surrounding them; the backdrop of the clear blue sky only makes the colors more vibrant. It's gorgeous here. My mom would have loved it. I can see her here, holding her arms out wide, telling us all how lucky we are to be living near such a beautiful place.

"Also boring," he says. "I'm so tired of training."

"Thank goodness for my clever texting."

"Yes. Couldn't survive without you." He turns his aviator-clad gaze on me, giving me a bright smile.

We chat as we follow the trail as it wraps and weaves around large boulders. We end up walking single file on a narrower part, a wall of red rock on one side and a pretty big fall on the other. This part is starting to feel more like a hike, with the smaller trail and the uneven terrain.

It's just as I'm starting to wonder if we'll ever reach the swimming hole, sweat dripping down my back from the workout and the heat of the noonday sun, that we come upon it. The trail lands on a flat rock of sandstone, and when we get to the edge, below and across from us are various platforms of flat stone, and at the bottom, a crystal-clear pool of water. It's … amazing.

"Wow," Chase says as we look down at the oasis below. It looks like a crack in the earth with all the rock surrounding the water. The name makes more sense.

There are only a handful of people around. Some lying on towels on flat rocks under the sun. No one is swimming in the hole, but I watch as a couple jumps from the highest rock, plunging into the water. They're screaming and gasping when they come up for air. Must be cold water, which makes jumping sound even more appealing after the heat from the hike.

We make our way down to one of the lower sandstone pads, closer to the water. We find an empty area and lay our towels out, claiming the spot.

If anyone was paying attention to us, we'd look like a couple that's been together for a long time. Sitting here on our towels, Chase reaching into his backpack and handing me a water, me reaching over and tousling his hair after he makes another joke about the Crack.

THE ACCIDENTAL TEXT

There's a level of comfort with Chase that I'm not sure I've experienced with another human before. Certainly not with Dawson.

"You ready to do this?" I ask him.

"Hell, yes," he says. That half-grin back on his face.

I really do love that smile of his. It makes me feel like everything is right in the world. My stomach takes a dive again. He's leaving. Going to London for six months. I really don't want him to go. He's become such an important person in my life. I think about him all the time, wondering what he's up to, what he's thinking about. The great thing with Chase is that when I get those thoughts, I just text him. I don't overthink anything or try too hard. It's so easy with him.

It's nothing like what I experienced with Dawson. All those sweaty pits and palms. All that anxiety.

A thought jumps out at me that makes me freeze in place. Do I have feelings for Chase? Is that what this is? Was Dawson right?

"What's wrong?" Chase asks, a look of concern on his face. "You look like you've seen a ghost."

I take in a breath. "Totally fine." I'm being an idiot. That's not what's happening here. And yet ... "Should we jump?" I say, the words rushing out of my mouth.

He gives me a strange look. "Sure."

We stand up and I take off my shorts and tank in a hurry, leaving them on my towel. I decided to wear a one-piece today since jumping off cliffs can cause lots of wardrobe malfunctions with a two-piece. I don't know this from experience, but Chelsea does.

Chase gives me an appreciative look. A double eyebrow raise, that half-smile on his face. It makes my stomach do a weird diving thing.

I just need to jump in the water. All this heat has gotten to my brain.

Chase takes off his shirt and, for the love of all that's holy, my mouth goes dry at the sight. He's very ... fit. There are abs—not the kind that are super defined, but they are there and, wow, they are *pretty*.

I swallow and move my gaze away, trying to act relaxed, like his shirtless shape didn't have any effect on me at all. Chase is handsome—I already knew that—but he just went from attractive to ... well, hot.

"Do you want to jump together or separate?" I ask him. I must focus on the task at hand and nothing else.

"Together, of course," he says, giving me that slight smile again. "Wouldn't do it without you."

Together. Right. I can do this.

We make our way over to one of the lower rocks that we've seen plenty of people jump from. I keep my focus on not hurting myself as we climb up to the spot. I walk to the edge and look over. It's a good twelve-foot jump. No big deal.

"Okay, let's do this," I say to Chase when he comes to stand next to me. "Three, two—"

"Wait," Chase says, grabbing my hand and pulling me back from the ledge. "Where's my kiss?"

"Kiss?" My mouth goes dry again.

He pulls his brows inward. "For good luck?"

"Oh, right." I lean over and give him the barest of kisses. Like, he might not have even felt it, it was so light.

"That felt unlucky. Better do it again."

"Fine," I say, acting more annoyed than I really am. I lean in and kiss him on the cheek, this time letting my lips linger just slightly longer than I normally would. Somehow this is worse. It feels too intimate, and my brain is sending off thoughts that I'm not sure I want to be thinking right now. "Happy now?" I ask, making my tone extra sarcastic.

"Very," he says. "Okay, on the count of three."

We walk to the edge, he counts down, and we jump. Down, down, down into the water.

It feels like jumping into ice, the water is so cold compared to the heat we were just in. When I come up to the surface, I let out a little scream.

"It's freezing," I say when I see Chase bob up. I'm kicking my legs around, trying to get my blood pumping again.

Chase whips his head back to get his hair out of his face. "It is," he says, his words coming out breathy.

We swim over to the side and pull ourselves out of the water, the heat of the day having little effect.

"Oh my gosh," I say, feeling shivers from head to toe. "Are my lips blue?"

"They're a little blue," he says after examining my lips. "Come here." He pulls me into him, wrapping his arms around me, my cold wet body up against his. I'm too cold to wrap my brain around this, being in his arms. But I'm coherent enough to know I like it. It's not long before our bodies, with help from the sun, start to heat back up.

"I don't know if I can do that again," I say, my cheek up against his nice firm chest. I'm warming up but still not warm enough to pull away from him. I also kind of don't want to. I kind of want to stay here forever. Crap.

"We have to do the thirty-foot one," he says. "We came all this way."

"I don't really feel like dying today."

"How about this," he says. "Let's go back to our towels, eat lunch, lie out and get nice and hot, and then see how we feel."

I agree to this and allow Chase to take my hand and guide me back to our spot. Once there, I wrap myself up in my towel and sit on the warm sandstone, letting the heat of it work its magic on my body.

"I love heat," I say.

"Me too," says Chase. He's lying out on his towel, his eyes closed. He's drenched in sunlight from head to toe, making him look almost as if he's glowing.

"I need sunglasses. Your butt-white skin is blinding me right now."

He doesn't even open his eyes. "Like what you see?"

"No," I say, but it comes off a little too emphatic, especially since I was staring at him and I did like what I was seeing.

Better go douse myself in cold water again.

THE ACCIDENTAL TEXT

"I can't believe I let you talk me into this."

After an hour of lying in the sun and then eating the lunch Chase packed, which consisted of a yummy ham sandwich and some chips, Chase works his charms on me and convinces me to do the tallest cliff jump the Crack has to offer.

"You can do this," he says.

"I know I can do it," I snap back. "I just don't want to."

"Come on," he says, grabbing my hand and pulling me toward the edge. I use my weight to try to keep my body in place, leaning away from him, but somehow he's still able to get me closer to the ledge.

"Do you want to count down, or do you want me to do the honors?"

"I don't want to do this at all," I protest, removing my hand from his.

"For me?" he asks, and pushes out his bottom lip, giving me the same look Alice gives me when she's trying to manipulate me into doing something. Works every time with her. I'm falling for it this time too.

"Fine," I say, shaking my head and rolling my eyes.

"Thank you." He gives me a broad smile.

We walk toward the edge, our toes nearly hanging off the side of the smooth sandstone. I look down, and it's a pretty significant drop.

"You ready, adrenaline junkie?" I say, looking over at him.

"I need a kiss for good luck first," he says. Pointing to his cheek.

"You don't really deserve one," I say.

"Just give me a kiss, woman."

I'm standing so close to him, I barely have to lean in to kiss him. Just as my lips are about to meet his cheek, he swings his face around, and instead my lips meet … lips.

It's a quick kiss. Just slightly longer than a peck. It's the second time this week that a man has stolen a kiss from me. But unlike the one with Dawson, I find that I wish this kiss were longer; I want there to be more.

Chase gives me a devious little grin after, his nonverbal reply to what I'm sure is a very deer-caught-in-headlights expression from me. Then he turns, counts down from three, and we jump.

Chapter 26

He never kissed me again. I thought there might have been a moment after the second frigid plunge, when he held me again to help warm me up. That time, it wasn't just his body heat that helped—his nearness had my heart beating double time and my blood pumping again.

As we hiked back to the car, the sun setting along the way, I started to wonder if it was all in my head. Chase never said anything about it, never once brought it up. I almost asked, but then didn't. It was just a kiss … that I still keep thinking about.

It's now Sunday night and he's been texting me all day, just like old times, and it kind of annoys me. I think I want him to think of it as more. I think I want it to mean more. How did he go from Chase to *Chase?*

Hannah and I are currently sitting in our mostly dark apartment, *The Real Housewives of Beverly Hills* playing on the television. Trashy reality TV is one of our favorite things.

"I think I like Chase," I blurt out during a commercial, no longer able to keep it in.

"Oh, yeah?" Hannah says. "Glad you finally caught on to that."

I swing my head to her, the light from the TV dancing around her face. "What?"

"It's been obvious to me for a while," she says.

"And you didn't think to tell me?"

She reaches over and pats me on the hand. "Oh, sweetie," she says, her voice full of faux condescension, "you needed to realize it for yourself."

"Well, I do now. And … he's leaving." I slump back in my seat.

"Only for sixth months."

"That's a long time."

"You're also assuming he likes you back."

I whack her on the arm. "You're supposed to be my best friend. My cheerleader, remember?"

"I'm just keeping it real."

"Do you think he does?"

She contemplates this for a second. "I don't know. I haven't spent all that much time with him."

"That's true."

She pats my hand again. "What does your heart tell you?"

I pull my chin inward. "Since when do you care what the heart says?"

"Well … I have one. I'm pretty sure."

I take a breath. "What do I do?"

"Tell him," she says. "See what happens."

THE ACCIDENTAL TEXT

I feel a tiny jolt of anxiety at the thought of telling him, though it's not the heart palpitations and sweaty pits I used to get around Dawson. It may not even be anxiety, what I'm feeling now. It's more like ... excitement. I *want* to tell him. And I don't know if he reciprocates, and I don't seem to care all that much. Why is that? Shouldn't I feel the same as I did with Dawson? I tell Hannah as much.

"I have a theory," she says.

"Do tell."

"I don't think you really liked Dawson. Like-like, I mean."

I eye her, dubiously.

"Hear me out." She holds up a hand. "Maybe you could never tell him because, deep down, you just weren't that into him."

"Are you serious?"

"Serious," she says, and then gives me a shrug.

That seems ridiculous. Of course I liked Dawson. He's the most beautiful man I've ever seen.

"I know he's the most beautiful man," she says, and I wonder how she just read my mind. "But ... maybe that's all he was to you: a beautiful man."

"I'm not that shallow."

"What else do you know about him?"

"He's thoughtful, caring, and hard working."

"He also picked Natasha for a girlfriend."

I twist my lips to the side. "He does lose points for that."

"I'm just saying: it's something to think about."

She's not just saying that. She's made up her mind about it.

My phone beeps in my lap.

I look down and see Chase's name on my screen and open up the app. My heart does a little speeding-up thing.

> **Chase:** I just found a wolf howling at the moon on my ceiling.
>
> **Maggie:** Very nice. You should make a wish on it.
>
> **Chase:** Is that a thing?
>
> **Maggie:** No

He sends me a laughing face.

> **Chase:** We're running out of adventurous things to do around here. We'd have to drive 4 hours to bungee jump.

I say a prayer of thanks for that. I do *not* like bungee jumping. Once was enough for me.

> **Maggie:** Bummer

I send him a frowning face. But really I should be sending him the one with the star eyes.

> **Chase:** I never realized how boring Phoenix is until I decided to be adventurous.
>
> **Maggie:** Yes, you've got to travel to do the really crazy stuff.
>
> **Chase:** Tell me something you've never done.

THE ACCIDENTAL TEXT

> **Maggie:** Hmmm
>
> **Chase:** How to impress the girl that's done everything …

I try not to read into that, although my hormones did not get the note. Neither did the butterflies in my stomach.

> **Maggie:** Short of hiking Everest, I don't know what to tell you.
>
> **Chase:** Everest it is!
>
> **Maggie:** Hard pass
>
> **Maggie:** I've actually never tried heli-skiing.

I send him one of those shrugging emojis.

> **Chase:** I don't even know what that is.
>
> **Maggie:** Helicopters that take you up to remote places to ski. It was on my mom's list.
>
> **Chase:** Might be a little warm for that.
>
> **Maggie:** Wait. I've got one. I've never been in a hot-air balloon.
>
> **Chase:** Really?? Seems kind of lamesauce.
>
> **Maggie:** You're lamesauce! Always seemed kinda romantic to me.

I throw that line out there. I want to see if he catches it. *Romance, Chase.*

> **Chase:** Yes, with a third wheel. Someone has to fly the balloon.

Line not caught. But also, he has a point.

> **Maggie:** Well, maybe you should save up all your nerves until your big jump.
>
> **Chase:** But I want to do something else. Just one thing more. With you.

I feel a fluttering in my belly. I could tell him I've got a perfect adventure for him: return my feelings and let's see where it takes us. Feels like a daring thing to do for both of us.

> **Chase:** I'll think of something. Be ready on Saturday.
>
> **Maggie:** I'll be ready.

Chapter 27

"You were right," I say, standing in front of Dawson. It's Monday evening and I was just about to leave work when he came into my office to say hi. It was good timing because I needed to talk to him and I had been avoiding it all day. Like the chicken that I am.

I didn't jump right into it. First, I asked him how his day was, and we went back and forth with the small talk. And then I took a breath and told him he was right.

"Right?" He crinkles his brow.

"I might have feelings for Chase," I say. Not might—I definitely do. But Dawson doesn't need to know that.

"Ah," he says, giving me rueful smile.

"I'm so sorry, Dawson, I—"

He holds out a hand. "It's on me," he says. "Maybe if I'd had the chance to dance more with you at the party."

I think back to the party—it feels so long ago, like a different part of my life. What would have happened if Natasha had never shown up? Would it have been me walking hand in hand with Dawson toward the parking lot at the end? Strange how life works.

"Maybe," I say.

"So, have you told him?"

"Chase?"

"Yeah."

"I … haven't yet," I say.

"Well, you should," he says. "Guys are dumb. We need you to spell it out for us." He gives me a knowing smile.

I'm having such déjà vu right now. Wasn't it not that long ago that Chase was giving me the same advice about Dawson? This is quite the odd turn of events.

I twist my lips to the side. "So … how do you go about doing that?"

"Doing what?"

"Telling someone you like them."

"Right," he says, the apples of his cheeks turning just the slightest bit pink.

I shake my head in little quick motions. "I'm sorry, that's … I shouldn't be asking you that."

"No," Dawson says. "I don't mind. I'd say you can either just straight up tell him, or … do what I did and steal a kiss."

It's my turn to blush now. "Well, he sort of did that."

"Then he probably likes you."

Yeah, this feels so weird. I'm currently getting man advice from the man that I was previously getting man advice for. But now for the man that was originally giving me the advice.

I'm just going to stop this thought train. I'll get a headache for sure.

"Well, thanks, Dawson. That's helpful."

THE ACCIDENTAL TEXT

He turns to go but then turns back. "I don't like to play second fiddle, but ... if things don't work out with the other guy, maybe I could get another shot?"

I smile at him. "Absolutely."

***

Later that night after Halmoni has filled me with *bulgolgi* and rice and lectured Hannah for not dating, I walk over to my dad's house to see how he is. I haven't talked to him much since the whole dinner fiasco. I've seen him at work a couple of times, and we've talked on the phone once or twice. But not about anything important.

I want to see how he is ... to see if he's still looking at me like I'm fragile or need mental help.

I knock on the door this time, so as not to interrupt anything. I don't need to learn that lesson twice.

My dad answers the door; he's wearing khaki pants and a Cooper's polo, even though he never came into the shop today.

"Hey, Magpie," he says, opening the door for me.

"Hi, Dad," I say. I stand on my tiptoes and give him a kiss on the cheek after walking inside. "Is June here?" I look around the front room to see if there are any hints of her. Shoes? Jacket? I don't see anything.

"Nah," he says. "She just left."

I smile. It feels a little fake, but I keep going with it. The truth is, I don't mind June. She's actually really sweet, and I think she and my dad dating is ... okay. I mean, it still sometimes feels like a punch in my gut, if I'm being honest. But maybe … less of a punch. More of a pinch.

At any rate, I'm glad she's not here today. So that I can speak with my dad freely and not feel like I have an audience.

"How are you?" I ask as I follow my dad into the living room, a news station on the TV. My mom used to hate it when he'd watch the news. She said it was like poison, listening to all that doom and gloom. He's probably watching it to spite her. He probably leaves his socks all around too. Another pet peeve of hers.

"Oh, you know, just doing my thing," my dad says as we sit on the couch.

"Didn't see you at the shop today."

"I was busy around here. I figured you all got it covered."

"We have a good teacher." I reach over and pat his leg.

"What have you been up to, Mags?" he asks. "I haven't talked to you in a while."

I take a breath. Time to be straight, no matter what conversation it brings up. "I've been hanging out with Chase, actually."

"Ah," my dad says, rolling his lips together and nodding his head. "What have you been doing?"

"Oh, you know. Just the odd zip-lining, ATVing, some cliff diving. Stuff like that."

He turns to me, his lips now turned upward. "Oh, really?"

"Yep," I say. "I think I've found Mom's long-lost twin."

THE ACCIDENTAL TEXT

My dad chuckles. "Well, that sounds like fun. Pretty funny, how you two met."

"Yes, I know."

"I was worried about you, you know." He pauses, looking like he's trying to get his words in order. "But then June made me realize what you did was actually pretty healthy."

I pull my face back, lowering my chin. "Healthy?"

"You found a way to get your feelings out. You didn't keep them all locked up inside of you. I've had June to talk to, and Chelsea has Mark … and I'm not sure who Devon's talking to, but he seems to be handling it okay. And you … you had a different way you needed to express yourself."

"It's okay; you can think it's weird."

"No, no, I really don't. I'm just sorry I was a cheap old man and turned off your mom's phone."

I giggle. "You really are cheap."

"Your mom loved that about me," he says, and gives me a wink.

"Oh, sure. That's why she sometimes had me hide her shopping under my bed."

"Yeah, your mother tried to hide that stuff. But I always knew. I never cared. I would have bought her the world, if she'd asked."

I feel that lump in my throat. It's weird that it's not a regular occurrence anymore. "I miss her."

"Me too. Every day. Sometimes every minute of every hour." He puts an arm around the back of the couch and gives my shoulder a little squeeze.

"Well, I'm glad you turned off her phone."

"Are you?"

"Yeah, I would have never met Chase if you hadn't."

His eyebrows go upward. "Oh … really?"

There's a lot of insinuation in that "really."

"He's been really great. It almost feels … meant to be. That sounds dumb to say out loud."

"It's not dumb," he says. "Didn't he lose his mom too?"

I look down at my hands. My fingers are intertwined, my thumbs twiddling. "He did; it was a car accident."

"That's terrible."

"Yes. Sort of makes you appreciate that at least we got to say goodbye."

"I do appreciate that. And that we also got to tell her how much we loved her."

The lump is back. *Hello, old friend*. "That too."

"How old was she?"

"Fifty-nine."

"Too young to go."

"Yes, it is." I look down at my lap again. "Does June talk about her husband?"

"Oh, sure … sure. We talk a lot about our spouses. She's been doing this much longer, though. But she has a lot of stories to tell about Roger. He was a great man."

I have vague memories of Roger. I'd see him jogging around our neighborhood—that's how I remember him the most. He was so healthy, a heart attack at the age of fifty was such a shock to the neighborhood.

"So, how does dating in your fifties work?"

THE ACCIDENTAL TEXT

"We do a lot of texting," he says.

"Sounds familiar."

"In fact, she sent me one today." He reaches over to the arm of the chair and grabs his phone, which is perched there.

He pulls up the app and clicks on her name. I'm reminded of Devon, Chelsea, and me snooping on his phone, finding their song. I wonder if it still is.

"She said: 'I've got a lot to think about. I hope you do too.'" He looks to me after reading me the text. "What do you think she meant by that?"

I tilt my head to the side, eyeing him. Is my father asking me to break down a text with him?

"I don't really understand the context," I say.

"Neither do I," he says with a chuckle.

So the reality is, dating is the same no matter what age you are. That's … disheartening. I tell my dad this.

"Well, it's not as hard as it was when I was your age. There's not a lot of figuring out what the future holds, like how we'd raise a family, or stay on a budget, and whatnot. It's mostly about companionship. Having someone around."

"But doesn't it feel strange? To be talking and sharing feelings with someone that's not Mom?"

"Not really," he says. "No one will ever top your mom; I married up with her." He smiles in that way that makes his eyes do that endearing crinkling thing. "I'd like to think that if it was me that went first, that your mom would have found some way to be happy, however that was."

I nod my head. She would have. But it may not have been in the same way. Or maybe it would have been. I'll never know the answer to that. But I do know she would have been happy. She used to tell me that it was my job to make myself happy. No one else can do that. I think I understand that more, now that I'm older.

"Do you think you'll marry her?"

"June?" he asks, his eyes going out of focus as he contemplates what I've just asked.

"Yeah," I say. I picture us coming over here for dinner, June running things. It feels ... strange. Even worse, would my dad sell this house and move in with her? What would I do if I lost the home I've known for most of my life? The place where most of my memories were made? I'm not sure I want to think about this right now.

"I don't know. I've just started dating. Maybe I want to play the field a little more," he says, giving me a mischievous grin.

"Dad," I say, whacking him on the arm. Now I'm having defensive feelings on June's behalf. He can't do that to her.

He chuckles. "Life is short, this I do know. You have to find happiness where you can. That's all we really have in the end."

Chapter 28

"Okay, I feel bad for saying Phoenix is boring," says Chase.

He should feel bad. Chase and I are back in the Sonoran Desert, this time in the dark of night. Stars everywhere. You can barely see city lights on the horizon. No sounds of the city, only the light wind through the brush can be heard.

"It's pretty amazing," I say.

He's standing close to me, our arms touching. If I just stretched out my fingers, I could reach his. I feel mine flexing, like they want to, like it's the natural thing to do.

For our last adventure, Chase took me on a night desert tour on fat bikes, which are bicycles with fatter tires that help with balance and give you the ability to go over uneven terrain. We're wearing helmets with bright headlights so we can see the trail.

It's a perfect night, temperature-wise, and the cloudless sky is putting on an excellent show, the stars twinkling above us and the moon bright. I think of all the things we've done, this might be my favorite.

It's quiet out here and it feels like we're separated from the world. There's just our guide, Jeff, and two other people here. We take breaks now and then for water and snacks.

We're on a break right now as Chase and I stand near our bikes, our headlamps off, taking it all in. My mom would have absolutely loved this, and I feel a tinge of sadness that this was something she missed out on, that she never got to do. Still, I can picture her standing near me, her head tilted upward as she enjoys the experience. She'd probably tell me about how big and small this makes her feel. Big because she's part of something so huge, and small because she's just one person in this grand universe. It was something she'd told me once when we were standing at the top of Diamond Head in Hawaii, looking over the ocean that went as far as our eyes could see. She was known for her deep thoughts while we adventured. We used to tease her about it.

I might be loving this, but there's also a weight in my gut. Chase is leaving in less than a week. I want to tell him how I feel before he goes. I don't know why, but I need him to know. I just do. And unlike how I felt with Dawson, where it was so hard to say anything, the words I want to say to Chase are there, at the tip of my tongue, waiting to come out. I just need a good segue. Some kind of opening. I don't want to just blurt it out.

The thing with Chase is, I know there's something there. He didn't steal a kiss tonight when I gave him a peck on the cheek for good luck, but there have been other signs. I also just feel it. Like there's something between us, and there's supposed to be something between us. I'm supposed to know Chase. It doesn't feel like coincidence to me.

Right now is not the time to say anything, though, as Jeff just told us the break is up and we get back on our bikes and back on the trail, the quiet, dark desert all around.

I've been keeping my eye out for critters, but we've unfortunately not seen many. There was a jackrabbit, a few scorpions, and one snake off to the side of the path that I got to see the tail end of before it slithered its way back in the sagebrush. We searched out the scorpions. Jeff brought a black light to find them and they looked otherworldly under the purple-blue hue.

The light breeze whips through my hair as we ride. I can hear Chase behind me, his tires moving along the dirt trail in tandem with mine. I feel free in this moment. In this dark, quiet desert.

"That was my favorite adventure," I declare as we get into Chase's car after returning our equipment and trying to dust ourselves off from all the trail dirt. I pull the sun visor down on the passenger side and look at myself in the lighted mirror. I try to brush my fingers through my wind-whipped brown hair and then give up and twist it into a low-hanging bun.

"Really?" Chase asks while putting his seat belt on.

"Did you not like it?"

"Loved it," he says. "I think the Crack was my favorite, though."

"If it wasn't for the cold water."

"I kept you warm," he says. I feel his head turn to look at me; there's a flirty tone to his voice and I feel my stomach do a flipflop.

The conversation is light as we travel the hour back to my place, where he'd picked me up earlier today. We talk about all the things he has to do to get ready for his trip, and, surprisingly, he's yet to do many of them. He's usually so prepared for things.

"I guess I won't see much of you next week," I say, my tone conveying my disappointment.

"What makes you say that?"

"You've got to get ready."

"You can always come over and help," he says.

"I do want to get my fill of my boyfriend, Oscar, before you leave."

"Exactly," he says.

We pull into the parking lot of my apartment, Chase taking a space next to my Jeep. The lot is fairly empty, as most of us living in this complex are single and out doing things on a Saturday night.

He puts the car in park and sits back in his seat. He turns his head toward me and then reaches over and grabs my hand, holding it.

"For our official last adventure before I leave," he says, "I just wanted to say thanks for coming with me and keeping me company. I appreciate it, more than you know."

"I'll be there tomorrow too," I say. Tomorrow is Chase's big jump. What all this has led up to.

THE ACCIDENTAL TEXT

He has to attend an hour training since he's going tandem for his first time. But I told him I would come and sit with him while he waited to go up. Sometimes the wait can be long. Then I'll be on the ground when he lands.

"I've had a lot of fun," I say. "More than I've had in a long time."

"Do you—" he says at the same time I say, "I was thinking—"

He chuckles. "You go."

This is it. I reach up to grab on to my necklace but then remember I didn't wear it tonight. "I was thinking that ... I could come visit you, in London."

It's hard to see Chase's expression with only the dashboard lights of the car and the streetlamp giving us light. He looks ... surprised.

"Yeah," he says, his voice emphatic. "I'd love that."

"I'm going to miss you," I say.

He squeezes my hand. "I'll miss you too."

I take a breath. "I know how we met is strange. But don't you kind of feel like it was supposed to happen?"

I see the corner of his mouth lift up as he nods his head. "Yeah, I've had that same thought."

"I don't want you to go to London and forget me."

His eyes shoot to mine. "I could never. You ... you're ..." I will him to keep going with his line of thinking. "We'll still text, and you can come see me."

That wasn't exactly what I was hoping for, but I forge on, ignoring the not-quite-pleasant feeling swarming inside me.

"I just need you to know, before you go, that you've become more to me ... than just a friend. I ... I want you in my life, Chase."

I keep my eyes on him and watch as his gaze moves from my eyes down to my lips and then to our adjoined hands.

"I know you're leaving, but I need you to know how I've been feeling lately."

I wait for him to say something, to tell me to continue. He doesn't, though—he just keeps his focus on our hands. How much more is he going to make me spell this out for him? And if I have to, does that mean he doesn't feel the same? My stomach does a sinking thing.

Chase's eyes jerk up to mine and I feel something like hope wash over me. This is it. "Jump with me tomorrow."

"What?" I say, confused. I try to pull my hand away from his, but he tightens his grip.

He changed the subject. He just did to me what he does when I bring up his mom. An unwelcome feeling starts to swirl in my belly. He doesn't feel the same.

"Come with me and do the jump tomorrow." His words have a desperate sound to them. Like he's pleading.

I shake my head, slowly. "Chase, I ... I can't."

He lets go of my hand and angles his body so he's looking forward. "Why?" He wipes a hand down his face.

"Why?" I can't help my frustrated tone. "You know why."

"Because you're scared?"

THE ACCIDENTAL TEXT

"Yeah, I'm still scared." I'm also super pissed right now. I think I'd have rather him just say he didn't feel the same than change the subject so abruptly.

He turns his body to me again. "I don't get it. I just watched you do a bunch of adventurous things." He throws out his hand toward the window. "I know how brave you are, Maggie."

I roll my lips and close my eyes. "None of that was like jumping out of a plane," I say. "You'll see when you go."

He turns his head back toward the window, toward the lit-up dashboard.

"I'm not going with you tomorrow. I can't. I'm hoping I have one jump left in me, and I have to use that next Saturday with my family." I'm getting that feeling — the one where tears aren't far away. I close my eyes, trying to push it all back.

"You realize how silly that all sounds, right?"

"I'm sorry?" The teary feeling is growing. I'm angry, and disappointed, and sad.

He looks at me. "Do you think … maybe it's not the jump?"

"What?"

He looks away from me again. "I don't know … maybe it's more than that. Maybe you're avoiding something. Avoiding feelings or something."

I turn my head to the side, away from him. My mind is absolutely swimming with thoughts right now. "Are you seriously asking me if I'm avoiding feelings?" I turn back to him. "Me?" I point to myself, jabbing a finger into my chest.

"I don't know." He lifts a shoulder and lets it fall. "Maybe?" he says.

I can't help myself. I let out a sardonic laugh. "This is so rich, coming from you." I reach for my necklace, remembering again that it's not there. "How could you even ask that? I've been a freaking open book to you since the beginning. I don't hide my feelings … that's what you do."

He doesn't say anything. So I keep going. "I've just followed you around for weeks, Chase. Helping you avoid your feelings."

"That's not what that was," he says.

"That's exactly what that was. And I didn't say anything because I thought you just needed time or something."

He's silent again. I've never seen Chase mad. I'm learning that he's the quiet type when he's angry. It's my least favorite kind of anger from people. I'd much rather them be loud and say what they're feeling. But that's par for the course with Chase.

"You don't know what you're saying," he finally says, his eyes on the dashboard.

I slap my hands on my thighs. "You're right. How would I know? It's not like I've recently lost my mom too."

"I didn't mean that."

"And how could I know? You don't talk about it."

He doesn't say anything again. He just sits there.

"You're just going to sit there? Tell me what you're feeling right now, Chase. Anything."

No words. His eyes stay on the dashboard.

THE ACCIDENTAL TEXT

I let out a breath, shaking my head. "You know what? I'm—" I stop myself from saying what I want to say. I'm hurt, and I'm angry, and I'll say something I'll regret—I know I will. I may already have. Instead, I go for passive aggressive: "Have fun in London, Chase. I wish you all the best." I open the door and get out of the car.

"Maggie."

I hear him say my name, but I don't care. I slam the door shut and I race up the stairs to my apartment, taking two at a time. I use my keys to get in and open the door to find an empty, dark apartment. It's probably for the best; I don't know if I want to talk to Hannah right now.

I don't bother turning on lights. I just go to my bed, where I fall face-first and cry.

Chapter 29

"I take it last night didn't go well," Hannah says, standing over me. I'm lying on the bed, my face focused on the ceiling.

"What gave it away?"

"Your face looks like you've been crying all night. Unless I've got it wrong and they were tears of joy?"

I scoot over on the bed and she lies next to me. "Not good," I say, my voice breaking up.

"What happened?"

"He … rejected me."

"What? I'll kill him," she says, exasperated. "What did he say?"

I take a ragged breath, tears falling down the sides of my face. "It's what he didn't say."

"Talk to me."

I tell her the conversation, the one that's been playing over and over again in my head, on repeat, like a broken record. He doesn't want me. He only used me.

That's what it feels like. All the texts we sent back and forth. All that time together. That was just him distracting himself from his loss, him trying not to feel.

THE ACCIDENTAL TEXT

"Wow, he's got a lot of nerve," she says.

"Yeah," I say.

My phone, which is down by the end of my bed where I threw it, beeps. I just lie there, ignoring it.

"Do you want to see who that is?"

"Not really," I say.

She sits up and grabs my phone, then looks at it and lies back down. "It's Chase."

"Yep," I say. I knew it was him. Like some stupid sixth sense. It's not the first text I've gotten from him since I heartbrokenly left his car last night.

Chase: Please call me

Chase: Can we talk?

Chase: Please talk to me

Chase: Please, Maggie

I'm sure the one he sent just now is just a repeat. Or maybe he's at the jump, telling me he wishes I were there with him. To hold his hand, or whatever he needed from me, like the safety net that I was to him. I could help him not feel his feelings there too.

It doesn't feel like me to not text him back. It feels weird. Like an itch I refuse to scratch. But I'm not ready to talk yet.

I sniffle, needing a tissue. "The part that hurts the most was his rejection."

"Did he actually reject you?"

"Not with his words. He ... changed the subject."

"Oh, gosh."

"I know."

"I'm sorry, Mags. I'm honestly surprised."

"I am too. I guess I shouldn't be."

"Maybe ..." Hannah says.

"Maybe what?"

She lets out a breath through her nose. "If he was doing all that to avoid his feelings, then maybe he's avoiding how he feels about you too?"

I sigh. "I don't know. I want to think that, but I think it would just give me hope. And I need to not hope right now."

"I'm sorry, Mags," she says again. She reaches over and taps me twice on the arm. All the comfort I'll get from her. I'm grateful for it.

We lie in silence. My eyes find the heart on my ceiling and it doesn't bring me any peace. I see it for what it is: an accidental shape made by a texture gun. That's all it's ever been. Maybe I should stop with all this fanciful thinking that Chase was meant to have my mom's number or that all this was some sign or something. I need to grow up. I need to get real.

"I think he's just not that into me," I say finally. My words sound weak with a dash of pathetic.

"Guys don't spend that much time with girls that they aren't into," Hannah says.

"I don't know if I believe that. Anyway, he's going to London next week. He'll be gone, and I can just ... do ... I don't know."

"Dawson?" Hannah says, and then lets out a giggle.

"Right. Dawson. Too bad I told him no last week."

THE ACCIDENTAL TEXT

"That was dumb of you. You should have kept him around just in case."

"That sounds like a sweet thing to do," I say, with an eye roll, my voice full of sarcasm. "Anyway, now that I've had all these feelings for Chase, I realize that all it ever was with Dawson was lust."

"He's easy to lust after."

I snort laugh.

"Ready for a hard question?" Hannah asks.

"No."

"If you knew it wasn't lust with Chase ... was it ... love?"

"I said I didn't want the hard question."

"How long have you known me?"

"Too long."

I let my body feel heavy, sagging into my bed. Tears spring at the corners of my eyes and I feel them roll down the sides of my face and into my hair and ears. "I don't know what love feels like."

"Well, I fancied myself in love with the Cheating Douchewaffle, but I'm not so sure about that now. So, I can't help you there."

I think about it for a few seconds. "I don't know. It's definitely the most heartbroken I've ever felt. At least compared to other relationships."

I've felt a lot of heartbreak this past year ... watching my mom fade away, watching her take her last breath. This feels different than that. It's like a different part of my heart this time.

"What's the saying?" Hannah asks. "The bigger the jump, the harder the fall?"

I side-eye her. "Pretty sure it's 'the bigger they are, the harder they fall.' Not sure that's what you were going for."

She sighs. "I was trying to make it a jumping-out-of-a-plane metaphor. Like, bringing it all together."

I reach over and give her a couple of her signature impersonal pats on the arm. "Good try."

She turns her body to the side so she's facing me. "What are you going to do?"

"Nothing," I say. "I'm going to go to work tomorrow and just live my life."

"That sounds so boring."

"It sure does."

Chapter 30

I haven't heard from Chase again. Not since Sunday morning when all he said was "Please call me." I never texted him back. I just need more time.

It's Tuesday now and I'm at work, trying to focus. It's been hard to do that. I feel kind of lost right now. The irony is that the person I would have texted right now, to tell him how lost I feel, is the same person who's causing that feeling.

Life feels hard right now. It feels like too many things coming at me at once. I feel like I've lost so much in the past six months. My mom, texting my mom, and now I feel like I've lost Chase.

Maybe I shouldn't have said anything. Maybe I could have just kept things the way they were.

I keep thinking about what Hannah asked … her hard question. Is this love? Is what I feel for Chase … love? It kind of feels like it. Hannah's quote she used—the wrong one about the bigger the jump, the harder the fall—kind of works in a different context. Like the bigger the feelings, the harder the heartbreak. It feels like that. My feelings were big, and now my heartbreak is equally big. Or bigger.

I feel tears prick in my eyes and I do that rapid blinking thing to get them to stop.

"Are you going to be ready for Saturday?"

I look up to see Devon standing in my doorway. He's got on dark jeans and a Cooper's polo. "What?" I say, as I reach up and dab the corners of my eyes with my fingers.

"Saturday? You're not going to chicken out again?"

"Did Chelsea send you?"

"Of course." He comes in and takes a seat in the chair opposite my desk.

"Of course," I echo. "Well, I hope I don't."

"I can't report back with that answer. I need a firm yes."

"Go away, Devon."

He smiles. "What's wrong with you?" He gestures with a hand toward me.

"Nothing."

"Your eyes look all watery or something."

"Just … having a rough day."

"Right," he says. "Mom?"

I give him a sad smile. "Not Mom this time. Surprisingly enough."

"Then what?"

I already know that Devon will not offer me anything I need right now. This is our MO. I've tried to talk to him about feelings, and he's never been a source of advice or comfort.

"Boy troubles," I say, hoping that will get him off it.

"Try me. I'm a boy." He points to himself.

THE ACCIDENTAL TEXT

"You're also my brother." I should have gone with lady problems. Devon has no ability to deal with that.

"What are your boy problems, Mags?"

"Okay, fine," I say, expecting little from this conversation. "I have feelings for Chase."

His brow crinkles. "The guy that I gave a ride to? The one with Mom's number?"

"The very one."

"I knew it," he says.

"What? You know nothing."

"I could tell when you told us at Dad's. There was something going on."

"Joke's on you, because nothing was going on then. These are ... newer developments."

At least, I'm pretty sure they are. I try to think back to that night, the night I'd busted out this info like I was confessing a crime or something.

Were the feelings starting then? We'd already been ATVing, race car driving, zip-lining, and spelunking. I remember sitting on his couch, with Oscar in my lap, feeling like myself ... a feeling I hadn't had in so long. Had I been feeling this way for a while and just didn't recognize it?

"And?" Devon asks, his voice carrying notes of impatience.

"He does not reciprocate."

"Ah," he says. "Well, he's a jackass."

I might have been wrong about Devon. That actually makes me feel a little lighter. Just that one sentence.

"What did he do?"

"It's kind of a long story."

"I've got too much ADD for a long story. Give me the shortened version," he says.

I chuckle. "I thought he liked me. We spent a lot of time together, but I told him how I felt the other night, and he did not feel the same."

"Did he say that?"

"Pretty much."

"Can I punch him?"

This time I laugh. "Sure," I say. "He's leaving for London on Friday for six months, so you'd better act fast."

He punches a fist into his hand. "Tell me where to go."

We both smile at each other now.

"There's clearly more here than you're telling me, which my ADD appreciates, but just so you know, I think whichever guy finally gets you is going to be pretty lucky."

I blink rapidly again. "Thanks, Dev."

"No problem."

"You're a pretty great brother. And I guess a pretty great guy too."

He shrugs. "I try."

"Hannah's still off-limits."

"Damn," he says, looking to the side.

"So's Robin," I say.

"You ruin all my fun."

I wink at him. "Now you sound like the brother I know."

THE ACCIDENTAL TEXT

Later that night as I'm lying in my bed, my phone beeps. I grab it and look at it. It's Chase. It's been so long since I last heard from him, I'd thought maybe that was it. That he'd given up. No such luck.

I look at the text because I feel like I'm in a mood to torture myself. Can't wait to see which version of *Can we talk?* he decided to send.

Chase: You were right

Well, that's new. *You were right.* I go to text back, but then, what could I say? *Yes, of course I'm right* or just *Duh.* I could send him one of those emojis with the eyes rolling.

My phone beeps again.

Chase: I'm sorry.

I don't know what he has to be sorry for. It's his own feelings he was avoiding. He needs to apologize to himself. Or maybe he realizes that I was also part of his subconscious plan to avoid his emotions. I guess he could apologize for that. Or worse yet, he's apologizing because he doesn't reciprocate my feelings.

Maybe he's sorry for telling me that I was avoiding my feelings. But I've had a lot of time to think about that … and he could be right. It does seem like the anxiety surrounding the jump is shielding me from feeling something else. The problem is, I don't know what it is.

I could text him back that I'm sorry too, but I'm not sorry. Well, I'm sorry that I told him how I feel, and that I got so many things wrong with that.

The truth is, I'm still not ready to talk to him. Maybe I'll get over all these emotions I'm having right now. Maybe when the dust settles I'll want him back in my life. As a friend, of course. But I'd have to be okay with that, and I just don't know how long that will take.

Chapter 31

On Thursday morning I wake up to six texts from Chase. Now I *am* starting to feel a little annoyed. *Come on, Chase, you're a smart guy.*

I open my app anyway and click on his name.

> **Chase:** Hi, Mom. A wise person once told me that writing out your feelings can be therapeutic, so I'm going to give it a shot. I'm not exactly sure how to do this, but here goes. I ... miss you. You left so unexpectedly. I didn't get to say goodbye. I've never felt so hurt, or heartbroken. I've never felt so sad about anything in my life.
>
> I've been avoiding my feelings, trying anything to just not feel. Don't worry, I've stayed away from the wrong stuff. But I've still been avoiding. I've been coping in other ways. You'd be impressed by the list of adventurous things I've tried ... I've become a bit of an adrenaline junkie.
>
> Or maybe you wouldn't. You never got into that stuff.
>
> I just want to say that I'm sorry, Mom. I'm sorry I couldn't do anything. I couldn't save you. I felt so helpless in that hospital room, seeing all those machines hooked up to you. I'm just so sorry.

This is really hard. Feeling my feelings.

Chase: Hi, Mom. Dad is not doing well. I'm sure that's to be expected, but I don't know how to handle it. And what I've been doing so far—ignoring it all and hoping things will change—is not working. He hardly ever talks to me or Kenzie. He just sits in that house, in his robe, watching TV. Kenzie has been checking on him. I need to.

Speaking of Kenzie (I don't want to be a tattle, but), she didn't want to get married after you died. She wanted to cancel it. But Trevor talked her around. I'm glad she has him. Someone she can talk to. The wedding is still happening in February, by the way. So all that prep you did was worth it. Kenzie is happy that you were there when she picked out her dress. But we both agree it won't be the same without you. None of this life is the same without you. I hate that feeling.

You're the glue, Mom. You're what kept us together. Without you, it feels like we're all a little lost. I know I am.

Chase: Hey, Mom. Remember that time when Kenz and I were younger and you came home from work to find the paint peeled off that kitchen cabinet? And no one would admit to it? It was me. I'd found a piece of paint that had gotten wet in the corner, and it just … peeled off. It was really fun. I'm sorry I didn't tell you. But I guess you probably knew. So thanks for not calling me out on it.

Also, that goat in the lunchroom my senior year? Also me. I know you found that funny, but maybe you wouldn't have if you'd known who did it.

THE ACCIDENTAL TEXT

I have more. SO much more. Maybe you don't want to know. It feels good to tell you, though.

Chase: Hi, Mom. I just called Dad. We talked for 30 minutes. It was good to hear his voice. I should have been talking to him more. I hate that I avoided him so much. It hurts to admit that—to write it to you. I have to face it, though. I have to own it.

I can see you looking down on me now, shaking your head the way you used to when you disapproved of something I'd done. I deserve the disapproval. I'll make it right, Mom. I promise.

Anyway, it was good to talk to Dad. He … he sounded better as the conversation went on. We talked about you, and about Kenzie, and about me leaving for London. I promised I would go over there tomorrow and see him before I left.

I also told him he should come visit me in London, and for the first time, I heard a bit of lightness in his voice. Maybe? Like that thought—him coming to see me—made his day a little lighter. I hope he does come to see me.

Chase: Hey, Mom. I saw Dad today. Kenzie came too. It's one of the few times we've been together since the funeral. It was horrible to realize that. I've been selfish. I'm trying not to beat myself up about it. What good would it do? That's what you would tell me—what good would it do? I can still hear your voice in my head. So perfectly.

We talked about you a lot … and cried. It was good. It was good to talk about you with the people who love you the most in this world.

You are missed, Mom. So much.

Chase: I've been writing these in my notes app on my phone for the past few days. Thought you might want to read them. Or maybe you don't. But either way, you were right … it feels like therapy.

I stare at my phone, feeling so many things in this moment. I've been crying as I've read his words, the tears flowing freely down my face. I feel all this — everything that he's written. I know exactly where he's coming from.

I send him back a text.

Maggie: I'm glad it helped.

Then I send a heart emoji.

❦

"What are you going to do?" Hannah asks that night over *gamjatang* that Halmoni made us. It's a spicy soup with pork and potatoes, and it's amazing. I'm on my second bowl, which got a pat of approval on my head from Halmoni.

I've just told Hannah about Chase's texts. I didn't let her read them — it felt like betraying a trust to do that. I just gave her general information.

"What can I do?" I ask.

"You could … talk to him?" She tilts her head to the side, giving me her best sardonic glare.

"I could," I say. "But what do I say?"

THE ACCIDENTAL TEXT

She doubles down on the glare. This time with a touch of annoyance. "I don't know, maybe tell him your feelings?"

I pull my face back. "I did that, remember? I got shot down. Why would I want to do that again?"

"He's clearly telling you all this for a reason."

"Yeah," I agree. "He's just showing me that I was right about him avoiding his feelings. That's all. It's not like he was declaring his love for me or anything."

"That's true," she says, swirling her soup with her spoon.

"He's leaving for London tomorrow anyway."

"Also true," she says. "I'm sure you'll hear from him again, though."

"I'm sure," I say.

"And maybe when he gets back …"

I wave her insinuating words away. "I can't think like that, Han. I'll make myself crazy if I do. Too many what-ifs."

"I guess," she says. "I just hate seeing you like this."

I give her a sad smile. "Me too."

Chapter 32

"Who are you texting?"

I look up to see Chelsea standing in front of me, a paper cup of coffee in her hand, wearing her white jumpsuit. The one with the black-and-pink detailing.

I chuckle to myself. So many familiar things with this scene. I'm sitting on the same bench, tasked once again with watching our rigs, in the same hangar, in the same jumpsuit I was wearing three months ago. And my sister is, like last time, snooping.

But I'm a different person than I was three months ago when I was here last. I feel it. I'm … stronger. Not as strong as I need to be, but I'm definitely better in that area. I'm also not trying to hide anything anymore.

I hold up my phone so she can see it. "Hannah," I say.

Chelsea glances at my phone and then back at me. "What are you telling her?"

"That I'm still not feeling this," I say, giving Chelsea a sad smile.

She sags her upper body. "Again?"

"Yes," I say holding out a hand. "But this time, I'm not going to try to stop it. I'm doing this."

THE ACCIDENTAL TEXT

Chelsea takes a big breath. "Good, because I was going to throttle you."

I'd had a small hope that the weather would be my saving grace, but the sky is clear and the wind is perfect. It's like all the stars are aligning. If only I could get myself to align. I just want to feel happy about this. I want to feel good.

Chelsea sits next to me and puts an arm around me. "Love you," she says.

"I love you too."

"Fifteen minutes. We need to go queue up," my dad says as he approaches us. He sits down on the other side of me. "You ready for this, Magpie?"

"As ready as I'll ever be." Translation: nope.

He holds up the cylinder urn, the one holding my mom's ashes. "I guess it's time, then."

My dad yells for Devon, who's been flirting it up with some girls for the past fifteen minutes. He says goodbye to them, but not before one of them types her number into his phone. Devon, it would seem, hasn't changed all that much in the last three months.

We put our stuff in a locker, take our rigs, then head out of the hangar and stand with our group to wait for our plane.

"Kiss for good luck?" Chelsea asks as we wait, her voice breaking on the last word. She gives us all a kiss on the cheek, and I think we're all feeling so many emotions right now.

I take a couple of cleansing breaths because I still feel anxious. But because I'm resigned to do this, I just push it away. It's probably not my best move, but it'll get me through.

We load up on the plane, a group of ten going up, and buckle in. The most dangerous part of this entire thing is the takeoff. Before I can freak out or back out, we're off, speeding down the runway. I wasn't really going to back out. But I did entertain the thought for just a few seconds.

We climb up into the sky. It takes about twelve minutes to get to thirteen thousand feet. I look out the window I'm sitting next to, watching the ground below us get farther and farther away.

I realize something as I watch the buildings and the cars get smaller. The ashes that my dad is currently holding in his hand, in that white cylinder container, are all I have left of her. This is it. When my mom's ashes go up into the sky, that's my one last tether to her. My one last connection. I wonder if this has been my problem all along. Maybe I wasn't really worried someone would get hurt—maybe I couldn't deal with the finality of what we're doing.

I'm crying now—big fat tears. I look over at Chelsea and she's crying too. I reach over and grab her gloved hand and squeeze it.

About a thousand feet before we reach altitude, we start getting ready. Taking off our seat belts, putting on our helmets, doing a final gear check. Then we do this thing that everyone does before a jump; it's like this little hand slap

THE ACCIDENTAL TEXT

thing. It's happened on every jump I've ever done. Like a good luck tradition.

Once at thirteen thousand feet, the pilot gives the signal to open the door. We let the other group go before us so we can exit the way we need to link up.

The feeling washes over me again. This final jump with my mom. This is all I have left. I want to stay on this plane and refuse to do it. But I know that I can't. I have to do this for Devon, for Chelsea, and for my dad. I can't let them down again.

When it's our turn, the four of us squeeze out the door together, our backs facing outward. We're each holding on to the inside of the doorframe so we can jump at the same time, so we can do it just like we practiced with Mom. It feels almost like clockwork. If only I didn't feel so empty right now. So … sad.

Once we're all leaning out of the plane and ready to go, my dad nods his head and we let go.

And then we're falling, though it doesn't feel like falling. It feels like you're suspended in air. I'm close enough to Chelsea that I can grab on to her by her gripper. Devon has Dad by his, and we easily link up, Chelsea grabbing on to Devon. Just like we practiced. Mom—if she's watching this—would be so proud.

We all look to my dad and he nods his head just once. Then he opens the top of the cylinder urn, and we watch as my mom's ashes fly into the sky. It's beautiful and heartbreaking and we did exactly what she wanted us to. I feel happiness that we were able to pull it off, but also such sadness. It's over. That was it. The tether is gone.

My dad gives us a thumbs-up and we drop away, giving each other enough space to deploy our parachutes. I let mine go first and feel the tug as my drop slows. I watch as the rest of my family's chutes deploy.

I'm by myself now, just me canopying through the sky, the world coming closer to me by the second. I guide myself toward the landing.

"Love you, Mom," I say. I can't help but feel close to her right now, up here in the sky. I can picture her, in her favorite teal jumpsuit with white detailing. Her grin wide as she flies through the sky, giving me a thumbs-up as she does one of the things she loved most.

And then an overwhelming realization comes to me. It's a ton of information at once, but I feel it in my bones, like I've known it all along. I haven't wanted to do this because of the finality of it all. But … it isn't over.

I've been such a fool.

This is the tether. It's still here. I can feel her right now, flying beside me. Smiling at me. Cheering me on. She's been there when I was ATVing, zip-lining, cliff diving, and riding a bike through a quiet desert night. She's there in every hug from my family, every kiss for good luck, every time I touch the necklace with her initial on it. The connection isn't gone; she'll always be with me.

She will *always* be with me.

I smile at this realization. I smile, and I laugh, and I cry.

THE ACCIDENTAL TEXT

After our landing, when we've gathered up our chutes, my dad pulls us into a family hug. I'm sobbing as we hold each other. We all are.

"We did it," Dad says, tears rolling down his cheeks. "I love you all so much. Your mom loved you all so much."

We hug each other. There are tears and laughter, and it's just how she'd have wanted it.

Once we've pulled ourselves together, we go inside and drop off our rigs to be repacked. Devon grabs our stuff from the locker and brings it to us while we wait for our gear.

My cheeks hurt from smiling, and my nose feels raw from crying. I feel happy and tired and grateful. What a day it's been. And it's only nine thirty in the morning. But I feel like I've experienced so much, so many feelings in the past hour, that it feels like it should be the end of the day, like the sun should be going down.

Devon hands me my phone and the first thing I see is that I have a text from Chase. I smile. Despite everything that's happened between us this past week, I'm grateful for him. For remembering today.

I picture him sitting at a café in London. Or maybe he's at a pub. He's got that signature half-smile on his face. I miss him. I miss texting him, miss talking to him. Maybe I can get over all these feelings and we could be just friends. I hope.

I open my text app and click on his name.

> **Chase:** Hi, Mom. I've been wishing you could have met someone. Her name is Maggie. And she's pretty amazing. I think you would have liked her … I know you

would have.

I could really use your help right now—maybe you could send me some guidance. See, I think I'm falling for Maggie, and I'm not sure how to tell her. I think I've been feeling this way for a while, but I didn't realize it fully. I've been keeping myself from feeling a lot of things lately.

I wanted to tell her before I left, but I felt selfish. I didn't want to ask her to wait for me while I'm in London. But I don't care that it's selfish. I just want her to know. I need her to.

Chase: Oh, by the way, I'm waiting by her car right now. So, I'm planning to tell her this in person. Wish me luck, Mom.

My breath hitches and I look up from my phone. Is this for real?

"Where are you going?" Chelsea asks as I make a mad dash for the parking lot.

"I'll be right back," I yell back at her.

I exit the hangar and run toward my car. I don't remember where I parked—it was so early when we got here, and I was feeling so many things. Now I'm frantic to remember; I need to know he's really here.

And then I see my car, and there's Chase standing by it. He's looking down at his phone, wearing shorts and a charcoal-gray T-shirt.

"Chase," I say when I'm just ten feet away from him.

THE ACCIDENTAL TEXT

He looks up and his lips pull up into a big smile. A grand one. It's a sight to behold. *He's* a sight to behold. And he's really here, standing next to my car.

I run the last few feet and stop just in front of him.

"You're here," I say, still not fully believing it. "Why are you here? You're supposed to be in London."

"Changed my flight," he says, his smile morphing into that half-grin I love so much.

He takes a step toward me, so we're now just inches away from each other. "I couldn't leave without seeing you. I tried, but I couldn't do it. So I changed my flight, and here I am."

I don't know what to say; all I can do is stare at him.

"I'm sorry for … everything," he says. "You were right about me, about what I was doing. I never realized how bad I was at feeling things. I'm working on it."

"Your texts," I say.

"Cheesy, right?"

I tilt my head, looking up at him. "I was going to say that you're a copycat."

He shrugs his shoulders. "Imitation is the greatest form of flattery." He smiles.

"I'm sorry too," I say.

He scrunches his brow. "Why are *you* sorry?"

"You were right. I was also avoiding things. With the jump."

"But you did it?"

"I did," I say, smiling and gesturing toward my jumpsuit. I'm sure I look windblown and my face is a little puffy from all the crying.

"How did it feel?"

I feel the tears prick behind my eyes. "It felt … amazing."

Chase wraps his arms around me and pulls me into him. I bury my face in his chest, the tears flowing once again. I feel him kiss the top of my head.

I pull my face back so I can see him, still not believing he's here. He reaches up and rubs one of my tears away with his thumb.

"Did you mean what you said … in your text?"

He smiles. "I did. Every word."

"Good," I say. "Because I'm falling for you too."

Chase doesn't hesitate; his lips find mine. There's no precursor, no heated glance, no eyes searching my face beforehand. No tiptoeing or testing the waters. It's his lips on mine, and it's full of hunger, and wanting, and needing. It's all the many things we want to say but aren't ready to say yet. And I feel it all as his mouth parts mine and the kiss deepens.

We are all hands and lips and tongues up against my car. And it's, hands down, the best kiss I've ever had. The most passionate kiss I've ever felt. I'm not falling for Chase — I've already fallen.

The kisses start to change into something more slow and tender, and then Chase pulls his head back and leans his forehead against mine. We're both out of breath, both feeling the heat from this midmorning desert air.

THE ACCIDENTAL TEXT

"That was …"

"Yeah," I finish. There are no words, really.

He pulls away and looks at me. I smile at him and I know: this is it. *He* is it. All I've ever wanted and needed. The stranger who was on the other end of my texts. This man. Chase.

I think he feels it, too, because now we're both smiling, and hugging, and kissing, and laughing.

It's the best feeling in the world.

Epilogue

May

Chase: London is boring without you

Maggie: Phoenix is even more boring. I didn't think it was possible.

June

Chase: Two weeks until you get here. Can't wait.

Maggie: Me either. Saw Oscar today. He told me to tell you hi and that he likes me better than you.

July

Maggie: Phoenix is a million degrees. I should have never left London. I miss you so much.

Chase: I'm sorry … who is this?

August

Chase: This meeting could be the end of me. You can have Oscar if something happens.

THE ACCIDENTAL TEXT

Maggie: Yes! I have this in writing. This would stand up in court, right?

September

Maggie: Next week!! I can't wait.

Chase: What's next week? Oh, right. Bad news. I'll be in Phoenix, but Oscar has already filled up my schedule with belly scratches, walks, and Frisbee throwing. Sorry.

October

Chase: That was a sexy picture—can you send me more?

Maggie: The one of my shoe? Or the blurry one of my arm? Avery sends her love.

November

Chase: Two more days

Maggie: Oh, right. This is awkward. I should probably tell you now that I've met someone else. His name is Oscar. We're running away together. I didn't want to tell you like this.

Long-distance relationships are hard. I can tell people that now, from experience. I wouldn't recommend it. Chase has been home for three months, and I still sometimes get that sinking feeling that he has to go back, that he has to leave again. It's silly, I know.

The only good part about it was that we were so far away that all we had was talking on the phone and texting. We know a lot more about each other—about what we both want in life and how we feel about certain things, like politics and religion and whatnot—because that's all we had. There was none of the physical getting in the way. I feel like I know Chase better because of it. Even if I hated every second of being away from him.

Visiting him in London was amazing. We took in the sights and Chase got to finally skydive, since he never did it back in Phoenix. He had to go tandem with a guy named … well, Guy *was* his name. Guy's accent was so thick and he mumbled his words. I think Chase was more scared to jump with Guy than he was to actually jump.

It was after the jump, full of adrenaline, that he told me he loved me. It was easy to say back.

He took me on a hot-air balloon ride while I was there, and despite the third-wheel pilot, it was as romantic as I'd hoped it would be, floating over the English countryside, his arms wrapped around me. Chase's, not the pilot's.

He came back to Phoenix for two weeks during September, and it might have been the best two weeks of my life so far. I spent every possible minute with him, kissing him, staying up late talking. It was hard to let him leave. I may have asked him to quit his stupid job.

Before Thanksgiving, he came home for good. I cried when I picked him up from the airport, so happy to have him back with me. I also felt stupid for crying. I've become

THE ACCIDENTAL TEXT

this ridiculous lovesick person. I hardly recognize myself. Hannah says I make her want to vomit.

Now we're sitting on his couch in his living room on a lazy Saturday evening. We're watching TV, Oscar's head in my lap, Chase sitting right next to me. So close that it feels like we're glued together. His arm is around my shoulders and he's making lazy circles with his fingers on my arm. I love this moment. I don't care if I'm a cheesy person now.

We've had a lot more of these lazy days since he's been back. Gone are the days of one adventure after the other. We still do them—it's just only once in a while. We've settled into a real relationship, a real adult routine. And I love every second of it.

"Do you realize it's been a year since I got that first text from you?" he asks.

I chuckle. "Has it really?"

"I'm pretty sure."

I do the math in my head and I think he's right.

"Well, I'm not sorry for it."

He turns his head toward me. "Me either," he says. "In fact, I'm really, really glad." He leans in and kisses me softly.

He sits back. "I've got an idea for another adventure." He gives me a mischievous smile.

"I told you I'm not bungee jumping."

"Not that," he says.

"I'm also not hiking Everest."

"You've already made that clear."

"So what do you want to do? Volcano surfing?"

Chase pulls his head back skeptically. "Is that a thing?"

"I read about it the other day."

"Would you want to?"

"Probably not."

He chuckles this time. "I actually have a different adventure in mind."

"Tell me," I say.

He taps a closed fist on my leg and I look down. He turns it over and lets his hand fall open. There's a ring. A round diamond set on a gold band.

I take in a quick breath and then look up at him. His eyes are searching my face, looking for answers.

"Marry me?"

I look back down at the ring and then back up at him. "Are you … serious?"

"Would I have a ring in my hand if I wasn't?" He smiles that half-smile, but this time it's tinged with something else.

"Are you nervous?"

"I am a little, yeah," he says, now tapping on my leg with his hand, the ring in his palm looking blingy and shiny.

"Are you seriously worried I'll say no?"

"Well, I mean, I hope you'll say yes. Would you just answer my question?"

I smile. "Yes."

"Yes?"

"That's one hundred percent yes."

We both smile now. Big and wide and bright.

"I love you," he says.

"And I love you," I reply.

I hold out my hand for him to put the ring on my finger. I feel so many things in this moment. But mostly I feel peace. This is right; this is where I'm meant to be. I picture my mom looking down on me — on us — giving me that big reassuring smile of hers. I think she'd approve of Chase. I sometimes wonder if Chase getting her phone number was somehow her doing. It's a silly thought, but one I like to entertain.

Chase stops himself before putting the ring on, and I look up at him.

"Kiss for good luck?"

I smile. "Well, it's the rule."

THE END

ABOUT THE AUTHOR

By day, Becky Monson is a mother to three young children, and a wife. By night, she escapes with reading books and writing. An award-winning author, Becky uses humor and true-life experiences to bring her characters to life. She loves all things chick-lit (movies, books, etc.), and wishes she had a British accent. She has recently given up Diet Coke for the fiftieth time and is hopeful this time will last... but it probably won't.

Other Books by Becky
Thirty-Two Going on Spinster
Thirty-Three Going on Girlfriend
Thirty-Four Going on Bride
Speak Now or Forever Hold Your Peace
Taking a Chance
Once Again in Christmas Falls
Just a Name
Just a Girl

Connect with Becky
www.beckymonson.com

Printed in Great Britain
by Amazon